19
SOULS

19
SOULS

A SIN CITY INVESTIGATION

J.D. ALLEN

MIDNIGHT INK
WOODBURY, MINNESOTA

FIRST EDITION
First Printing, 2018

Book format by Bob Gaul
Cover design by Shira Atakpu
Editing by Nicole Nugent

Midnight Ink, an imprint of Llewellyn Worldwide Ltd.

Library of Congress Cataloging-in-Publication Data
Names: Allen, J. D., author.
Title: 19 souls: a Sin City investigation/J.D. Allen.
Other titles: Nineteen souls
Description: First edition. | Woodbury, Minnesota: Midnight Ink, 2018. |
    Series: Sin City investigation; #1
Identifiers: LCCN 2017029345 (print) | LCCN 2017039585 (ebook) | ISBN
    9780738754505 | ISBN 9780738754031 (alk. paper)
Subjects: LCSH: Private investigators—Nevada—Las Vegas—Fiction. | GSAFD:
    Mystery fiction.
Classification: LCC PS3601.L4188 (ebook) | LCC PS3601.L4188 A616 2018 (print)
    | DDC 813/.6—dc23
LC record available at https://lccn.loc.gov/2017029345

Midnight Ink
s2143 Wooddale Drive
Woodbury, MN 55125-2989
www.midnightinkbooks.com

For Allen.
Your beautiful mind encouraged so many.
Without you, none of this exists.

1

HER BLOODY FINGER LEFT a translucent smear on the phone screen as she glanced through the list of private investigators in Vegas. There were more than she'd imagined. Most had important-sounding names like Blackman Private Investigation or United Investigative Services. Big firms. Not what she was after. Her stained nail came to rest on Sin City Investigations. She tapped the link for the web page.

It was sparse—only two pages. One was a long list of qualifications. The other was his contact info. One cell phone number and one email meant a one-man operation. How corporate could a guy named Jim Bean be? She pictured a string-bean thin man with glasses and a crooked tie. Perfect.

She tapped the number, cleared her throat. The phone rang.

"Bean." The voice was deep and breathy, but not gruff.

"Hello, Mr. Bean. My name is Cynthia Hodge. I'm looking for an investigator to help me track down my brother."

She paused, but he didn't immediately speak.

She continued. "He's been missing for several months. He took off with most of my mother's nest egg. You know the type."

"Drugs?" More labored breathing. He was doing something.

"Have I caught you at a bad time?" She was ready to get on with the plan. She didn't have time for his drama.

"In the middle of something." Somewhere in the background a man groaned and then came the scratching, rustling sounds of a struggle. "Hold on just a moment, Ms. Hodge." A loud noise pierced her ear as the phone clattered to the ground. The definite sound of a punch, that smacking of skin on skin, possibly the crack of bones snapping. There was a grunt, then a second of silence. Visualizing the scenario made her pulse jump again. Maybe this Bean guy had more mettle than his name gave on.

"Are you okay?"

"Fine. Just needed to get someone's attention."

"Do I need to call you another time?" Not that she would. There were plenty more PIs in the area.

"How long since you've seen your brother?"

She wanted to tell him the truth. That it'd been seven long years since she'd seen Dan. It almost slipped out, but she managed to catch the words on her tongue. She wasn't sure how long one would go without searching for a missing sibling. Seven years seemed too long. "Almost two years for me. Mother, a few months back."

"What makes you think he's in Vegas?"

"I'm not sure he is. He's been here before, staying with some card players for months on end. But I can't find him this time. I need to see if he has any of the money left. To confront him. Try to talk him into rehab or something. My father's passed. My mom's heartbroken and not able to pay her bills. Knowing Dan stole her money is killing her. She's not so strong these days. I need your help, Mr. Bean." She tried for tears. None came. She thought she managed the appropriate amount of despair in her voice.

"It's a hundred an hour, plus expenses. If any experts need to be brought in, they get their own fee on top of mine. Finding druggies can be slow. Expensive."

He was direct. Unconcerned with her mental state. She had chosen wisely. Jim Bean would serve her well. "I have the resources to make payment."

"Five thousand up front to get me started."

"That's fine."

"This is a Vegas number. You live here?"

"I do now, yes."

"You know the Coffee Girl diner?" He didn't give her a chance to answer. "Meet me there at nine a.m. with the retainer. Cash or credit only. No checks. No Discover cards."

Yes. He would do nicely. "Tomorrow, Mr. Bean."

"Nine a.m."

The phone chirped that the call had been ended. She took a cigarette out of her pack. Lit it with a match from a book she'd taken from the dive hotel she'd been forced to endure for the last two months. She blew out the flame. Let the burnt cardboard stick go, watched it flutter, the smoke leaving a crooked path to the floor. It landed next to the dead woman at her feet. Pooled blood was darkening under her head. Her once perfectly coiffed blond bun was now a bloody red mess.

"Did I sound like you, Ms. Hodge?" she asked the corpse and felt obliged to give it a moment in case there was a response. There was none. She shrugged and tucked Cynthia Hodge's phone in her own pocket. "Let's see if this guy can find your brother."

Don't get cocky.

Her own voice, young and angry, echoed in her head. Condescending. Always judging. Sophie Ryan Evers blew out a large puff of smoke. "Quit your worrying."

If Sophie was the type of woman who giggled, she would now.

"THEY'RE NOT *THAT* BAD."

Sandy, his favorite morning person, maybe his only favorite person, had stopped just shy of pouring his coffee. He eyed the pot as she held it just above the rim. A tease, so close to filling the empty mug. His coffeemaker at home had broken months ago and he'd not bothered to replace it.

She was young, cute and blond, midtwenties, a pro at sarcasm. Sandy had been taking classes at the University of Las Vegas for *forever,* she'd groan. Jim guessed closer to five years judging by how long she'd been serving him breakfast. She'd yet to declare a major. Like many kids, Sandy had no idea what she wanted to do with her life. Waiting tables at this joint was good enough for now. Or so she said.

Her quip was referring to the eggs, but the whole plate was suspect. Everything she'd put in front of him was mustard yellow. The organic substitute eggs, the shredded cauliflower that was supposed to replace hash browns, and the toast that was some kind of gluten-free cardboard shit that crumbled if you attempted to hold it. Even the plate itself was yellow. He was certain it was exactly *that* bad. "How does he make it all the same puke yellow?"

"You come here almost every day and order the same thing. Either quit your complaining or pick somewhere else to have breakfast and conduct your business." One eyebrow rose, daring him to argue further.

"I wasn't exactly complaining. I was trying to figure out the percentage of yellow foods in that kitchen. I thought all healthy shit was supposed to be green."

"You want green eggs?" Sandy grumbled like she was tired of his shit. But she was half smiling, half smirking. The exchange routine. He went to great effort to get her face to make just that expression every morning.

Jim thought on the green eggs for about one and half seconds. "Nope. I do not. I want a real egg that I can order sunny side up. And soft white bread to soak up the yolk." He pushed his cup closer to her. "I know you don't have those either." The pinko bastards had turned his greasy spoon into a vegan something or other *food oasis* over a year ago.

She poured. Turned on her heels. "One of these days ... " She walked away, shaking her cute, too-young-for-him ass. He smiled. Banter with Sandy was a great way to start the day.

He took a couple bites and, once again, he was correct. It was *that* awful. He took a swig of coffee. A well-dressed woman pushed through the glass front door and stopped at the counter. Sandy greeted her and pointed to Jim. Had to be the new client. Good. She'd showed. He needed the funds. The cat food supply was getting low and Annie was not a happy kitty when she was hungry.

The woman was tall, red-headed, and well put together. Her hair was pulled back in a loose knot, her clothing snug and professional. Her face was a hint softer than her clothing. "Jim Bean?"

He nodded and motioned for her to sit. She sneered a little as she checked the vinyl seat. Snob? Maybe he'd read the light makeup and relaxed lips too soon. The place was old but, as was posted in the window, the menu progressive. She didn't seem convinced. He noted the lingering hint of cigarette smoke on her. She'd eaten a mint, but it was still in the clothes. An inspection of his plate didn't ease her expression.

"How's the food?" She slid into the seat gracefully considering her footwear had tall, pointy heels.

"Not bad once you wash it down with the equally horrible coffee."

She smiled. Wow. That made a big difference. She was a beautiful woman. Nice to have a client with cash and a pretty face. He sat back, pushing his yellow plate aside.

"Ms. Hodge. Nice to meet you."

She nodded. "Thank you for seeing me so quickly." She folded her hands in her lap over her bag.

Okay. Down to work. He pulled out his notepad and little golf pencil. "Your brother stole from your parents and you want him back?"

She nodded.

"Why not the police?"

Sandy brought Ms. Hodge a mug and set it down. The redhead nodded again, this time to Sandy. She poured. "Would you like to see the menu?"

Ms. Hodge eyed Jim's half-eaten plate with that same repugnant look. "I think not."

Sandy left without filling Jim's cup. Evidently she didn't care for the uptight woman. Jim wasn't sure he did either, despite the amazing smile.

He looked at her and waited for an answer.

"Oh. Sorry." She cupped her hands around the cup as if she was cold. "The police will be more aggressive than we'd like. We're sure he's got a meth problem. With his history, god knows what else. I want him in rehab, not prison."

Jim nodded. He'd heard that before from families looking for lost children in Vegas. "Where was his last known residence?"

"He quit college years ago to rodeo. Bronc riding, I believe. Last I could find was Texas. He had a camper on the back of his truck."

"No real address?"

She shook her head.

"And the last time you spoke to him?"

She looked down. Her face tightened for the first time. "I haven't talked to him in years. I know he used to come see our mother. But after he got her to sign those papers, nothing. Not even a call on her birthday." Her gaze was on the cup. She didn't look at Jim.

"What papers?"

She glanced up. "Giving him access to her accounts so he could help her manage her money. She's got Alzheimer's and it's getting pretty bad. She needs full-time care. That's why I need to find him."

Jim shook his head. This was not going to be a pleasant conversation. "Addicts aren't big on maintaining savings accounts, Ms. Hodge."

Her arrogance was momentarily replaced with sadness, it danced quickly around her brilliant green eyes. She nodded. Recovered. "Call me Cynthia, please." She tilted closer, put her hands on the table. "It's more about Mother knowing he's okay than the money. When she's lucid, he's all she talks about. When she's not, she screams for her boy."

"You have his phone number?"

"No."

"Have his social security number?"

"No. Mom can't remember it. I can't find any paperwork in her belongings with it listed, either."

"You're not making the job easy on me."

"If it were easy, I would have found him myself. I tried all the avenues you're asking about. Nothing. Otherwise, I wouldn't need you, would I?" She flashed that killer smile again.

True. "Anyone else know where he'd go off to? Any other family members or distant relatives he may have made contact with?"

"We have a cousin somewhere in the northwest, outside Seattle maybe. I called. He said he hadn't heard from Dan."

"Full name?"

"Daniel Kent Hodge. Born August 1st, 1985." She fished a snapshot from the small clutch purse she carried. Small bag. Not much room for a cash down payment. That meant she'd be paying by credit card. He'd have to factor in the bank charges in her fee. He jotted down the DOB. Glanced at the picture. It was the two of them together. The pair were smiling. Dan had his arm around her. "Not very recent."

"Most recent one I have." For a wordless moment she was fixated on the snapshot.

Please don't cry. Crying women made him uncomfortable. He should be more empathetic in his line of work. But he wasn't. Everyone had their troubles. Every client brought theirs to his door. Those became his troubles. If he got emotional about it, he'd be in the nut house. Detachment Island was his happy place and he planned on retiring there.

She tossed the picture onto the open notebook. "He won't look so different."

"Drug addicts always look different." He watched her eyes. She'd flinched as he said it. "Side effects of the toxins."

"You're probably right. I hadn't thought of that."

"Anything else you can think of?" He'd ask her about fraternities, clubs, or other social activities, but if Dan was using meth, that was his whole life. Jim would start looking at the arrest records. Probably find him relatively quick that way.

"Not really. Like I said. I don't want him arrested, just found."

"Got it." He scribbled a few more thoughts. "The number you called from a good one?"

"Yes."

"This could take a while."

"Can you keep me apprised of your progress and what you find out?"

"Always do. The retainer is five thousand. I will have to travel to Texas. If I find him quick, any monies not billed to my rates or the cost of the investigation will be returned."

Cynthia took a stack of hundreds out of her little black bag and tossed them on the table. It skidded across the laminate surface, stopping beside his notepad. The bank band wrapped about it had *fifty* scribbled on it next to a pair of initials. A withdrawal. Neatly bundled. No need to count. Easy to deposit and pay all his bills with. Thank you, Cynthia Hodge.

She was all business. Easy and clean. He liked that. Liked that a lot.

He handed her a standard contract. "You agree to pay me what I need to find Dan and I agree to do my best to recover your brother."

She signed without reading it.

"There is a chance we won't find him, or that we find out he's died. I've seen it happen more than once. I just want you to be prepared." He hated this speech, but it had to be put out there. "When you're dealing with addiction, it takes people into some very dangerous places. Both with the drug use and the people who live in that culture."

"Are you trying to prepare me for that eventuality? You think he's dead?" A few strands of red bangs fell lose and dangled in her eye. She made no move to push it aside.

"It's a possibility you need to be aware of."

"He's not dead." She fidgeted with the corner of her bag.

He'd heard that before too. But it wasn't his job to be her shrink. "Okay."

She stood. Held out her hand. Jim took it. Her fingers were cold. Her grip surprising. Strong. "Please keep me up to date when you find anything. I like to know where my money is being spent. Remember, don't contact him. Just find him."

Not an unusual request. But she needed to know the reality. "I'm happy to do that. But know that this could take some time. I don't have much to go on here. Some of the process is a waiting game."

"I'm not so good with patience or being in the dark." She turned to leave.

"Mind if I ask how you got my name?" Most of his business came from referrals. Jim liked to know if he needed to thank someone, or pay them.

She headed to the door. "Your yellow pages dot com ad." She said it over her shoulder, not bothering to slow the swing of her hips in that creamy mustard yellow skirt.

Maybe yellow wasn't so bad after all.

3

SOPHIE PEELED OFF THE clothes she'd taken from the dead woman's closet. They were tight and not at all comfortable. She'd never been a slave to fashion. Even for work, comfortable slacks, a loose jacket, and flat shoes were her usual uniform. She sat on the side of the bed and rubbed her feet. The mattress felt good under her weight. Much better than the hotel she'd occupied for the last few weeks. She pulled her jeans back on and padded barefoot into the living room. She paused at the end of the short hallway.

Danny's sister's body still lay where Sophie had dropped it. The thing had to be moved. If someone came to the front door, they might catch a glimpse of her ugly feet sticking out from behind the couch. The layout of the little ranch was a simple T with the guest bath far enough away from the bedroom to prevent Sophie from living with the impending smell.

She rummaged through the hall linen closet and found a tattered plastic tablecloth with strips of the plastic peeling away from the fabric liner. Red checked. Rather quaint for the task. She rolled the body onto the plastic, wrapping it like a burrito. Then, using the top corners, she dragged it down the hall and into the muted pink tiled bath. Obviously seventies, but the lighting and nickel fixtures helped to modern it up a little.

She heaved the wrapped body into a sitting position against the side of the tub. After a deep breath, she squatted over it. Needed to have the power of her legs to lift. The woman was small, but dead weight was dead weight and Sophie didn't want to wrench her back. She grunted with the upward force. Teeth clenched as she hefted with all her might and the body flopped ungracefully into the tub.

She looked in the cabinet under the basin and found several cleaning products. Clog remover. She read the label aloud. "Sodium hydroxide and lye. Perfect."

The tablecloth had slipped under the body and exposed a good bit of flesh. Carefully, she reached around the *thing's* legs and pushed the stopper down. She emptied the bottle over *its* length and ran enough water to cover *it*.

The foaming clog remover created an unusual mix of blue swirling with the scarlet red seeping from hair and clothes. The trashcan was overflowing with rumpled tissue, so she dropped the empty bottle in the tub.

Sophie washed her hands under hot water at the vanity. "Don't look in the mirror." The instruction was given to the thing in the tub, but Sophie wasn't about to glance into the looking glass either. Mirrors brought opinions and commentary from the past, from a time before she'd messed up her life. When there was hope, maybe even a time or two she felt joy.

With this messy job it was likely to have something nasty to say. That bitch in her head loved to pick apart Sophie's inadequacies.

Doubtless, it looked down on this performance, would preach at her for being impatient and leaving a body lying around the house. But Sophie had no desire to get it into the car and drive out to the desert. For now anyway. Maybe tomorrow.

She had promised the voice to learn something each time she killed. To look past the way it made her *feel* and find ways to make the task easier, faster, or cleaner. After all, she had to be perfect when the investigator found Dan or he would still find her unworthy. Spurn her again.

Memories of his mocking words the last time she found him made her chest tighten, her blood pulse. Trying to find Dan had caused her much anxiety, but it was worth it. He was hers. Anyone who tried to stop them this time … She tried to swallow past the bile in the back of her throat. Reminded herself she needed to take her meds. She needed to be in control.

She dried her hands and ducked out of the bathroom without looking in the mirror. She'd already covered the other three in the house.

She grabbed a big blanket from the linen closet on her way back to the living room. Folding it over twice, she spread it over the blood the body had left on the floor. Only a small bit peeked out near the counter.

You should clean that.

"No one's coming here. It's not a problem."

Her stomach grumbled from lack of breakfast, but there was no way she was eating the tree-hugging fare in that diner. It reminded her of regurgitated baby shit. Come to think of it, Bean really didn't look the type to eat it either. And he did not match the impression she'd had of him. Instead of a skinny nerd with thick glasses, Bean was at least six-two, and if she had to guess, he was every bit of two forty, two forty-five. It would take a big dose to put him down. She'd keep that in mind.

One of the reasons she hated people was their unpredictability. She liked things to have a certain amount of the expected to them. Made decision making easier for her. A PI punching people yesterday and eating vegan mush for breakfast today. Who'd have thought it?

Sophie grabbed some cheese slices out of the bags she'd set on the counter. She'd made a quick stop for cigs and snack food. After all, *the body* in the bathroom wouldn't have had much food on hand, now would she? Cynthia Hodge had thought she was going to an accounting seminar in L.A.—all expenses paid.

"Brilliant." Sophie marveled at her mind at times. She'd set up the trip. Going as far as to buy an airline ticket and express it to this address so *the body* would be packed and all ready to leave. And more important, take plenty of time off work. No one would miss her for days. "Brilliant," Sophie said again for a verbal back pat.

She lit a cig and took a long drag. In her opinion, nicotine was more help than her Prozac. Sophie had done her part now. The final leg of her long-term plan was in motion. All she needed was for Bean to find where Dan was living in a hurry, before *the body* would be expected back at the office. He had a week at most. Sophie would monitor *its* emails and calls in the meantime to keep *the body's* friends from becoming worried. But the charade would only be sustainable for so long.

She stuck one of the supposedly lean frozen meals in the microwave. It took her a moment to figure out the unfamiliar controls. When the turntable started spinning, she stood over the couch and picked up the remote control neatly waiting on the armrest. The noon news was on. A perky weather girl detailed what any moron could figure out with just the graphics. "Fucking hot all week." She muted the sound.

Two other bags sat at her feet. Not from the grocery but an earlier excursion to the hardware store and the pharmacy. Easing onto the couch, she carefully opened her little black suitcase on the coffee table. Her fingers traced the foam compartments. A long time went into the planning and arranging in there. Her knife drew her attention as she sat on the cream-colored cushions of the sofa. Good thing she'd not gotten blood on it. The leather chair looked far less comfortable.

The gleaming batwing switch with an English staghorn handle had been a present to herself after Number One. The switchblade she'd used on that bitch had been cheap. The handle had cracked, almost snapped, and it slipped in her hand. Sophie rubbed a small scar at the base of her thumb. Fortunately she'd managed not to leave any DNA around. Or if she had, she didn't think the police had found it.

"Pays to be prepared." So she'd invested in some proper tools and this beauty. It was heavy, thirteen inches with the blade extended, and finely sharpened. It had never let her down. Never bit back. The blade felt like magic under her light caress. The pleasing light hazelnut–colored staghorn was textured just enough to help keep a firm grip.

Next to it was a foam cutout big enough to hold several pairs of gloves. She double gloved most the time after that first incident. New knife, yes, but she couldn't be too careful. It wouldn't do to have someone search for her DNA now. Now that the plan was in action, now that she was so close to Dan.

A cell phone rang. Sophie jumped, even squeaked. She needed to calm her nerves. Take her meds.

The ringer went off again. *The body*'s phone. Sophie let it go to voicemail. She didn't want to talk to any of *the body*'s friends or co-workers. But she would text them back if she felt like they needed placating. She'd check it later. Work then play.

Her attention swung back to her case. Below the knife were auto injector pens set into the foam so she could get to them easily if need be. Seven. All had been preloaded with a strong animal tranquilizer—

ketamine. Easier to obtain than the human equivalent and just as effective. She'd used one on the body in the bathroom.

When Sophie, disguised as a cabbie, had come to her door for the ride to the airport, there was a cab running in the drive. Sophie had stood there in dark jeans, a dark long-sleeved shirt, and a cap. She'd offered to get the luggage. *The body,* his sister, had been happy for the assistance, even turned her back to get her purse from the kitchen counter.

That was the magic moment. That instant when Sophie knew all would be well. Easy peasy. She'd hit *the body* on the back of the neck with the injector and held *the body* in a headlock from behind until *it* started to falter. Then she'd used her staghorn knife. Thirteen inches of beautiful steel to cut a precise six inches. Most people say ear to ear when they talk about a slit throat. But the sweet spot was lower, about two inches on most average-sized adults. So she sliced from artery to artery. *The body* fainted from the drugs before a good fight or bleeding out. *It* then sagged to the floor at Sophie's feet with nary a struggle. Quite sad really, for her life to go out in an instant when she had spent the week expecting a great trip and conference.

Not Sophie's concern. Cynthia Hodge was a tool. Just like the items in her case. A nice clean kill, that was. She'd retrieved a tiny syringe from the fresh box she'd bought with a forged 'script and filled it with the tranquilizer from the amber bottle nestled inside a bundle of gloves for protection. The ketamine. She plunged the needle in and sucked out the tranquilizer. She loaded it into the disassembled auto-injector. With a quick twist and a compression of a spring, she had the Epipen-type auto injector back together. Only this brand was smaller, slimmer. Admiring her ingenuity and skill, she returned it to its proper place in the kit.

A square cutout in the corner of the case housed a roll of green plastic-covered garden wire, a small pair of wire cutters, a few bandages, a spare pair of contacts, and a trash bag. Her tools were ready. Calmness tingled through her body. She was ready.

4

BEAN POURED A SHOT of very good scotch he'd bought using the top Benjamin from the stack of Cynthia Hodge's bills. He'd been drinking cheap rot-gut brands over the last few weeks. Annie was chomping happily on her indulgence as well. *Tuna Feast* the can had read. He thought the picture of the white longhaired cat on the can was the perfect negative of his little black Annie.

He popped open a spanking new laptop. The new computer was part of the reason his funds were dangerously low this month. He'd been watching a thug for an insurance company and the mark had caught on, bum-rushed Jim's car at four in the morning with a two-by-four, and swung away. His computer took the brunt of one of the blows. Jim used it to protect his face as the wooden weapon crashed through the windshield. Shock resistant...my ass.

It had been cheaper to get his head fixed than replace the computer. Sadly, he'd needed both. Got a new laptop a week later, but he was stuck with the same old skull. He sipped the scotch in lieu of more pain meds. Only hurt occasionally now. Couldn't discern the pain from his normal morning headaches anymore. On top of the cost of replacing the hardware, he'd lost the revenue from not getting the information for his client. They'd fired him. Asshats.

The screen opened for the INtellix database. He typed in Dan's full name and hit search. Little bubbles swirled in a circle as the software searched nationwide for criminal records on Daniel Kent Hodge. Several hits returned. Oregon, Texas, Florida, and Michigan all listed individuals by that name. He clicked the one listed for Texas. That click costs him eight bucks. Three more listings appeared on the screen. Possible relatives and associates. Cynthia, his mother, and another male in his sixties, deceased, with the last name Hodge. And another man named Halbert Winters.

Arrest record was pretty short for a junkie.

Forth Worth, 2006, Drunk and disorderly. Fined $200 and time served.

Austin, 2007, Drunk and disorderly. Resisting arrest. Fined $350. Time served.

Neither of those would be pled down from a drug charge. Chances were he hadn't started using while he still lived in Texas.

Jim popped over to another database. Financial trail. Harder to trace, but it might even generate him a sweet social security number. That would be a help. Again, all of Dan Hodge's records disappeared after 2009.

Cold trail. Not looking good for evidence of life. Hopefully he wouldn't find a death record. The stack of cash was burning a hole in his pocket. Finding the kid dead in two hours meant giving most of it back to the redhead.

Jim let another sip linger on his tongue. Annie jumped onto the table and settled beside the laptop to begin her grooming ritual. The cat was so predictable. Always started with her paws gently rubbing over her eyes like a tired baby, ended with her ass. Next step was to try to rub his face.

He scratched her head. With an annoyed, chirping meow she turned away but didn't deviate from her routine.

Jim tried another search tool. The results closely mirrored the INtellix information. How does someone drop off the face of the earth and still manage to come see or call his mother? Maybe he'd snail mailed her. Bank accounts needed socials, credit cards needed socials. This kid had no marriages, no liens, no judgments, no back taxes, and no death record. Not on file anyway.

He Googled. Found one picture of Dan standing next to Halbert Winters. He saved the pic and zoomed in on the banner in the photo's background. *Party on the Porch ... Texas Circuit Finals Rodeo.*

He typed in Halbert Winters. Hal was a veteran of the Pro Rodeo Association. If he was, maybe Dan had been too. He looked up the history page on the association's website. Sure enough.

Annie finished with her ass and padded her way to him, purring, wanting attention. "No way, stinky butt. You're not kissing me with that mouth." He directed her away from his computer.

He scanned the pages. D. Hodge and H. Winters traded the top spot in the saddle bronc events from 2006 to 2009. Both made pretty good money for the finals. Dan had had some cash back then.

The association had an event this coming weekend in Fort Worth. "Maybe Hal is still around."

Annie meowed her agreement at him.

In the meantime, Jim decided to pop in and see what Dan's momma had to say about her baby boy. Maybe she would remember something. Jim was good with talking people into doling out facts. Sometimes facts they didn't even know they knew. It was his talent. Besides, old ladies liked him.

5

"**GET YOUR SKINNY BUTT** outta my room." The command was almost a shriek. Serious enough to stop Jim in his tracks.

He looked to the open door at his back. Nothing but empty hall. Who was she talking to? He was just shy of 230 pounds these days. No one would call him skinny.

The woman faced away from him, silver hair shining in the late-afternoon sun. The glow was the only thing in the room that looked warm. Beige walls would have made it a bit warmer, but almost every inch below about the five and a half foot mark was haphazardly covered in newspaper articles.

Momma Hodge's retirement suite was little more than a hospital room. A beige couch that might seat two people was jammed into the space between the window and a cinderblock wall. No other seating but the rolling chair Mrs. Hodge currently occupied as she faced the open window. He doubted she could see out from her low angle, but a collection of scuffs on the floor indicated her attraction to the location.

A hospital-gray bed frame with a knot of tangled white sheets was the only other furniture. A small stand held a lamp, a glass of water, and a mirror. Beside the bed at Jim's feet was a two-foot-tall stack of newspapers. Jim glanced at the front page of the one on top. Older than a week.

"I said…" She spun the swivel chair and rolled it several feet until directly in front of Jim. She nudged her glasses closer to her eyes. "You're not Stephen." She chuckled. Shook her head, apparently amused. "But I suppose you knew that, didn't ya?"

"I believe so. Last I checked I was Jim Bean." She was a feisty one to be talking to the staff like that.

"Beam? Like the whiskey? Could sure use a snort of that at the moment. You bring me any?" Her face was painted with hopeful anticipation.

Jim smiled. There it was. Several times a week he answered this question. Used to piss him off. Not so much anymore. He was the one who changed his name. He should have given it much more consideration at the time. He thought it was kind of cool when he did it. He'd been holding an expensive cup of joe from a fancy place down the block from the courthouse. A bean was roughly painted on the cardboard sleeve. Behind him a loud talker was jabbering away on the phone. He was in coveralls, like the mechanics wear. *James* was scrolled across a patch on his chest. James Bean. Good enough. He'd shortened it to Jim as he filled out the paperwork for the change. And Jim Bean was born.

These days he used the question: "Jim Beam? Like the whiskey?" as a way to judge character. The more uptight or nervous a person was, the less likely they were to bluntly ask him.

He shook his head. She was pretty out there. "No, ma'am. Like green. Green bean, Jim Bean."

24

She didn't crack the slightest hint of a smile. "Don't know no Bean either." That hope turned to a suspicious glare and a raised lip. "You're not dressed like one of the morons who works here." She was not holding back, more wary.

"Nope. And I suggest you be a little nicer to the people who bring your food." Jim smiled. He didn't want to say the word *investigator* unless he had to. Might upset her. He wasn't sure if Cynthia told her mother she'd hired a PI.

"Ha. I can make my own way to the food lines, mister. Don't you worry."

He scanned the articles on the wall. Lots and lots of them. Nothing seemed to connect at first glance. Entertainment, sports, political. More obituaries in one place then he'd ever seen. Few had pictures. Most were bold headlines and story copy. They gave him an idea. "I was wanting to do a story on the residents here. One of the morons said you were a firecracker. Told me you'd be a good interview."

"Me? In the paper?" She used the heels of her scuffed black shoes to scoot the chair a bit closer.

He hated to lie to the old girl, but he didn't want to upset her. Given most his life was lived in a lie these days, what the hell? Nothing like the fluidity of ethics. "Mind if I sit?"

"Heck no."

She seemed bright and alert. Cynthia had given him the impression the old woman would be out of it. This exercise may garner him better intel than he'd hoped. He started with how long she'd lived in the facility.

"I've been here almost seven years, best of my recollection. Since right after Kennedy died."

Jim nodded. "Kennedy, huh?" His hopes of accurate information faltered almost as fast as her smile.

"Sad day."

"It was." He'd best get to the point then. She wasn't going to give him Danny's last address. "Heard you have a son, Mrs. Hodge. Daniel?"

"I do." Her face was unreadable. No longer smiling, but not exactly unhappy. "He's a cowboy."

"I heard that too." Jim leaned in, glancing behind again. Never liked his back to the door. But in this case it was to make her feel like he was secretive, that she could trust him. "You know where he is?"

"Out riding horses, last word I got."

"You've heard from him?"

"Not directly. Not in a while. Cindy says he's busy." Her face fell. "But he's promised me cake for my birthday next week. Tuesday. And a clown face. He always wore the best clown faces." She scrunched up her face and rolled her chair to the wall on her right. She plucked down an article. "Five hundred and seventy-five words." She handed it to Jim and grabbed another. "Fourteen hundred and seventy-five words." She pushed herself out of the chair, teetering on the brink of disaster. Jim braced to catch her. She swerved and twisted, grabbing one of the highest and longest sheets taped up. "Three thousand six hundred and seventy-five."

He looked over the long wall coved with the newsprint. "They all end in seventy-five?"

"That they do, mister. You'd be wise to remember that." She tapped her temple and winked.

He smiled down at her as she resettled in her rolling chair. "I'll do that." He sucked in a deep breath. "Anyone else come asking questions about Dan, Mrs. Hodge?"

"My name's Lynette. And only girls come round. But you know how handsome my boy is. Just like his father." She worried at a loose

thread from her sweater, inspected it, and then let it fall to the lino-
leum floor. He'd give her a moment. See where her thoughts went.

She refocused on the paper in her hand. "My Andrew's last article
was two hundred and seventy-five."

Jim remembered the name listed on the database. Andrew Hodge.
Daniel's father.

She closed her eyes. "Obits ought to be short."

6

JIM PARKED THE BLAND Japanese rental among jacked up pickups and horse trailers the next afternoon. He'd thought it was hot in Vegas, but the oppressive Texas heat and humidity had him sweating before he made it five feet from the car and its robust air conditioner.

He'd parked behind the arena area on purpose, guessing that would be where the riders and pros hung out. And as he suspected, there were several guys working horses and moving livestock toward the action.

He looked like a cop in this environment even with his jeans and hiking boots on. Three men stopped what they were doing to watch him approach.

He pulled out his ID. "Name's Bean. I'm looking for Hal Winters."

As expected. No answer. Three blank stares from three thin men in tight jeans and boots. They all had the same look. Pressed bright shirts with patches all over them, big buckles, and dusty well-worn boots. These guys were riders and had been around a while to pick up so much sponsorship.

"I'm hoping he can help me find a missing guy. He's not in any trouble."

The information brought little change of expression. Jim stood his ground and stared at them. The rather short one on the left finally looked down. He was the one who'd spill.

Jim addressed him. "Really, man." He tried to look like he was harmless. "I'm looking for Daniel Hodge. His sister hired me to find him. Their mother's sick. Help a guy out, would ya?"

Shorty nodded and tipped his hat back a bit. "I remember Dan. Haven't seen him in a few years. But you're on target with Hal. If anyone knows, he will."

"And he's here?" Jim was hopeful. Long trip if he wasn't. The circuit standings online had ended with last season. No way to know if Hal was riding the same one this year.

One of the quiet men spit. It landed close to Jim's feet but if it was directed at him, he'd have known. Jim ignored it.

Shorty pointed to a building off to the left of the covered arena. "Having a Coke in the AC would be my guess. Broncs don't go off till later."

"Thanks." AC sounded good to Jim.

Inside the cafe Jim didn't garner as much attention. There were all kinds of people there to watch the rodeo with families, people working the snack bar, even a couple cops in the corner. The seating area sported three long rows of white plastic folding tables. It would maybe hold a hundred people. There were only about thirty scattered around now. No tablecloths. No pretense. The food smelled like a summer baseball park at dinnertime. A huge whiteboard displayed the handwritten menu. Empty bottles displayed the choice of beer.

A couple dozen cowboy hats dotted the room. Jim scanned the faces of those turned in his direction. A cute blonde was smiling up at him as she spoke to her friends. Working. He moved on. A behemoth of a man in a pressed white shirt stood from the table closest to Jim and gathered a plate of fried chicken remains. He nodded. Jim took that as an invitation.

"Hal?"

The man hesitated.

"He's not in trouble. I owe him money." There's a lie that almost always works.

After another once-over the guy evidently agreed that Jim wasn't there for trouble. He pointed to the far corner of the room. No subtlety. Good thing Jim didn't need to sneak up. "Black hat talking with that lady in the green shirt."

Not to mention the guy had a mustache the size of Dallas. "Thanks."

Jim walked straight toward Hal. No surprise to Hal since he'd seen the big fucker pointing his way. Jim still had his ID in his hand. He flipped it open to Hal. The blond girl looked a little frightened. "I'm a PI from Vegas. Cynthia Hodge asked me to help her find her brother, Dan Hodge."

Jim gave the guy a quick minute to think on that. Wanted him to relax. Understand Jim was not there to find him for any troublesome reason.

After about four seconds he said, "I haven't seen Dan in a few years."

"Last time he beat your ass in the regionals." The blonde laughed. Her face was over-tanned from the Texas sun and over-coated in Maybelline. Lips the color of a fire engine. Eyes painted up cornflower blue. A look Jim was used to on the showgirls. Intentionally overdone for the lights and the stage.

Hal smiled. It made it to his eyes. Genuine. "It was."

"You two used to pass that title back and forth from what I could see online." Jim slid into a folding chair uninvited. The blonde turned more his way.

"He was a great rider," Hal said.

"Was?"

"Up and disappeared one weekend." Hal's accent was thick and rolling. He used his index finger and thumb to smooth his handlebar mustache. "Last day of regionals, 2012. His entry fees were paid. He was sitting in first place after the first go round. Never missed a ride before that. Never seen him since."

"Unusual for a guy to disappear in the middle of a competition?"

The blonde tapped an unlit cigarette on the table to pack the tobacco. "I've never heard of anyone else running out like that. I always thought he had to be dead to miss out on the buckle." Jim let his eyebrows rise as she elaborated. "I mean, he was in the money all the time. Had a decent truck but kind of lived out of it. We're on the road a lot, but most of us have a home base. Dan didn't."

"You think he could have gotten mixed up in drugs?"

"Oh. Hell no." Hal straightened, offended by the idea. "This is a real sport, mister. You have to have a clear head to strap yourself to a twelve-hundred-pound animal and hold on. We all get behind it at the bar every now and then, but he took this shit serious. Was saving to move to Montana and buy his own land."

Interesting. Montana's a big place to get lost in. "You guys know any other riders who did that? Move up to Montana?"

They both shook their heads but Hal answered. "I don't know anyone who could save his money like Dan."

If the man had some cash and no drug problem, there had to be a money trail. But why would his sister think he was a druggie? "Could he have started the drugs right before he disappeared?" Jim asked.

Hal pressed that mustache down again, stretching his lips into a frown. "Don't see Dan like that. He was smart. Hardworking. The guy you'd trust your sister with."

"Drugs change people."

Hal shrugged. "I think you're throwing your rope in the wrong direction."

Jim stood and nodded. "I appreciate your time." He said it to Hal but made eye contact with the blonde as well. "One more thing. Anybody else come looking for Dan after he went off?"

"Not that I can think of," Hal said as the woman shook her head.

"Great." Jim had a thought. "I need to get some cash out of the bank. Want to hit the bar myself tonight. What's the biggest bank around here? Don't want to pay too many fees."

"There's a First Texas Fed on Highway 377. I use them. Got an All Points ATM. No fees no matter where I go."

Another leather-faced woman stepped up behind the cowboy. "You best get to the chutes, Hal."

"I'll get out of your way. Have a good show … ride?"

"Go."

"Go. Have a good go." Jim headed back into the Texas heat.

Follow the money.

7

JIM SAT AT THE bar, his reflection directly below a buffalo butt the size of his first car. The rust-colored, stuffed rear-end was once part of a whole bison merrily roaming the range. Where the hell ever a range might still be these days. Now half a dead bison hung from a bar-back mirror in tribute to the house labeled beer, Buffalo Butt. Jim opted for scotch to accompany the rare piece of meat in front of him. No butt beer.

He pressed his shoulders back and cranked his neck to the side for a crack and stretch before cutting into what might be the end of his almost-decent cholesterol score.

Twelve ounces of marbled perfection. It sliced like butter. Tasted like heaven. The texture of the aged beef was flawless. The seasoning minimal. Perfect. Jim was dog-tired from the late flight last night. A beautiful meal and the scotch was exactly what he needed before an early night and a dawn flight tomorrow. It'd been a good trip. Fast and efficient. Just the way he liked it. One interview and he had a good lead.

Jim stopped chewing when he caught a glimpse of himself in the mirror. His dark hair was too long, spilling over his ears, his gray eyes looked gaunt above dark circles. The haggard appearance in the reflection made him wonder what had made Dan go so far off course. The kid was in college, then quit and joined the rodeo, and then turned junkie.

Jim's own life had been buffalo kicked too. His derailment was caused by a co-ed and a false accusation of assault and rape. He'd lost his scholarship, his spot in the FBI training academy, and a good deal of his mother's retirement to make bail. The following scrutiny and mistrust had sent him to Vegas. He'd changed his name and put out his plank declaring himself a PI. Started all over.

In the beginning he'd drunk enough to kill that buffalo hanging above his reflection. He counted himself lucky no one had offered him heavy drugs. He closed his eyes to the darkness that lingered from the self-loathing and anger of his past. Yeah. He'd have been happy for that kind of chemical-induced escape from reality. Maybe Dan had come across a need to indulge, to bury pain, life.

Someone maneuvered into the stool next to him even though there'd been plenty others open along the bar. Slowly he opened his eyes and looked down at the steak. He was in no mood to chat with a local.

"Well, Mr. Bean." His gaze snapped back to the mirror. The voice was smooth. The face familiar. "Did we find anything today?"

He blinked a couple of times, letting the confusion of seeing someone completely out of context ease out of his brain. He slowly took another sip of scotch. Catching his tongue. He didn't like being surprised ... or followed. He needed to edit his thoughts before he vomited out words he'd wish not spoken to a client. He silently counted to ten to hold his tongue. So the court-mandated anger-management class had paid off. This time.

"There was no need to come all the way to Texas, Ms. Hodge. That's what you paid me for."

"Call me Cynthia." She'd crossed her legs and angled herself to face him. Her elbow was casually draped over the dark-stained wood of the bar. She tilted her head and loose red locks tumbled over her shoulder. It was longer than he had imagined when he met her. That grin was mischievous at best. But damn, she was hot.

"I told you I wanted to see him as soon as you found him. So I figured if you were coming to Forth Worth, why not?"

"Shouldn't have." It came out more of a growl than he would have liked.

Cynthia's spine straightened, her face hardened, and she glanced around as if to make sure no one heard his harsh tone. "Please don't think I'm questioning your prowess as a PI. I'm just anxious."

That didn't help. "You wasted a trip."

Relaxing back onto the bar, her body language changed, softened. Jim got the feeling this woman rarely lost her poise for long. "He's not here?" She eased over even closer. He could smell her perfume. Something exotic. Not fruity or sweet.

"I really didn't expect him to be. But I do have a lead." He decided to hold off telling her his thoughts on Dan having cash at this point. He had no idea how long his techie guy would take to find the money trail. If there was one left to follow.

"Oh?"

"Old friend says he talked about Montana a lot."

"Montana. That sounds about right for Dan. Always loved the thought of the West. He thought Texas was too … not green."

"His rodeo buddies find it hard to believe Dan got into drugs."

She blinked hard. Swallowed. "So did we. It happened so fast. Seems like he was visiting one day and he was fine and then he missed his next planned visit. After that, he was always flighty and we got calls from a hospital once. He'd almost OD'd."

"I didn't find any arrest records."

With that she sat up and recrossed her legs. Jim tried not to notice that they were long and lean. He took another sip.

"I don't find that surprising. I did a criminal background thing online as well." She twisted and glanced around then nodded to the back of the restaurant. "I have the corner booth" She picked up his plate and handed it to him. "Join me. You can buy me dinner with my retainer money." Before he could answer she grabbed his drink. "Sir." The bartender looked up from his phone as Cynthia continued. "I'm moving Mr. Bean to my table. Is that okay?" She urged him out of the stool with a flick of her wrist.

Dammit. He really wanted a quiet evening alone. Sinking into bed in a scotch haze. Like most of his evenings.

He fell into the booth. She said something to the waitress before leaning back to the bartender. With her back turned and the angle she was leaning over the bar, he could see the shape of her ass in that tight denim skirt. He let his head fall back and hit the booth. It was not soft, as the upholstery made it appear. Dammit. A clock to the head would do him good right now.

She turned back to him holding two glasses—his close to empty one and a full one. She showed a good bit of cleavage as she set them in front of his plate and eased into her place behind her plate, which looked remarkably like his. Rare beef and vegetables.

With a wink she raised her wineglass and offered a toast. He groaned internally as he raised his glass. The evening reminded him of a very bad prom date. Wrong place. Wrong girl. Again.

She chatted about Texas and accounting through the meal. She smiled a lot. Even touched his arm a couple of times.

Cynthia was a knockout, but he would never get involved with an active client. She blasted him with that amazing smile again, this time with the head tilt thrown in for a murderous effect. The last gulp of the scotch did seem to help. He felt it. Woozy. Must be the traveling, because two drinks would never make him this relaxed. Damn shame too. Would have saved him a stack of cash during the years he was drowning the reality of his trashed life and bad choice in women.

The waitress stopped by and filled the water glass in front of Cynthia. "You two okay?" The waitress cleared the plates.

"One more?" Cynthia asked.

Jim felt the back of his teeth. His litmus test for years had been to stop when his top front teeth felt a little numb. They were still there and still hard. That little exercise was pretty danged effective. No need to worry. No driving tonight, as the saloon was attached to his hotel. All he needed was to stumble up the stairs to his room. She was buying and he was beginning to enjoy the company. "I think so."

"Good." She turned to the young girl. "I think I'll have a different glass of wine." She picked one off the small list she was handed. "Well, Mr. Bean. What's your story?" she asked when the waitress was out of earshot.

He let out a laugh that sounded a little too feminine in his head. "It's long and sad and I'm in no mood to go down that road right now." And he wasn't. He was feeling light. Happy. Strange.

"Okay. Life history is off limits. How about music? I'm guessing this country music is not your favorite."

She hadn't pushed. He liked that. "I'm a classic rock guy. Grew up with it in the house."

"I would have guessed that." She tossed her hair off one shoulder and scooted around to his side of the booth so she was sitting next to him. She pulled out her phone and tapped into the music section. "Love the classics." The play list was rather fuzzy but he made out ZZ Top and CCR.

With a little twinkle in her eye, the waitress set down their new drinks. The night was looking more and more like a first date. He took another drink. A big one. He needed to back away from his client. Cynthia got her lipstick out of her bag and touched up her lips.

No need to waste the good stuff. He would finish the drink and be on his way.

"Not so fast, big guy." She grabbed the glass and pushed it away from him. "We should have a toast before you slam that down."

Jim looked from the glass to her face. His head felt like it took too long to make that short distance. He blinked. Also sluggish. Travel must be kicking his ass this trip. Not usual, but the bed in this joint felt like sleeping on a fresh doughnut. Soft and unsupportive. He'd tossed all night. "What toast?"

"Here's to you bringing Dan home to me?" She pushed his glass back to him. Then she let her pretty nails trail up over his fingers oh so slowly. The delicate movement mesmerized him.

His gaze took the path up her arm, across that sexy spot just where her neck curved into her shoulder, and then found her recently re-reddened lips.

"You are amazingly pretty in this light." The words were out and he hadn't even thought them. He chuckled to himself. It should be embarrassing. Inappropriate. Client. Bad juju.

Her hand slid over this thigh.

But...

"You're very handsome yourself."

Client. Stop. His thoughts spun to the toast. Dan. "I may not, you know?"

"You may not what, Jim?"

"Find … find him." His lips felt dry. Licking them only seemed to spread the condition to his tongue.

She inched her fingers up the seam inside his jeans along his thigh. It tingled, burned. Nails grazed over his zipper. "You will."

For a moment the sexy smooth lines of her face hardened. She gripped his package. He sucked in a larger than normal breath of scotch-flavored air. Her touch seemed hot. His body jumped to react. "Yeah."

The waitress slipped the bill down. Cynthia opened the vinyl folder and signed it, all with her right hand. Her left was working him through his jeans. He was melting to her touch. His bones had deserted his being. The music in the room picked up in tempo. He felt the melody twisting and turning around his head like he could visualize dancing notes. Humming. He felt like that when he'd had a contact high at his tech guy's house once. Ely was a Viet Nam vet and prone to smoke without thought or care of who was around. He felt that way now. Like he'd been too long in front of Ely's computers while the man puffed away. Floaty. Comfy.

Her hand changed pace. He liked the rhythm.

"What's your room number?"

8

CYNTHIA WATCHED AS JIM worked diligently at his jean button. He pulled at the fastener with the finesse of a man wearing mittens. The continued failure to achieve his task didn't appear to upset him in the slightest. Rather, he seemed amused by the activity. How long would it continue if she didn't intervene?

Tonight's little game wasn't the first time she'd used GHB. The first foray had left the man vomiting and completely unwakeable. She read on the Internet the next morning that he'd died. Number Four.

She didn't get upset because the experiment failed. The supplier had warned her that the date rape drug produced a very ugly overdose. He was correct. No real loss, him being an over-cologned stranger from a sleazy bar. He was already falling-down drunk and in horrible shape when she'd found him.

She shuddered at the thought of the unappealing naked man on the lime green motel quilt and took a sip from her wineglass.

The fourth time she'd played around with this shit, she managed to overdose another one. Not to the point of danger or passing out, but he couldn't maintain an erection or concentrate on the task at hand. Dead weight. And he remembered too much the next day. She'd messed up that time. Picked a target who was too close to home. And, as should have been expected, it turned into a big mess. That experience cost her a great job and she had to change towns again.

She slipped off her shoes as Jim chuckled at his efforts. He looked younger without all the stress. When she'd first approached him at the bar, he'd looked beaten down. Maybe even sad. Now, playing with his zipper like a nervous teenager, his gray eyes danced with delight.

Sophie tossed away the memory of that past faux pas. Now she had a better job, made more money, and had greater flexibility with her schedule. She was ready for Dan. The house was ready. The plan in place to find him was moving along nicely.

She eased up and kissed Jim's neck. He froze for an instant. He left off working on the button and slowly responded with a deep, if sloppy, kiss. She enjoyed the scotch on his lips and the rough feel of his hands as he dug his fingers hungrily into her hips. Now, this was workable. The mix of GHB to alcohol was perfect. The experience would be useful research for when she got Danny to the house. He would need some coaxing the first time or two. Until he understood.

She let her hand slip back down to the PI's crotch. He was still as hard as he'd been in the bar. The drug was lasting. Maybe he was even harder now. But his rugged breathing worried her.

"How does that feel?" She wasn't sure the cause was the drugs or his excitement.

"Amazing." That sounded strained as well, but she was vigorously stimulating the man. She was sure he would deny her without the drugs. Not because of her looks—no, she had that covered—but because she was a client.

Yet here he was with his baser needs overriding rational thought. She'd provided the catalyst for his actions, but men were low-minded animals, really. They all turned on her eventually. They used her. Always had. Starting with her foster father and all the way through her life, until she got older, smarter. Not soon after she was out of that fucking house, Sophie started turning the tables, using men how *she* pleased. If she could gain something from it or if she thought they would wound her or detract from her mission, she'd use the blade. Simple plan.

But right now she was enjoying the outcome of this spur-of-the-moment party. Risky in that he might remember, but she felt this one wouldn't talk to anyone about it. He had far too much pride to whine about a drunken sexual encounter with a client. Men rarely cried rape.

He staggered back a little as she twisted the fabric around the metal button. He looked down at the jeans as if she'd accomplished some huge physical feat. His smile was boyish, even charming. Caution tingled her senses. Maybe she shouldn't play with someone she knew again.

She supposed he could get upset and stop looking for Danny. Then she'd have to start over with another PI. But she'd decided on this course as she watched him stalk into the restaurant and pull himself up to the bar. He was a good-sized man. His muscles thick and powerful and he wore a kind of arrogance mixed in with his confidence. He may not know how appealing his masculinity was. But maybe he did outside of work. Maybe he played games with women. Probably did. She liked to take men like that down a notch.

"Take it out."

"Huh?" He pulled his T-shirt off with only a minor amount of flailing and unsteadiness. Jim stood before her bare-chested, his jeans unbuttoned and hanging low on his hips. His eyes were glassy and unfocused. His balance seemed to disappear and he stumbled backward a few steps. Fortunately, the bed was there to stop his progress and catch him before he hit the ground.

This was perfect. He was happy as pie to be there. To be with her. And she was sure there was some rule in his profession that said don't sleep with clients. One he clung to. One she was able to strip away with ease. She could see it on his face just after she'd put the GHB into his glass. Mr. Bean was not happy to be joining her for dinner. Not that she'd given him a chance to argue. In such a short time, he was very happy to pull his penis out of his pants for her.

She chuckled to herself as she stalked closer to the bed. In this state, the PI was compliant and excited.

"Come to papa." He propped up onto his elbows. "Did I just say that?" His brows drew together.

She slipped off her shirt and apparently all thoughts of his last comment were washed away. Simple. Base. Flash a smile and bit of flesh and they fall all over themselves to give her what she wanted.

She'd managed to accumulate a small fortune with that tactic, conning and stealing and killing. Three pimps died when she'd hit Dallas with her plan to get off the street. Not that anyone missed them.

The plan had been to kill the lowlife fuckers for seed money. Maybe save a working girl's life in the process. Then she took the money, the drugs, and the guns they all hoarded. It was easy enough to sell the stolen shit to make a nice profit. Sophie thought of herself as an entrepreneur, after all. Hadn't taken more than a couple months to get where she didn't have to sell her own body or take out the drug dealers or pimps anymore.

She reinvested almost every dime into the plan. Hard work and savings paid her way through school and earned her a degree. Back then she'd had more money in the bank than any two people her age. Over time she bought several sets of identification. All with real social security numbers. She was smart. Determined. Danny would be impressed.

She eased to the edge of the bed and tugged on Jim's jeans. He did his best to lift his hips and she slid him out of his pants. Commando. "Yay me." She was getting excited as well. Jim Bean was a very nicely built man—defined muscles, nice abs, all without looking vulgar. She liked it. Big and just enough body hair to accentuate his physique. Reminded her of an Italian model she used to drool over.

Jim was mumbling, shaking his head. He'd lost his ability to voice his opinion on the upcoming amusements.

The thrill of taking someone against their will was almost as good as a kill. It was best when she could see the aftermath. The anguish that men suffered at having been violated. It was usually a woman's territory to be used. It gave her such a jolt to turn those tables. No one used Sophie Evers anymore.

She crawled up Jim's naked body, touching and teasing as she went. His muscles flinched and skin twitched as she tickled or stroked. "Are you always this sensitive?"

9

"USUALLY WHEN A GUY looks as bad as you, he's leaving Vegas, not heading into the party." The man's voice was at least one octave higher than Jim's current tolerance level.

Jim nodded but didn't respond or look his way. No way he wanted to chat with the high-talker for three frickin' hours.

"I take this flight a few times a month," the guy went on as the plane finally settled into its course and quit floundering around the airways like a wounded bird doing its best to make Jim hurl. "These nonstops are hard to get. Sure am glad to have it today. It's my girlfriend's birthday."

The rumbling of the jet engines was like a team of Clydesdales running a long-distance race in Jim's head. He leaned forward and used his thumbs to hold pressure on his temples, hoping for some relief. Nothing. His eyes squeezed shut trying to block out the morning light. The closed plastic window shade wasn't cutting it. Too many others in the cabin were wide open. He hoped this man didn't request that he open it back up. Jim needed what little respite from the glare he could manage. Might have to punch the high-talker in that flapping piehole if he didn't shut up.

Fuck, he didn't remember drinking that much. He couldn't remember drinking enough to feel like this in *years*. Maybe ever. Not that he remembered much after his *client* had started rubbing his junk while he stared at the taxidermied buffalo ass. He eased his thick head against the seat back as the plane banked north to head away from Dallas and toward Nevada. The sensation and a tiny bit of turbulence made him swallow hard. Bile. How the hell did he manage to get himself into these situations? Do the job and get paid. Easy. No need to add a fat layer of drama on top. Women. Of course it was a woman. He had to have the world's worst luck when it came to the fairer sex. Maybe he should consider only taking cases involving men.

Those cases would all be men looking for proof of cheating or lying wives. Although, he made a good bit of cash from women looking for proof of cheating husbands.

Behind his closed eyes he saw choppy images of Cynthia in the dark. Flashed moments of the night. The restaurant. His hotel room. Her bare shoulders looming over him. Long red hair in his face. Soft thighs pressed against his. Her breasts caressing his chest as she moved. The silent mental video of her talking to him as she dressed. But those memories were as cloudy as an abandoned fish tank. Hazy. Green. The sound dampened.

"You visiting Vegas?"

He shook his head. "Local."

"Me too. I'm in poker table sales. I'll be glad to be back home. A lonely casino out in the Texas sun was not for me."

The plane jumped again. Usually, turbulence didn't bother Jim much. Hell, he'd jumped out of planes a couple of times, but this time his stomach felt as though the big plane had taken a five-thousand-foot drop in altitude. He swallowed hard. Fighting what quickly was becoming a losing battle. Maybe that famous rare steak was bad. Could have been actual buffalo butt for all he knew. Food poisoning. Maybe that would account for his memories of Cynthia naked. Could it be hallucinations? Fantasies? He hoped so. There had been no real evidence of her stepping foot in his room this morning. No abandoned underwear or lipstick stains.

He searched the seatback pocket for the airsick bag. None.

"Jesus ... here man." The high talker shoved the bag from his seatback pocket into Jim's hands. Just in time too. Fortunately, it was just bile. The tiny bag was enough to manage until he shuffled down the aisle to the lavatory. Many eyes on him as he went. He had to stop himself from planting his fist into the face of one guy who gave him the *you pussy* smirk. Then again, the constant throbbing in his head egged on a burning desire to punch everything. He tried to think back on his anger-management class. They hadn't covered anything about working through the world's worst hangover.

The cramped quarters made it hard to puke into the metal john. He was listing back and forth with the sway of the plane. Public restrooms suck. While he balanced, he considered the thousands of bare asses and men with bad aim who had come before. His best hope was that the minimum-wage cleaning crew did a decent job before he boarded. No other choice.

Fuck. He hated being sick. Felt weak. Out of control.

It ended.

His shoulder banged the wall as he splashed water on his face. He paused to consider the state of his innards. No rumbling. No cramping. All seemed calm. For the moment.

He pushed the door to the side. "Not feeling so good this morning, Mr. Bean?"

She was standing right there. A foot from his face. The shock of seeing her made him almost stumble back. He had to catch himself on the folding door. Her voice echoed around in his skull. "No. Seems not."

With a little pout, she handed him an opened bottle of water. "Drink this."

He choked on the first swallow. Bitter. Fake limes and something spicy. He inspected the half-empty bottle. "What the hell is it?"

The plane bounced over another air pocket. He fell against her. His body responded to the feel of hers even though his head felt like it was being melted by sulfuric acid. Dammit. He hated this situation. No denying it. Hated himself for breaking his own code of ethics. Bright eyes and an impish flash of her dazzling smile convinced him the snippets were memories and not hallucinations. At the moment, drunken fragmented fantasies would have been much better.

"It's aspirin, Alka-Seltzer, and a secret ingredient. Family recipe. My college friend called it the Wings of Angels." She turned to walk back up toward the front of the plane. "Drink it, Bean. You'll feel better by the time we land. Trust me." She glanced over her shoulder and winked.

He watched her walk past his third-row seat, back to first class, and slide in. Right-hand aisle seat.

He took another swig. It was horrible, but what the hell? The only other choice was scotch. The stomach did a little complaining at just the thought of it. He waited another few seconds before making his way to his seat. This time he passed pity-filled faces. The contempt had felt better.

He settled in, chugged his liquid remedy, and then tried to close his eyes and sleep. Within seconds the frayed images from the previous night replayed like a bad horror movie preview. No hesitancy on his part. He could tell that. But the rest was unclear. Out of order.

He'd woken to an alarm set on his phone. He never set his alarm. Didn't usually need it. Maybe Cynthia had done that. But how did she unlock it? He twisted in the seat, searching for a spot on his head that didn't feel as if it was propped against a bed of nails. He didn't remember if he'd felt like he'd had sex this morning. His body was as groggy as his mind.

The guy next to him started to snore. The erratic, guttural snorting was far better than his voice had been.

10

HE HESITATED AT THE gate. Paced a small circle in the midst of the gathered throng anxiously waiting to board the plane he was very happy to have just disembarked. His head was no longer pounding, but his chest was tight. Was she waiting up ahead to speak to him? As promised, Jim felt much better. He wasn't sure he wanted to deal with her right now. Breaking his own rules and the issues it would most likely cause going forward angered him. By all rights …

"Aww. You waiting to walk me to my car?" He turned to see her maneuvering around someone's overturned bag. Didn't slow her down a hitch. She moved with the grace of a tiger.

He shook his head and bit his lip at the thought of the sleek line of her hips. "Not really." He squared his shoulders. "I should drop this case, Ms. Hodge. I have the names of a couple other capable investigators in the city. I can get any of them up to speed in an hour." He realized he was looking at the stained terminal carpet instead of her. Coward.

"What happened between us last night…" He raised his head to meet her gaze. The amused smirk on her face was demoralizing. He deserved it too. There were a few lines he just did not cross. Seducing a client was one of them.

"Don't be silly. It's not like you took my virginity, Jim." She leaned in and gave him a peck on the cheek. "You follow that lead you got. Let me know what you find."

"I think it would be best if you contracted with someone else. I apologize for my behavior in Fort Worth."

"Jim, I really appreciate your commitment to being moral or following some PI's ethical code. But we had a few drinks and we had a good time. We're both past the age of playing at making a good time into a lifetime. It was fun. It was in Texas. Today we're back here and you have a job to do. A job I'm paying you very handsomely to do."

"I…"

"Really. I won't become some love-struck teenager over this. I expect you won't either."

He really needed this job. And was genuinely curious as to what happened to Dan. So far, the facts didn't line up. Nothing pointed to drugs being the reason this boy went into hiding.

He wasn't sure he was relieved to be keeping the job and the cash or worried that she was more of a shark than he suspected. "Ms. Hodge. Please allow me to pursue the leads without following me. If I find your brother, you'll be the first to know."

Her shoulders fell and she let out a huff that reminded him of a teenage girl not getting her way. "Are we really going back to this formality, Jim?"

He didn't answer.

"Fine. I will take your request under consideration, Mr. Bean." The cold eyes and aloof look of the businesswoman from their first meeting returned. Good. He could manage that. Naked and beautiful, not so much. "However, this is *my* case, *my* brother, and *my* money. If I choose to be involved, I will. Now, go do your job."

With that, she turned and stalked down the terminal with nothing but a small carry-on bag.

11

"**YOU NO LOOK SO** happy, my friend," Ely said in a fake second-rate Mexican accent as Jim disconnected his call. Ely often did strange things, so an acute-onset accent was not a real shock.

"Strange client." He turned to see Ely talking to Annie as she sat on his counter. The cat glared at Jim's friend. Beside the fact that he was the best tech guy Jim knew, Ely was gracious enough to watch Annie when Jim was traveling or spending days on a long stakeout. Ely's urban loft was her second home.

The guy had served in Nam. A POW. He let small bits of experiences of his tour and his time in the hands of the enemy slip every now and then, but he never told the whole story. He was a badass then and a smartass now. And he was the best hacker in Vegas. The guy was older and weirder than any of the young bloods in the tech game and many lawyers didn't like Jim to use Ely because he wasn't a reliable witness. But even stoned, he was the best, and most of his cases never saw the inside of a courthouse. Jim knew when to use Ely.

Annie ducked Ely's attempt at physical contact. "I was talking to her. Don't so much care about *chew*, man." That cat loved to play hard to get. She darted up the counter just out of Ely's reach and then plopped back down to stare blankly and twitch her tail at the two men. "But now that you mention it, you do have the look of a man *wid* bad hemorrhoids."

"Annie's just hungry. *I* have a missing man that is really missing and his sister is a serious control freak."

"She the client?"

Jim knew what Ely was getting at. He gave him a shrug.

"She have the cost of admission, *hombre*?" Ely poured Annie's food from a container kept under the counter. The bowl was a permanent feature on his countertop. While eating, she let Ely run his skinny fingers down her back.

Jim put his phone in his backpack. "Yeah. Cash."

"Then you got no beef with telling the *chica* what you doing with her money." He gave Jim a creepy grin that showed way too many stained teeth.

If only it were just the giving of information. Jim still felt a little off from his drunken liaison with Cynthia Hodge. His head no longer hurt but his lack of concentration lingered like a bad odor.

"You here to take Annie home?" Ely asked.

"Not yet. Let's see if we can get anything from First Texas Federal on Daniel Hodge. Savings, ATM card, anything."

"Shit. I hate bankers, man. Almost as much as jowers. But not as much as creepy cable guys."

"What is a jower?" Jim was sure the man was stoned out of his mind. He checked for the smoky haze that hung around the high ceilings. The place was an abandoned lawyer's office. Ely bought the run-down building several years ago. It was one of the few pre-seventies buildings in the area that had not been demolished and replaced with a huge hotel. Trump must have missed the listing. Vegas loved the new and shiny. The upstairs to this unique place sported two rooms that now served as bedrooms and a gallery that was—in the past and still today—a library.

Jim's guess was the literature wasn't original to the law office. Who knew? He hadn't spent any time up there. From down here, a good part still looked like law books. The big change was artistic. Ely crafted disturbingly large metal sculptures of eagles and dragons suspended from metal and wood railings around the galley. It was a bit freaky from the ground floor to have them looming overhead all the time. But it was not his place, and Ely loved them.

Enough pot smoke to give Jim something of a contact high lingered. Maybe he could use the buzz to clear the cobwebs.

Ely held up Annie. "Jowers. You know, attorneys." He shook his head, kissed Annie. "Sorry, girlfriend," he said to Annie and put the cat on the floor. "Got to work for *the man.*"

Jim wasn't sure if he was trying to imitate a Mexican accent or if he'd done a Cheech and Chong movie marathon again. Probably the latter. "Can we drop the Spanglish?"

Annie let Ely scratch under her chin one more time before she darted for the stairs. Ely slid behind one of the terminals on his wall of servers, routers, processors, and lord knew what else. The man could find out what an FBI agent scored on their entrance exam. Tracking down a bank account should be fairly easy. It wasn't a local bank, so Jim had no connections to call upon.

Movement high and to his right caught his eye. Jim turned to see Annie circle then settle down in her favorite spot, right on the back of an eagle sculpture closer in size to a VW than the national bird. She loved the precarious position. It used to make him nervous, but Ely had moved a big cushy chair under it in case she ever rolled over in her sleep and took an unintentional dive. After all, she was hanging out near the smoke zone.

Keys clacked at the pace of Morse code. Green lines of text tracked across the screen. Ely grumbled. Jim made his way back over to the kitchen area and opened the fridge.

"I made margaritas this morning!" Ely sounded excited. "Have one. They're amazing, man. I got some Herradura from this dude for fixing his satellite feed. Good shit."

So that was the inspiration for the Spanglish this afternoon. "You got high-dollar tequila and decided it was a good idea to dilute it with juice and salt? No thanks." He was ready to be home with his own scotch and his own bed.

"Ding, ding, ding," Ely sang out and threw his hands up as if he'd scored a winning field goal.

"What you got?"

"I found a K. D. Hodge." Jim moved closer. "Utah, baby." He typed into a window and brought up the database Jim used to track people. They found two listings for K. D. Hodge in Utah. One was a small loan from a boat dealer. Paid in full two years ago. The second an account with First Texas Federal.

"Dude's got no car registration, nothing in that name. If that's your boy, he is playing a serious game of hide and stay hidden." Ely scratched the back of his head so hard Jim thought he'd draw blood.

"If he's a junkie ... " Jim started.

"No dammed junkie lives in Bryce Canyon, Utah. Seriously?"

Mountains, red rocks, tourists, and canyons are not the perfect place for someone with a serious drug habit to hang out, blend in. "There is a possibility."

Ely pulled up the Wiki page for the city of Bryce Canyon. Amazing nature shots of snow-covered rock formations and summer hikers neatly placed alongside the printed history, both natural and cultural, for the area. The last shot in the slide show was of happy travelers riding horseback through the spires and standing stones

"Of course. That's it."

"Dude's on a dude ranch!" Ely's sly giggle was more spooky than maniacal. "Gotcha."

12

THE BROKEN SPUR INN was just ten miles ahead according to the hand-painted sign Jim had recently passed. He'd rolled down his window a ways back as the elevation rose and the numbers on his car's thermometer fell. It was under 50 degrees at the moment. The air gushing into the car felt like heaven after forty-eight hours in Texas and returning to 102 in Vegas. Back home it'd still be 70 even after dark. His phone vibrated against his leg before he heard the ringtone. The number displayed on the screen made him grit his teeth. Cynthia Hodge. At least he was almost there. Too late for her to follow tonight.

"Bean," he fired.

"Where are you?" No greeting. She'd turned cold fast.

"In my car."

"Funny." But she didn't sound amused at all.

He hadn't meant to be. "It's best not to aggravate your investigator, Ms. Hodge. Slows down the progress of the case."

It was best not to sleep with clients too, but ...

She laughed. "Really? Well, I wouldn't think looking for an update would constitute aggravation. But you seem to dwell on being unhappy, Jim Bean. Maybe you should see a counselor to help with that pent-up aggression of yours."

Five years of counseling and his therapist was as done with him as he was with her sessions. "Shit doesn't work. I'm still angry."

"Maybe one day you'll tell me exactly what you're so angry about. Maybe I can help. You ooze hostility. I can feel it in the way you move, the way you look at people. Even the tone of your voice screams *asshole*. My guess is there's a correlation to the women in your life, but I'm no therapist."

Shut up. He wanted to snap it at her. But he was still spending her money in hopes of getting lots more of it. "I'm on my way to Utah. Actually, I'm in Utah as we speak. Weather's great. You *shouldn't* come."

There was a moment he thought the call had dropped. "Utah?"

"Lead on an old loan. The account was closed a couple years ago, but I'm checking it out. Gonna circulate his picture around the local dives." He saw another hand-painted sign on the right. It was in much worse shape than the last one. A splintered sandwich board only two feet high, tilted and half hidden in the red sand. White with black lettering. *Broken Spur This Way!* Under the words was a crude arrow missing more paint than not.

"Utah's a big place. What city?"

"Bryce Canyon area. Seriously, there's no sense you rushing out here, Cynthia." He used her first name, tried playing it calm enough so maybe she'd believe he wasn't hiding anything. "I'll call as soon as I know if Dan's here. I'll wait for your instructions once I know. Okay?"

Again the line was silent. The racket from his open window blocked any cellular noise from the conversation. It sounded empty.

For a second an eerie sensation crawled up his neck, tickling his hairs. Like someone was watching him. But the road was dark.

"All right, Bean. I'll give you this one. But I want to be alerted as soon as you lay an eye on him. Don't talk to him first. You got me?"

Jeez, pushy woman. "I got it."

She hung up. That time he was sure of it. The beeping of the call dropping. Cynthia Hodge was pissed. He smiled as he pulled up to the Broken Spur Saloon and Inn and parked in front. A second entrance for the saloon was on the left side of the building. More cars parked over there than out front.

He pulled the picture of his prey out of a folder and tucked it in his shirt pocket. It was dead-on midnight. A few people were heading in the direction of the saloon entrance. The rest of the night was dark and quiet. He had a sneaking suspicion Cynthia Hodge was packing her bag.

The lobby area was only populated with a couple swapping DNA on an overstuffed couch. As expected, the inn's decor was a stylized version of the early West. A carving of a howling coyote and two boot-shaped lamps sat on the front desk.

Romeo pried his lips away from his pretty little Juliet's lips. "Jay will get ya up at the bar."

Jim nodded. He headed toward the blaring country music off to the left, past the elevators. The saloon entrance was marked with swinging doors. He pushed in, wondering if people really enjoyed such over-the-top gimmicks in their travel accommodations. He just wanted a bed and bottle. Looked like he'd have both tonight.

Didn't take him long to track down Jay. She was the only one tending bar and her nametag was a dead giveaway. He was an investigator, after all.

After supplying a large number of long neck bottles to a tiny waitress, Jay turned to him. "What'll you have?"

"A room and a scotch."

"Reservations?"

"Bean, Jim Bean."

For an instant, Jay looked like she was going to say it. *Beam, like the whiskey?* But given she was a bartender, had bright intelligent eyes, and had possibly already seen his name printed out on her list of late arrivals, he correctly decided she would not.

She fingered through a couple papers next to her register, then handed him a key envelope. At least they weren't still using metal keys like in Texas. "212. Upstairs at the back. Nice view in the mornings." She poured the scotch without waiting for a reply. "Anything else, Bean, Jim Bean?"

"Kitchen open?"

She retrieved a small menu. "Just bar food. All full fat and all full flavor."

Jim glanced and ordered the burger without much thought.

She went off and attended to other customers. His stomach was as empty as the canyon out there and wasn't particularly happy about the scotch after the hangover from hell and the drive up here all in one day. He took another sip and turned to scan the room. From what he'd seen online there were only two real bars in the area. This was one. The other was a ways up north. His glance rested on each male face, trying to compare them to the picture of Dan in his head. None matched right off the bat, but the picture was old. Men changed. Grew facial hair. Went bald.

Jay set his food and a glass of water in front of him like it was a drive-by. She didn't slow a step on her way to service the small crowd. The plate was just as he expected. Burger too. Huge and dripping in cheese and barbecue sauce. The best he'd ever tasted. Given the state his body was in, boot leather would probably sate his appetite.

Jay came back to check on him.

"Let me ask you something." He slipped the pic of Dan and Cynthia onto the counter.

She looked down, blinked, and her gaze snapped back to him. Oh. She was good. Covered her recognition fast. But Jim had seen the glint for a half beat. She shook her head.

"You don't know which of the pair I was going to ask you about."

"Don't matter. Even if I did recognize them, you know we got a kind of doctor-patient confidentiality thing going in this business."

He smiled. "Nice. I'm looking for Dan. He's not in trouble. His mother's ill and his sister asked me to help find him."

She managed an eye roll in combination with the lash flutter. She was cute and smart and a hell of a bartender. "You think I'm green enough to fall for that?"

"I think you trust your gut." He pulled out his card. "I'm a PI, not a cop." He slid it over to her. "His mom's in a rest home outside Las Vegas. Her time is short." *That* might have been exaggeration. Anyone her age was short on days in his opinion.

Jay walked away again. Filled several glass mugs. Washed a few more. She glanced at him more than once. She knew something.

He finished the burger, leaving most of the fries on the plate. It was close to one a.m. when she slid him his third shot. His water glass stood full.

The place was still hopping, but the busiest part of the night was over.

"His mom's sick?"

"Alzheimer's."

62

"Damn." She huffed and then downed his shot. "You'll find him eventually, I suppose. We're a small town. He's out at Ruby's."

Jim raised his brows. As much for her taking his drink as for wanting more info on Ruby's.

"Ruby's Horse Adventures. It's north of here. He's the barn manager or head wrangler or something like that. Keeps to himself mostly. When he comes in, he's never as drunk as the rest of the bunch. Polite guy." She refilled the shot glass. "You better not be here to cause any trouble or you'll answer to me."

13

THIS PUZZLE WAS NOT coming together, and not for missing pieces. To Jim, the mystery had a couple wrong pieces in the mix. Like a puzzle of a cat with random pieces from an Eiffel Tower picture thrown in just to mess with your head. None of Dan's acquaintances had any knowledge of the guy ever using drugs. His existence was so far off the grid he was close to impossible to find. Took a lot of work to have an electronic footprint so light. No Facebook. No cell that could be traced to his name. No job on record. And yet, here he was, a head wrangler or something at a resort in Utah.

Jay had made it sound as though he'd been around long enough for her to judge his character. Bartenders were good at that. And his experience in Vegas had told him female bartenders were particularly talented at it. Jim had been tossed out of some pretty low places by some pretty tough ladies.

He drove the quiet road north the next morning, following a bus from the Broken Spur Inn. It pulled up to the opening of a huge barn.

Jim parked at the far end of the lot and watched as hotel guests filed off the aging blue shuttle bus.

He mingled into the back of the group as they made their way to be checked in by a couple of smiling young girls in tight jeans and dirty cowboy hats. He lingered as parts of the group were led off in different directions. Older and less-mobile to the wagon rides, younger and more-agile to the horseback rides. To the left side of the barn was a sign: NO GUESTS BEYOND THIS POINT. Looked like the path led to the main house and the back of a snack bar/gift shop building. No doubt the buggy rides let off directly in front of *that* building when finished. Like how theme parks now guide guests through gift shops after they get off the rollercoaster. Sales. Sales. Sales.

Farther along were cabins. Plain. Not for vacationers. Living quarters. Eight doors. If they all had two bunks, at least sixteen of these hands lived on site. Would explain why there were no real estate or rental records for Dan Hodge. Beyond those were wide open spaces, fenced paddocks with horses milling about, and another big barn. The closest was rugged, less painted than the one customers came through. Likely for working rather than impressing guests. A lot of people around in the Ruby's T-shirts but none were his guy.

He eased his way to the edge of the barn. Two horses were tied in the aisle between rows of stalls that lined each side of the building. Both were resting with one back leg relaxed and seemed content to be tethered and left alone. Better than pulling a wagon. Jim moved along the outside of the barn. It smelled like a horse ranch back here. He peeked around the corner. A tall, thin guy was giving instructions to a young kid with a clipboard. Jim's gut told him the tall cowboy was Dan. His jeans were clean and pressed, his shirt only wrinkled from where he'd sat down, nice crease still down the sleeve. The thing that confirmed what his gut knew was the name *Kent* stamped on his leather belt.

The horse tied closest to Jim snorted his displeasure at being ignored. Both men turned to look. Jim backed around the corner, but they'd spotted him. His choices were few—turn and run or face the music. They were close and knew this area. Nowhere to go out there but the parking lot or the wilderness. His instinct told him to stay put. Cynthia would just have to get over it; he was gonna talk to Dan first. Besides, this guy was no junkie. Jim's gut was talking to him, he just had to figure out what it had to say.

"Can we help you, mister?" Dan and the much younger man stuck their heads around the corner. Dan tilted his head a bit. "Insurance company says you can't be back here, sir."

They'd given him an out. He could leave and follow Cynthia's orders. "Sorry."

He felt that tingle on his neck again right before he was going to turn and walk away, following her orders. His feet stayed put.

"Are you the boss round here?" he asked, looking at Dan.

"Of the horses, yeah. That's 'bout it."

"I have a couple questions about running a barn, you have a minute?"

Dan looked at the other guy. "Don't worry. I'll get the meds from Doc Milton." With that the kid rushed off toward the main building and the parking lots. "I need to get these two out in the paddock. Can you walk and talk?"

"No problem." Ah, the needs of a workingman. This workingman was clearly *not* on drugs. Possibly never had been on drugs. What was Cynthia's motive for saying so? Jim would have found Dan for the money. He didn't need to be convinced to hunt someone down. Why the misdirection? And why did it matter to him now? He should back away, call the client, and get his money. Job done.

The guy unhooked the horse and spun it toward Jim. "Hold her." He handed Jim a rope attached to the animal's head. The beast had to weigh a ton, maybe more. She was sniffing his arm, her lips nibbling at his sleeve.

"Is she a biter?"

Dan walked past with the other horse. "Only if you bite first."

The horse followed right on her horsey friend's tail. Jim was along for the ride. He didn't want to bring up anything until he was not attached to a thousand pounds of animal that could kill him with her feet. Dan opened the gate and spun the horse around and took off her head strap. He took the rope from Jim and did the same with that one. It was impressive just how hard they ran to the open pasture, kicking and farting along the way. It was amazing to see in real life. He'd been a city boy most of his life and had never been really close to horses.

"Now." Dan latched the gate. "What can I help you with?"

"You ever ride rodeo?"

The man's eyes narrowed. "A thousand years ago. Yeah."

"In Stephenville, Texas?"

Dan's body stiffened. He took a step back. Boy was going to run.

"I'm not a cop. You're not in trouble."

"You say?"

"Didn't see any paper on you." No warrants, no tickets, no nothing.

"And who are you, mister?" Dan's hip cocked. It was not a fighting stance.

"Jim Bean. I'm from Vegas. A PI. Your sister hired me to find you."

Dan's face twisted up and he scratched his cheek. "My sister? I talked to my sister last month. What the heck would she hire you for?"

Jim's expression must have mirrored his confusion.

"What exactly did *my sister* say?" Dan's expression changed in a heartbeat from confused teenager to frightened child.

"That you'd been missing for a while." Jim leaned against the fence for support. His gut was screaming at him loud and clear. There was something wrong here. This boy was not a drug addict. Never had been. Cynthia had lied to him about her brother. She followed Jim to Texas, got him drunk and seduced him, probably to keep him off-guard. Keep him from thinking about her or the job too much.

If Dan was telling the truth that meant *Cynthia* was the puzzle piece he hadn't expected? The odd part that didn't fit quite right? "What... what does your sister look like, Dan?"

"Blond. Short, a little thin."

"Oh, fuck." This was as bad as bad got if the kid wasn't playing him.

"What did she look like when *you* met her?" Dan stepped a little closer trying to loom over Jim.

Jim had thought he had all his ducks in a neat quacking row and now the little bastards were scattering. The feeling of not being in control, not being sure of himself, dug in his side like a spur. That woman had followed him all the way to Texas to make sure Jim did not speak to Dan. Now he might know why. And to top it off, they'd...

"Redhead. Shapely. Green eyes."

"Sophie. Oh my fuck. Was she in Vegas? Did she talk to my sister?"

"Who is Sophie?"

Dan started walking toward the cabins. He cursed and shook his head. Jim caught up as he hit the wood porch. A single rocking chair sat next to the upside-down bucket that worked as a table. He stopped. "Sophie was a girl I grew up with. We hung out some. I grew up, moved on. She showed up years later when I was in college. The crazy bitch couldn't take no for an answer." He took his hat off, then ran his hand through his hair. "The girl I was dating at the time suddenly disappeared. I was investigated. Almost accused. None of us thought of Sophie as a suspect. I had an alibi. The case was never solved. Sophie disappeared again." He let his thin back slam against the wall. He slammed his booted foot backwards. Boards cracked.

Jim's FUBAR meter sounded the alarm. Dread churned with the acid in his stomach. Been a while since he'd screwed up *this* bad.

"When Sophie showed up next, it was at a rodeo. I was hooking up with some buckle bunny at a bar. Sophie got all pissed. Said I was cheating on her. Cursed out the girl. Poor thing was no one I'd even met before that night. The next day that girl went missing too. They found her with her throat slit two days later." He rubbed his eyes with enough force Jim heard the squeaking sound of it.

"So you've been living a cash-only life out here in the middle of Utah to hide from Sophie." And Jim had led the spider right to the fly.

"I wasn't sure what to do. I was ready to leave the rodeo circuit anyway. Not being where she'd likely be looking for me only made the idea more appealing. It's not like I was settled down in Texas. I drank too much, played too much, whored around too much." Dan's gaze went out to the stunning rock formations. The view from his porch was travel-magazine perfect. "Turns out the quiet life suits me right down to my Justins. I do my job. Read. Sleep. I don't miss the traveling or the partying at all."

Dan let his head fall back to the wood siding. "It's been seven years. After a couple without hearing word one from her, I was sure she'd gone off and found someone else to obsess over. Or maybe I was overreacting. Either way, Sophie needed some serious help."

"This your place?"

He nodded.

"Let's go inside."

Jim looked around the barn lots before closing the door behind him. The one-room cabin reflected Dan's words. A single worn, over-stuffed chair with a thick blanket sat in front of a fireplace. A pot hung over cold coals. Small table for two and an efficient little kitchen. The couch and chair that made up the living room were made of carved logs. Reminded Jim of a lodge in Montana he once stayed in when he was trying to forget his own past. No TV. No phone. Jim understood.

What a fucking mess. The kid had to be right. And that being the case, Cynthia—no, *Sophie*—had had overnight to catch up to him. He eased over to the thin curtains and peeked out the edge. She was not in plain sight. The day seemed eerily quiet out there. Only a few horses milled about with their heads to the ground, chomping what little grass they could find. No breeze moving their tails, not a soul in sight. Everyone must be on the trail ride by now.

"You're convinced she killed those girls?"

"I need to call Cynthia." Dan pulled a cheap throwaway phone from a kitchen drawer.

"Not a good idea. I think she has Cynthia's phone." Jim pulled out the old photograph. He had to know. If he'd brought danger to this kid, he would never forgive himself. And if that was the case, he worried over Sophie's current mental condition. Well, this was why.

How many times was he going to let his guard down only to have a woman blindside him?

"Is this Sophie?"

Dan sat back on the bed gripping the picture in both hands. They trembled a little. His mouth was a tight straight line and his brows drew in. "Yes, sir. That's her."

Crap.

Jim's mission had just changed.

14

SOPHIE DROVE PAST THE cluster of barns and parked in a little-used driveway to a ranch up the rocky hill from Ruby's Horse Adventures. The overgrown grass might be a result of neglect, but it looked more like abandonment to her.

She lifted the hood on Cynthia's car just in case someone came up the long drive. More than likely it wouldn't be a problem, but she didn't want to explain herself if someone stopped and questioned her.

Through her binoculars, she found Jim's car in the middle of the lot. Just about where the GPS locator she'd attached under his bumper told her it had stopped. After Bean got so upset in Texas, his forthcomingness with information was in doubt. So this was the easiest way to keep in the loop with instant updates. Follow him. So when she'd called last night, she wasn't far behind him.

The idea of tracking the tracker gave her a little thrill. She stretched her neck to the side. The audible pops told her it was time to relax. Bean was checking out a horseback riding business in Utah. It was a perfect place to find her Danny. She'd called around and asked at a bunch of them in Texas years ago when Danny first got lost. She'd had no luck. She would have never guessed Utah. Bean had been a good investment.

Sophie took a drink and patted her side, making sure her blade was in its place. In the event Bean called and confirmed Danny was there … She shivered. Always be prepared.

You learned the hard way, didn't you?

She shook her head. "That was a long time ago." When she was experimenting with the tranquilizer in the auto injectors, she didn't think she might need more than one per outing. After stalking a woman for hours through the garish bars in Dallas, Sophie broke the needle in her skinny neck before the shit could be injected. She'd had to fight the bitch before she could kill her. It'd been much more physical than Sophie would have liked. Number Nine.

Too much contact with her germ-laden skin. Excessive physcial contact could lead to DNA transfer to your victim as she pathetically tries to scratch her way free.

Sophie took pride in her strength. Working out five days a week ensured she could hold her own enough to get the job done, but the fight-or-flight response could make even a drunk socialite stronger than one would imagine.

You've made a few mistakes.

"Back then," she snapped at the voice in her head. Always critical, derogatory. But she was better now. She'd gotten exceedingly good at getting better. Of using her brains and her brawn to move ahead. She rubbed the back of her neck. She was sweating. Heart pounding. "Now I'm smarter."

Stealth, perfect. Danny would be so impressed with what she'd done to create a place where they could live happily.

She swept the binoculars around to the opening of the barn and all the activity of the unloading bus. She saw no sign of Bean or Danny. Something moved to the side of the barn. She'd found her PI. He was watching around the corner. The barn blocked her view of what he was looking at. Jim started back toward his car at a good pace but stopped short when Danny and another man approached him.

She gripped the plastic of the binoculars. Driving hard all night had not done her nerves any favors. "No! Dumbass. What part of *don't talk to him* didn't you get? Do what you're being paid for!"

Danny approached Bean. Her clenched jaw was so tight her grinding teeth echoed in the still air.

She closed her eyes and took in a deep breath, used her inner strength to calm. *Breathe in through the nose, out through the mouth* her yogi would chant during class. It kept her calm and she desperately needed that now. Rushing down there to throttle that PI, no matter how much pleasure that would bring, would do no good. She focused on the ultimate goal. Danny in her sights.

In through the nose. Out through the mouth. A moment of joy and excitement was well deserved. A scant celebration even, if only internal. There had been so much preparation, buildup, this was not the climax she'd hoped for. She'd wanted to come into his life by rushing into his arms. Bean had ruined that fantasy moment forever.

Anger is not your friend. Control is your friend. Anticipation had been growing, consuming her for the last year. And there he stood, as beautiful as he'd been ten years ago at twenty-three, still fit and looking good in those jeans and boots. He smiled for just an instant. A giddy rush of excitement washed though her. Soon they would be bound together. As it was meant to be.

Only Bean needed to walk the fuck away. She pressed the glass hard to her face and watched, not caring if there would be a round impression in her skin. The conversation looked light. Maybe it was just small talk. Why hadn't she taken a lip-reading class? She'd taken about everything else under the sun over the last seven years. An extended conversation between these two would ruin everything. It wouldn't take Bean long to figure out her story was a lie. Danny wasn't a junkie.

I told you that backstory would be a risk.

"Shut up. I know. But I needed a good excuse for the cops being left out of the search for a missing person." She shook her head and kicked a little rock at the stupid car.

Should have told him Danny was a thief.

"But then he may have insisted on police involvement. Or decided not to be involved in finding him without having him arrested after."

She marched about three feet and spun around. Hopefully Bean was just chatting, getting her precious information on her "brother." The asshole loser needed her cash. With any luck he wouldn't give two shits about the why of finding anyone. She looked through the binocs again.

Not really his business at all, is it?

"PIs would go broke if they only took cases that found out good things about good people."

They moved, and she found them in time to see them entering a cottage.

No telling what Bean's thoughts were until he let her know.

An hour later, they hadn't come out.

"Fuck." Sophie slammed the hood down.

There's always a plan B.

"Too soon for that."

15

DETECTIVE MILLER WAS ON the phone, running down what his guys intended to do, but Jim was distracted as Dan slammed a pair of boots into an old duffle bag. The thing was covered in rodeo patches and torn in two places.

Dan was making a living here, but it was simple. Cheap. Jim couldn't help but think of Dan as a boy who needed help, running from a past that was not in his control. Living on an as-needed basis. Using what was left of his skills as a rodeo star to be a ranch hand at a cheesy tourist trap. Spooky similar to Jim's running to Vegas and using what was left of his life to start his investigative agency.

Dan's face was beet red. The color spread to his neck. "I have to get to Cynthia. If Sophie…" Dan mumbled as his panic peaked.

Jim finished up his conversation with Miller. The guy was a good cop with the Las Vegas Police Department. The police worked *with* PIs most of the time, provided you weren't moving in on a case they were working. And provided you weren't a pain in the ass. Jim usually managed to break both those caveats.

"I talked to a detective in Vegas. He's putting out a BOLO for Sophie and sending uniforms to check on your sister right away."

Dan had convinced Jim that Sophie was, in fact, playing him. It took all of five minutes. Dan had pictures of both women. His sister looked just like her mother, Lynette, in the nursing home. Plus this client had felt odd to him from the beginning.

Clearly, Sophie had lied to him. Used him. Violated him? What if he hadn't just been drunk in Texas? What if she'd drugged him? Hard to wrap your head around being sexually assaulted by a woman. No way. It couldn't be. He'd wanted her. He remembered that much. Remembered the way she felt.

Then again, if he was not under the influence of alcohol or drugs, he would never sleep with a client. Wouldn't under any circumstance confuse the professional relationship. *Fuck.* He fought off a wave of bile threatening to bring back his breakfast.

And if she had really killed two people associated with Dan ten years ago, there was a bigger problem to deal with than what had happened in that Texas hotel room.

"Dan. Slow down. We need to think this through. She hired me to find you. If she was anxious enough to follow me to Texas, there's a good chance she's right on my ass now. Here."

Dan made a deep growling sound. "No one's called me Dan since I left Texas and right now all I can hear is Sophie saying my name." He slid a light straw cowboy hat onto his head. The mirror by the door caught his attention. With a quiet hesitation he said, "I'm Daniel Hodge."

He grabbed up his bag and shook it to make more room. "I want my name back. Sophie's a ghost I didn't want to tangle with, but she's back. I need this to stop. I've got to make sure my mom and Cynthia are okay."

"I get that." Jim had changed his name to run away from something he'd wanted to forget as well. One difference: he hated the sound of his birth name now. No going back. Never wanted it back.

Dan paused. "Did you tell her you were coming here?"

"In general. But not specifically." Jim caught the shaving bag Dan tossed toward the bed. "Look. Let me drive you to Vegas. We'll meet with Detective Miller. He's a friend of mine. A good cop too. We'll check it all out. We'll find her and settle this mess for good."

"I can drive to Vegas."

"I know you can. Fact is, if she followed me, she's got a line on you. I want to be able to protect you."

"She won't hurt me." Dan put his hands on his hips and looked up at the ceiling. "She wants me. She's had this fantasy of us being married and shit since she was a kid. I told her not to think that way a thousand times. It just got worse. She got more and more needy."

"Don't be so sure. I once saw a woman shoot her husband in the foot over a few bucks. Women are not afraid to do some damage. She's been looking for you for a while if she went to this kind of extreme."

Jim did the math in his head. She could have left right after their phone call last night. Time was running out if she had followed. "Listen, Dan. I hate that I brought this on you. I do. But it's done. I can help you. I have friends that can help you. The longer we stay here, the more chance she knows I found you. We need the time to get to Vegas before she does. That way, we can catch her before she does any more harm."

Dan jerked the zipper shut on the bag. "Fine. But she knows your car. We should take my truck."

Made sense. "Okay."

"I'm driving." Dan tossed his head to the back of the cabin. "Truck's out back."

They exited the cabin: there were three trucks sitting back there. Two were regular, base model, everyday pickups. They walked past those to a small lean-to shed. Inside was a fire engine red eighties Ram with twin pipes that shot up over the back glass and exhausted above the cab. It was jacked higher than a street truck, but not so much the thing would tip over in a tight curve. Chrome everywhere. Pretty thing. Dan walked up and tossed the bag in the back.

He got in and started up the truck. It roared like a bear on a mission.

"So much for living a quiet life."

"A guy's gotta have a hobby." Dan tilted his hat. "Consider it hiding in plain sight."

"I'll feel like a sitting duck in this thing. Might as well have a target painted on the tailgate."

"If you don't like it, you can ride on your own. I want to be able to do my own thing if I need to."

"Disappear again?"

"No offense, dude, but if I have to, I will. Right now, I just want to check on my sister."

"I need to grab a few things from my car." Jim didn't want the man going to Cynthia's at all. The drive was almost five hours. He suspected they'd get a call from Miller about Cynthia long before they hit the Vegas city limits. And then there was another soul to worry over. Dan had not mentioned her and Jim forgot to have Miller check on Dan's mom in the rest home.

"Wait here." Jim scooted back the way he'd come, ducking behind fence rails and water troughs. He eyed the surroundings. Only one good vantage point to spy on the open area and a car similar to the one Sophie had been driving was sitting right there next to an old mailbox. He didn't have his binocs, so he couldn't verify, but his intuition told him it was her.

He crawled along parked vehicles to his car. She wouldn't be able to see. He slowly opened the driver's door and pulled out his laptop bag and his small duffle. The rest would have to stay put for a few days. With any luck the ranch owner would have it towed. Impound's a safe place for a car to be.

He crawled back to the barn and made his way around the cabin keeping fairly good cover. With any luck, he hadn't been spotted. But everyone knew Jim's luck sucked.

"Go."

16

MILLER'S CALL CAME BEFORE the screaming red truck crossed the Nevada border. The detective's voice was shaky. "It's a fucking mess in there, Bean."

Not what Jim wanted to hear. He'd been holding out hope that this was all a nightmare. He wasn't sure his reputation could survive getting hired by a killer to help her find the object of her obsession. "Yeah?"

"Throat cut. Left to decompose in the tub with some drain cleaner to speed it along. Looks like Sophie has been staying in the vic's house with the body. She's been living in the space with the vic in that tub. Clear evidence she's been eating in the kitchen and she's slept in Cynthia's bed."

"Damn."

"More than damn. ME's doing his thing to collect her now. He'll probably have her out before you two roll into town, but I think it's best your boy doesn't come here until we've cleared out and there's been some clean up. Not how I'd want to remember my sister. Bring him to the station. I'll meet you there."

Now Jim really wished he'd not forgotten to tell Miller to check on Dan's mother. The acid in his stomach churned and his pulse sped up at the thought of something so horrid happening to an elderly woman. She was all alone in that nursing home.

"Check his mother. Silver Hills nursing home on North Buffalo."

"Ahead of you for once. Saw some paperwork on Cynthia's desk. Already tracked her. She's fine. Got a uniform outside her room."

The sense of relief was almost as good as the burning of a good scotch going down this throat. Would not have wanted to deliver that much bad news to Dan. Cynthia's death was going to be hard enough.

"Check in when you get in town."

"Will do. Thanks, Miller." Jim hung up and glanced over at Dan. His face was tight. Grim. He knew what the call was about.

"Why don't you let me drive for a bit? I won't scratch the paint, I promise." Jim looked straight forward, not wanting to see the pain in the kid's eyes. Not wanting to be the guy to deliver the painful blow. Jim glanced his way.

Dan was chewing on his upper lip. "She's dead?"

No real need to answer. Silence was the coward's way out and Jim was going to take it.

Dan screeched to a stop on the shoulder, slammed the truck in to park, and got out. At first he just looked across the cloudless sky with his hands propped on his hips and his shoulders sagged. He closed his eyes tight for a moment, chin trembling, and then he took in a long breath. Tears escaped the outer corners of his eyes. He made no move to rub them away.

Jim felt the anger and grief roll off Dan like steam as he lumbered a hundred yards or so down the shoulder of the highway. He spun and paced back, his boots scuffing the asphalt at a military pace. He turned again and stopped with his back turned. His shoulders shook.

Jim stood numb-footed next to the truck. Staying impartial over this case was no longer possible. Sophie had made sure of that. He internally raged at the thought of his night with her, wishing she was within reach so he could choke the life from her. Sooner or later his night with her would come out. He'd have to talk to Miller or someone about it. Maybe. If she'd drugged him and used him as a distraction from the case, or as a ploy to keep him off her track. Using his self-doubt and self-blame to keep him from seeing behind her deadly mask. He didn't know Cynthia or Dan, but their lives were forever changed by Jim's fuck up. Vetting customers who paid cash wasn't something he always did. He'd only run checks on the guys who wanted him to work on credit. That would change.

Jim made his way to the front of the truck.

Dan paced down the road and back once more. He used his sleeve to clean his face and sniffed as he met up with Jim and leaned against the hood as well, both facing south, toward Vegas.

"I'm sorry, Dan."

"How?"

"You'll get the details ... "

"How?"

He deserved to know. "Throat cut."

Dan's eyelids clinched shut again. Jim chose to leave the rest of the details for Miller to pass on. "Your mother's fine. They have a uniform outside her room to make sure she stays that way."

Dan nodded again. "Now what?"

"We go see Miller. They'll probably want to put you and your mom in some sort of protective custody while they trace Sophie."

Dan kept looking straight ahead, as if looking at Jim—at anyone—would cause him to break.

"Miller says the FBI is looking for Sophie as well. Got a flag when he ran her name. Not really a surprise, given the lengths she went to. She may have killed more than just those two girls you suspected."

One small nod. "Cynthia's dead. I can't believe it. I should have figured Sophie would use my family to get to me."

"No way you could know she'd go this far. Blaming yourself is counterproductive at this point. She's out there. We need to help the cops help you."

Dan stared down the perpetual white line toward Vegas.

"Let me drive you in. You relax. Think of anything you might be able to give the police that will help catch her."

Jim thought the man would argue. His body was stiff and his face tight, defensive.

"What's she like now?" His voice cracked slightly.

"Sophie?"

"Yeah." He looked at Jim, his eyes etched with grief.

"When she hired me, she was in a suit. Direct. Gave me cash. Not a lot of emotion. Just how I like my clients." He neglected to mention how much that changed the next time he'd seen her.

"I could rip that crazy daughter-of-a-boondock-whore to shreds with my bare hands. No remorse. No guilt."

"I'm no doctor, but I'm certain that's a damn normal reaction to the situation. We could make it a party."

"Are they going to find her?"

"Yeah. If LVPD doesn't, I will. That's what I do."

17

SEVERAL COP CARS AND a big van sat outside Cynthia Hodge's shitty little house as Sophie cruised by acting like a lookie-loo neighbor. Her scalp itched in the short blond wig, and the stupid dog in the back of the van wouldn't quit whining, but she would have to make do until she figured the lay of the land. Two men in street clothes with badges at their waists stood out front talking with a uniformed cop. Slacks and dress shirts meant those were the guys in charge.

A block away, she parked and got the dog out.

The scruffy-looking mutt had been tied up outside a roadside restaurant where she had stopped to pee on the road back from Utah. Seeing the squeaky little thing had given her an idea. On the way out, he was still there, and still eager for attention. Sophie baby talked as she slipped his leash off the post and absconded with the dog. Now he was happy as pie to be walking along beside her. A grand adventure, it seemed. They rounded the corner and walked causally down the street, directly across from the house with the dead body inside. Cynthia's

84

house. Sophie paused as the pup peed on a street sign and the big van pulled away. Likely the ME picking up her mess.

So *it* wasn't there any longer. Sophie cursed herself for not taking a photo or even a peek at the deterioration the drain cleaner caused before leaving the house. The decay would have been far from finished, but the melted patterns of her flesh would have been cool as hell. No matter.

She got a good look at the guy in the front yard. Men in charge were always easy to pick out. With cops it was even easier. They all felt they were better, special. This one oozed that hubris as others approached for instructions, information. Within a few seconds, he glanced at her. She gave him an uneasy smile and worried eye contact for long enough to get his attention, no more. The actions said she was just a curious neighbor. He gave her a curt nod.

Perfect.

No further interaction was needed and she urged the dog to abandon whatever smell had him so intrigued and move on. It had not been soon enough. Next thing she knew a uniform was hurrying up the street after her.

"Ma'am … Ma'am."

She stopped as he closed in. Without fear, the mutt jumped on his pants legs, wiggling his tail, begging for attention. She gave the officer a big smile. No need to make an attempt to remove the distraction.

"I'm … "

"Going to ask me if I know what happened at that house, right?"

He returned her pleasantry with his own smile. Guy needed dental work. Shouldn't the state have a plan for that or something? She almost asked but he spoke first.

"Do you know Cynthia Hodge?"

Hearing her name almost made Sophie cringe. That person was gone. But she kept the fake smile over her face. She'd used the same plastic mask to cover her emotions for years and it hadn't failed to fool yet.

"No. Sorry. I'm house sitting a block away." She pointed over her shoulder to indicate a vague direction. "I've only been in the neighborhood since yesterday."

The mutt was still jumping, whining for attention. The officer relented and bent down to give him a friendly little head rub. Frumpy brown hair flopped with the motion. "Cute dog. What's his name?"

Her mind was suddenly blank. Sophie had never had a pet. She'd never been allowed one when she was younger and never wanted the stinking things around since she could make that kind of decision on her own. An arbitrary pet name shouldn't be so hard to conjure. "Carl."

"Carl?"

That was dumb. But it was the best thing she had. She shrugged. "Like I said, house sitting. He's not mine."

"So, I guess that means you didn't notice anything unusual in the last couple days?"

"I wouldn't know unusual for this place. I live near the Strip. Not much around here would make it high on the unusual scale for me."

"Okay. Thanks." He handed her a card.

She tilted her head to indicate the crime-scene-tape-encased yard. "What's the detective's name? The one in the blue shirt."

"Miller, ma'am."

Miller was now getting in a navy blue Charger, unmarked. She memorized the plate.

"Would you prefer to talk to him?"

"Oh no. I really can't help you." She smiled at him and pulled the dog away. "He just looked familiar." She walked off, wondering at what pace one walks a creature that wants to stop and smell everything.

They're going to figure it out this time. You've left a mess, girl. All kinds of trace evidence in there.

"Shut up. I cleaned up good before leaving. Always do. Oxy bleach and a good wet nap makes short work of a room. No prints will be in there."

She turned the corner and circled around back to the main drag. Now she had two separate people to follow. If Bean brought Danny back to Vegas so that cop could put him in a safe house, Sophie would find him. Not exactly plan A.

I told you that lie was too weak for a paid investigator.

"The man was cheap and easy. His dead eyes said so. I always knew the motive was the weak part of the PI plan. No matter what I said, there was a chance he'd figure it out before delivering my Danny. But it worked out, didn't it?"

Not a sound from inside her head.

"Don't like it when I'm right, do you? Bitch."

She pushed on her temple. At all the nagging and hate.

I am what you are. Who you are. You can pretend all you want. But …

Loser.

Fat.

Ugly.

Stupid …

Hate. Hate. Hate.

She rounded the corner with the pup in tow and found the car down the street. No one behind her, no one around the car. She looked down at the dog. "Plan B is really not that bad." He wagged his curled tail at her. His little eyes were so cheerful and he seemed excited to be on the adventure.

She lifted him back into the car.

You're not going to bring that mangy animal with us, are you?

"No mange on this guy. Smells like flowers, means he's been groomed. So shut the fuck up."

Sophie drove off without a look back. All she had to do was figure out what they'd done with Danny. After driving a few blocks north, she pulled into a random parking lot behind a closed tire center. She searched her pack for Cynthia's cell phone. The dog jumped to the passenger seat and licked her hand as she fumbled. She'd have to stop and get him something to eat on the way home.

Tomorrow she'd find the dang safe house. Wouldn't be a problem at all, but there were so many players to follow. Following was her strong suit, not finding. That's why she'd needed Bean. Now she would follow him or that detective or...

"Silver Hills. How can I help you?"

"Yes. I'm looking for my aunt Lynette. Lynette Hodge. Is she available to chat?"

"I'll connect the room." It was likely both Cynthia's phone and the nursing home's phones were being monitored. But that was okay. For now.

The line clicked and then rang in the old lady's room. And rang. Seven. Eight. She hung up the cell phone and then turned off the power in case the police could trace the location. The TV shows said they could. Her research was a little wishy-washy. No matter. Better safe than sorry. Time to get rid of the thing. She tossed it as hard as she could toward a dumpster. It bounced off the side and broke.

Fingerprints!

Sophie squeezed the steering wheel. "I know. Damn it," she growled at herself in the rearview mirror, then got out and stomped over to the bin.

The stink reminded her of a hot South Dallas Friday night. Walking the streets, picking pockets and hooking. She felt no shame in the memory, just a satisfaction. That shit had been the foundation of everything she'd built for herself, and for Danny, the beginning of the journey, the first brick in her financial house.

She found the three biggest pieces of the shattered glass and plastic. She dumped a glob of hand sanitizer on the tail of her shirt and used that to rub the phone parts down as best she could, taking extra time around the mouth and ear sections to kill off or remove any DNA. The she tossed them off into different directions.

"All clean."

What would you do without me?

"Celebrate." She got back behind the wheel of the rental and drove southeast. The pup eased into her lap. Thing couldn't weigh six pounds and she found herself giving in to the urge to rub his head.

"We'd have a big old party to dance the night away in honor of her demise. Wouldn't we?" she said in baby talk to the pup.

Don't let it touch you like that. It's probably got fleas.

Sophie sighed. Carl turned his little head as if to empathize.

The sun was setting in the rearview. She lit her first cig of the day. The surge of nicotine would clear her mind. Yes. The PI had complicated things. But he was still useful.

Until he is ... expendable.

She blew out a puff of smoke, followed its path to the cracked passenger side window. The reflection of her face was clouded in the smoke, making her look young.

"Everyone's expendable."

18

DETECTIVE MILLER LED JIM and Dan past the front desk at the Boulder Area Command Center where a young officer awkwardly avoided eye contact with Dan.

Hard to deal with people in pain when you first start this type of work. Kid must be straight out of the academy. Didn't take long to realize that most civilians who come through the door of a station-house were suffering or in big trouble. The vics may have suffered everything from loss of a loved one to loss of property. Hurt and violation existed somewhere along a sliding scale that ranged from irritation to devastation. It all showed in the eyes.

The conference room came to an immediate hush as the door swept open and Miller led the young man in. A blown up copy of Cynthia's driver's license was pinned on the wall. A fact sheet with her vital info was tacked below it. Fortunately, no crime scene photos were pasted up. Yet.

"I'm sorry for your loss." Miller pulled out a chair facing the mirrored wall and set down a bottle of water. Dan took it. As usual, Jim opted to stand with his back against the wall, but this time he chose a spot close to Dan.

"I have coffee if you want it. The Command Center has the best in Vegas." Miller slid his fingers around his waistband to straighten his tucked shirt. Jim had seen him do it a thousand times. As if he needed to pull his pants up, but he didn't. The man was feeling for his gun belt, the one he no longer wore since being promoted to detective. Jim figured no matter how long the detective had been out of a patrolman's uniform, he wasn't used to missing the weight of a gear belt.

"Not now." Dan managed a sip from the bottle.

"The medical examiner is with your sister. We should have a better idea of time of death when he's finished. But the crime scene tells a pretty clear story." Miller looked back to Jim.

Jim would give his left nut to shield Dan from this conversation.

Miller put his hand on the back of Dan's chair. "Looks like she was planning to go to a convention. It came up pretty last minute, according to her boss. He saw her Wednesday."

"She travels to train people at other companies all the time. Accounting software stuff." Dan picked at a bit of the water bottle label, peeling it away from the glue line that held the cellophane wrapper around the plastic. He didn't make eye contact with anyone in the room.

"That's what he said. From her phone records, we can see she called a cab company. Then an hour or so later, Mr. Bean was called. Last we have on her is that. No credit card usage. Nothing."

Miller paused. "Cab company sent out a driver named Lulu Strong. Said she was closest to the address. Lulu only worked for them for about four weeks." Miller pulled a page from a dark green folder. The

91

contents were already a good inch think. The paper was a fuzzy copy of a Nevada driver's license. "You recognize her?"

Jim sure did. Her hair was pulled back in a messy ponytail, she was wearing a headband, and she had a bad makeup job going, but that was Sophie.

"Sophie Ryan Evers." Dan's hands trembled as he pulled more of the label away.

Miller twisted back to address Jim. "This the girl who told you she was Cynthia Hodge?"

"It is." Jim's skin itched with the need for another shower. Images of the night in his Texas hotel room played in his head like a bad music video. One of those catchy songs he didn't like and couldn't shake from his mind. Thankfully, the memories were vague. He wished them gone. But, wishes got only empty pockets and headaches. Nothing more.

"How do you know her?"

Dan huffed out a tired laugh. "She moved in next door when I was about fourteen. Lived with a foster family. Not a good one. Her real dad had killed himself. Her mother left her in a department store when she was a toddler." He pushed away from the table and leaned back in his chair. Crossed his arms. "I felt bad for her. So I hung out with her some."

"How old was she?" Miller took notes on a fancy electronic tablet. No more paper for the Vegas police.

"About nine or ten. I don't remember exactly. Her foster mom was a bitch. The dad was a drunk. I think he was abusing her, but she never would talk about it. Got real mad if I even tried to ask about home, you know? It didn't take long for her to get real attached to me. I knew it. But like I said, I thought the kid needed a friend. My mom would let her come to dinner and stuff, you know?"

"Sounds like a nice thing to do."

"It was. Until I hit high school and wanted to date and shit." Dan got up from the table and paced to the far corner. "Sophie didn't like that at all. She got mad if she found out I was talking to a girl. I tried to explain that she was too young. That she and I were just friends."

"Did she get violent?"

"With me?" Dan shook his head.

"With the girls you were talking to?"

"She threatened me and them, but I never believed she'd act on it. I mean, she was like twelve years old. Even with all that, I would still hang out with her some. But she'd gotten mean by the time she was sixteen or seventeen."

"Mean?"

"You know, liked to hassle cashiers in the super-mart or rush the old lady in front of her at Mickey D's. Sophie was always bitching about the kids at her middle school, and she cursed way too much. Once, she told me she wanted to chop the popular girls' hair off or cut up their faces so they wouldn't be so pretty and powerful anymore." He shook his head and then pointed a finger at Miller. "And she really hated the boys in her class. I think she got suspended once for beating up one kid. Hit him in the head with a rock in the parking lot."

Dan picked up the bottle as if to drink, then set it back down. "She'd gotten to be a real manipulator too. The chick could talk my mom out of cash. She easily got out of trouble with the teachers. I think she even talked her way out of getting arrested for *borrowing* a car once. And her grades were excellent."

Dan moved again. Just a few paces, as if to get away from the things he was saying. Not enough space in the conference room to walk away from those memories.

"She liked classical music when the rest of us were into country. Could have been opera too. It sounded so dark and depressing to me. She dressed like the girls down at the private school. In dark blue uniform-looking stuff. None of it looked good on her. It was as if she was trying to hide herself."

"You two ever in the same school at the same time?"

"No. I was off in college by the time she hit high school. Thank god." He took his hat off and laid it carefully crown-side down on the table. Rubbed his head. "Next time she found me was a couple years later at a rodeo. I had dropped out of college cuz I was making serious cash on the rodeo circuit. Saddle bronc. That's when I was seeing Beth."

"You made enough to quit school?" Miller offered him a cigarette.

Dan declined the smoke. "That's what I thought at the time." Went back to his stream of consciousness as if he'd forget if he stopped. "Sophie came out of nowhere. Damn, she looked great. Dressed to kill in tight jeans and boots, all grown up. Cowboy's dream. Even sounded normal for a short time. Talking about how well she was doing, and all. I was happy for her. Till she asked about my girlfriends."

He rubbed his eyes. "I said I was seeing someone. Sophie went from zero to bitch in two point five seconds. Screaming and crying, accused me of cheating on her. Said she had been saving herself for me. I yelled back. Said some mean things I shouldn't have but I was drinking a lot back then. She put a chokehold on me that night. It was crazy."

"You're a lot bigger than she is."

"I know. Bitch wrestled me to the ground with some kind of twisting move that damned near broke my wrist." A bead of sweat rolled down Dan's cheek. His hands were shaking again. Miller didn't interrupt him.

"Then she just froze in place for a minute. Staring into my eyes. I swear I could feel her anger. After a few seconds, she let me go. Started to cry. I was put on my ass in a parking lot by a little woman. I should have been embarrassed. All I could think of was that I'd never seen her cry. Even when stuff was bad when she was a kid—and I mean really bad—at the old house, she just got quiet. Mad. Never sad. She got up, started talking to herself. But it was one-sided like she was talking to someone else. Freaky. And then she walked away."

Miller stopped writing and looked up at him. "What happened to Beth?"

"The next day she didn't show up to see my rides. She didn't return my calls. I had to go to Austin for a few rodeos, was gone a couple weeks. When I came back, no one knew where she was. She'd disappeared."

"Did you suspect Sophie?"

"I thought Sophie had gone and found Beth and scared her off me. I didn't think anything too bad right off the bat. But after Amanda Pen, well, I tried to tell the cops then that Sophie had to have been involved."

"Amanda Pen?"

"Yeah. Months after the Beth thing. I was, well ... I was *with* Amanda in the bed of my truck."

Miller nodded his understanding.

"I look up and there Sophie was, standing beside the truck. Watching me and Amanda with that same freaked out look in her eyes. Scared the shit out of Amanda, and me. I jumped up and tried to talk but she only said one thing and then walked away."

"She threaten you two?"

"No. She asked why. I didn't answer. Had no clue how to. Wasn't sure what the *why* was for, exactly. Why was I living my life? Why was I getting some tail from a chick in the parking lot? I figured silence was the better part of valor at the moment. I didn't want to say anything to piss her off again. She walked away muttering about loyalty."

Dan slammed himself back into his chair and took a long drink. "Amanda scurried out of there. She was just a buckle bunny. No one I was dating or anything."

Miller half smiled. "I assume that's a cowboy groupie. Around here"—he nodded toward the door—"we call them badge bunnies."

"Yes, sir." A smirk crossed his lips. "Cowboys and cops." He shrugged. "Anyway, three days later, Amanda was found outside a different bar with her throat slit. The cops came to me. I told them about Sophie and about Beth. She was still missing, as far as I knew. They questioned me. Not as nice as all this either." He motioned to the room. "But I had a group of guys I'd spent that night with on the road to Austin. No way I could have done it."

"It was about two weeks later that Beth's body turned up in the woods. Throat cut, just like Amanda. And the cops came back. But again, they couldn't pin it on her. They said they found Sophie in Dallas and she was at work during the time of both murders. Not that I think they tried that hard to prove that fact. They didn't believe she could do that."

Miller closed his book. "Hard to picture an attractive female cutting someone's throat. Investigators are no exception. Today, I believe she's our guy."

Jim decided it was time his opinion was heard. Asked for or not. "I think this bitch is a lunatic. I have no doubt she'd take a knife to every one of us in this room." Why she hadn't knifed him in his hotel room was another question. Likely, because he hadn't found Dan yet.

All he could think at the moment was that he was responsible for leading that wolf right to the sheep. The sheep who'd done a fine job of blending in and hiding away until Jim Bean came to town. Jim had no option but to help this kid.

"We have your mother in a safe house with medical care and two uniforms on guard. I'll take you there."

Dan stood. "Can I see Cynthia?"

"Not yet." Miller looked him in the eye. "And when the medical examiner releases her, you shouldn't. Have her sent to the funeral home. See her after that."

Dan's eyes closed. His frame seemed to shrink a full two inches.

Miller put his hand on the man's shoulder. "I'm sorry."

Not much to say that would mean a hill of cat's asses to the guy at this point.

"Shit like this shouldn't happen."

Dan gave the slightest nod to Miller's statement.

"I'd like to go with him." Jim spoke up knowing eventually Dan would hear or read about the drain cleaner and the shape of his sister's remains. But he'd keep Dan from driving straight to the ME's office to see Cynthia.

"Not necessary. We've got it covered. It is a police matter now, Bean."

"I brought this on him."

"And we'll take it from here."

Jim didn't want to make a scene when the kid was suffering, but he could help stop Sophie. "I need this, Miller."

"I can't let a civi in on a homicide investigation. You know better than that."

Dan chimed in. "I'd just as soon have him around."

"It's against policy." Miller gathered his folder and headed for the door.

"Do I have a right to hire my own security?"

Miller's sigh was probably picked up on the recording. He put his back to the door and gave Bean a *fuck you* look. "Yes."

Dan looked back to Jim. Why he wanted a washed-up PI's protection over the police's, Jim would have to puzzle out later. "How much did she pay you?"

Not a conversation Jim wanted to have at the moment. Stupid facts like that eat away at a man. Like when his client wanted to know how many times their spouse cheated or what the girl's name was. The guy *cheated*. Move on.

"I mean, you're still under some type of financial agreement with her, right?"

"She gave me a substantial retainer."

"Any of that left?"

"A good deal."

Dan nodded. "Then I would like to hire you, Mr. Bean. Using the balance of that retainer."

That was a great way to spend the money. Better than Jim blowing it at the blackjack table.

Dan looked at Miller. "As my protection and an extra investigator."

"Dandy," Miller growled and glared at Jim. "When you stick your nose in my cases, Bean, people tend to get hurt and/or killed. You live in a bubble of bad luck and misery. Don't bring that into this situation."

Jim wasn't sure how to break it to him, but there was no way to turn that shit off.

19

"YOU FIND THE WHACK-JOBS like no one else, Bean." Ely tapped away on one of his many keyboards.

Jim rubbed his eyes so hard he saw spots. It was late. He was beat, the long drive with the distraught young man then the interrogations, and he was done for.

From Jim's angle the monitor Ely was reading looked like a wave of green static. The events of the past few days replayed, highlighting his inadequacies and his fears on one short mental film. Trusting the wrong person. No. The wrong *woman*. He'd been living loose and reckless for years. Since college when he lost everything. Lost it all because a woman lied.

His life altered, distorted by a false accusation. He'd quit really caring about people. Working on autopilot. Job to job. Bottle to bottle. Culminating in dead bodies because he was more interested in cash than seeing Sophie's intentions as she sat across that table from him and lied. Lied her ass off. There was a time he'd have read that like yesterday's comics. Known her story before finishing the headline.

"I do." He lifted his gaze to Ely. "A damned curse."

"Suppose you were marked by banshees at birth?" He said it in a hushed tone.

"Banshees?"

"I don't know. Whatever creature crawls into children's beds and marks them so the dark and devious are called to them." He looked up from the screen. "I'll look it up later. Know I read it somewhere."

"Don't bother. I don't want to know that shit. I want to know where to find Sophie Evers."

Annie wrapped around his legs and gave him a little half mew. He reached down and pulled her up so she could prop on his shoulder. Her approving purr vibrated against Jim's collarbone.

"Not sure why she still likes you. Was here more than she was at home this week."

At least the cat loved him no matter what. Well, as long as there was plenty of food around. "Absence makes the cat grow fonder?"

"I guess, man," Ely said. The screen changed from the green mess of characters to a browser Jim was more familiar with. "Here we go."

Jim wiggled his rolling chair a little closer. "Sophie Ryan Evers. Born in Grapevine, Texas. Father died of drug overdose. Location of mother, a Belinda Evers, is unknown. Sophie entered the foster system at fourteen months old."

Jim leaned over the records. "Aren't most babies readily adoptable?"

"She had some signs of fetal drug syndrome. Probably got her looked over."

"Doesn't have any retardation or signs of birth defects now." Drug dependency might explain some of her neuroses. Dan hadn't mentioned her ever doing any drugs. If she was getting away with murder, Jim suspected she was clean.

Ely clicked away. "Her foster records are going to be harder to get."

"Social services?"

"Yep."

Jim scratched under Annie's chin. "Arrest records?"

"Nope."

"Try Lulu Strong. She used that alias here."

He clacked away. A different page opened on the monitor. A Nevada license came up. Same as the one Miller had. Cab company registration. Address listed as the Crabtree Hotel, south Vegas. Not a nice place.

Jim paced to the kitchen counter. Annie leapt off his shoulder.

"Wait a second." Ely typed a little more. "Found something on Lulu."

An arrest record came up. The picture was a dirty young black woman. A mug shot after a bad night. Her right eye was swollen and red.

"Prostitution?" Jim asked.

Ely nodded. "And drug charges."

"My guess is Miss Lulu came to a bad end."

"If so, that makes four."

As Ely stood and stretched, about fifty bones cracked. The skeletal sound made Jim shiver. Ely had lived through a nightmare as a POW in Nam. The man had seen everything and done even more. It showed in his leathered face and his lanky frame. A very slight limp on his left leg was the only hint of any disability. Didn't slow him down or make him any less lethal. Jim would take him as a second in any situation.

"Correction: four that we know of. She's got a taste, Bean. Sounds like Sophie's drug of choice is violence."

"Not good." Jim's phone chirped in his pocket. He answered. "Miller, was about to call you."

"Yeah?"

"Dan settled?"

"Yes. His mom is a hoot. But that's not why I called." There was a moment of background noise.

Jim chose to take the opportunity to give his info first. "The identity Sophie used was a pro with an arrest record."

"We got that too. Sent someone to see if any of the other girls knew this Lulu or has seen her. I'm hoping she was paid to leave and not killed."

"Not likely."

"Yeah. I got a call from a Dallas FBI field office. An Agent Webb saw our BOLO. They will be here by eleven tonight. Wants a one-on-one with you and Dan while it's fresh."

"What's the FBI want with this?"

"Says there's more to the case. I'll bring them to the house."

"Great."

"I'll probably lose control of the situation at some point if this girl's got an open federal jacket."

"Got it." Jim did. And that made the prospect of his staying involved rather slim. The FBI didn't take to PIs all that well. Or maybe it was just him.

20

JIM APPROACHED THE ADDRESS of the safe house. It sat one lot off to the right of a tight cul-de-sac. New neighborhood. The kind with the low price points for first-time buyers. Cheaply made and so much alike it was hard to distinguish one from another. The development was far enough north to keep the price at casino worker level and still close enough to work on the Strip.

One unmarked car sat on the left side of the double drive, a black Crown Vic. Not too obvious, but enough that this smart-assed chick would see it as a cop car right off the bat.

Jim would have been happier if the place was a ranch. Two floors divided the area and made covering it harder. But it had a nice front porch and fake grass. Almost-middle-class quaint. A plainclothes sat on the porch swing smoking. He sized up Jim's car as he approached.

Jim swung through the cul de sac and parked past the house in front of the neighbor's. Ely's car was a gold, dull, no badges, late model whatever sedan. Easy to miss. Hard to remember.

The officer stood as Jim got out. He relaxed when Jim waved. Most officers had seen him on stakeouts or around the courthouse. PIs were not always the cop's favorite—Jim included—because most of their work came from defense attorneys.

Prosecutors had the entire police force to gather evidence for a case. The defense needed its own investigative team. Often Jim was it...if the case was being handled by a low-rent attorney with a tight budget.

Inside the house was as ordinary as the out. He scanned the layout as he followed the officer. A short hall led back to a larger-than-expected living area, open concept. He could see all the way from the front door to the kitchen and the back door. Sliding glass. Didn't care for that.

"Well. If it ain't the reporter again. You need a close up of me for your story?"

Lynette was in the same rolling chair from the nursing home. Here she looked younger. The non-florescent light gave her back twenty years. Jim now figured her for early sixties. Too young for this kind of memory loss. Not remembering this day will be good for her. Small favors.

Her fist balled up and under her chin, smiling big and pretty, ready for a portrait.

"How are you, Mrs. Hodge?"

"Fine as pie. My baby boy's here. He got us this swanky room for my birthday. Whatcha think about it?"

"It's a great spot for a birthday. It today?"

"Nope, tomorrow. He's bringing cake, you know?"

"And a clown face."

Dan came in. He shook Jim's hand and leaned close. "She knows nothing."

No mention of Cynthia. Got it.

Her medical assistant was the big guy from the home. The one she was yelling at the end of Jim's visit. He brought her a mug. "Lynnette, don't spill this one."

She giggled. "I will if I want, Steven, and you'll bring me another then too."

"I should go right on home and leave you to all this." He turned to Jim. "Not sure what I signed up for here. She's even more of a smart ass than usual. All excited to be out." He stuck a meaty palm out. "Steven."

Lynette barked at him. "And hang up my papers." Her chair rolled like she was on the ice rink as she crossed the tile floor. She skidded her feet to stop just short of the wall by the back sliding glass window. She snatched a couple of the articles out of an open box on the floor.

The leather furniture sat empty and uninviting around the fireplace. The tiles inside it were pristine ivory, the logs old and dry. That fireplace had never seen a spark. Like a show house full of rented furniture, cold and stiff. It reeked of Rental World.

Steven didn't seem worried. "When I can quit making you tea over and over again, I can do that. Sit still and drink that, old woman."

Dan chuckled. "They really do love one another." He patted Steven on the back as Lynette Hodge let out an indignant grunt. "Always felt good knowing you were there." He looked down and then back up to Jim. "But to know Sophie was in her room makes me sick."

"I've been with Lynette for a while now. Nothing's happening to her with me around."

This was Jim's chance to ask some questions before the Feds showed. He pulled Steven toward the kitchen. Dan followed. Lynnette was busy sipping her tea and looking about the window. Jim glanced over to see that it was locked and barred along the bottom. "Did you see Sophie when she was in Lynette's room?"

"I see everyone that comes into any of my patients' rooms, if I'm on my shift. Can't vouch for the others. Some don't care so much. Usually we see family, a few old friends, sometimes a pastor. I recognize most of Ms. Lynette's visitors. I knew there was a stranger there so, like I'm supposed to, I checked with the front desk. They said she was okay. Nothing looked threatening. A pretty woman making one of my patients laugh and smile generally is no concern. I kept to my rounds."

No help. "So you didn't talk to Sophie Evers?"

"No, sir."

"Steven." The distress in Lynette's voice made all three men turn to her. She was red-faced as she looked down into her tea-soaked lap.

"Good, glorious Lord Jesus. This is why I give you lukewarm tea."

Steven fussed with her skirt. Dan looked on, dark circles becoming evident under weighted lids.

Jim made a quick assessment of the rest of the first-level floor plan. Front and back door only. A stairway was evident from the back of the kitchen area. He followed the hall back to the front door. Master bedroom on the left. Master bath, one small window. Bedroom was smallish, two windows overlooked the side yard.

The hair on his arms twitched with minor air movement and he smelled the hint of dime store cologne as someone came into the room. He felt no threat. No reason to look away from his inspection of the latches.

"Upstairs are locked too. I checked. There's an officer up there sleeping."

"The night guy?"

"Girl." Dan had his hands buried in his pockets. "I want a gun."

"What for?"

"So I can protect my mom."

Jim hated guns. Never carried one. "Guns get people dead."

106

"Exactly."

He huffed. "Usually it's not the right people who get dead, Dan." He knew that for a fact. "You have two uniforms and me. Lynette will be safe until we find Sophie."

"What the hell am I supposed to do?"

"Relax. Spend some time with your mom. Read."

"Read?"

"Yeah. There were some classics on that bookcase. Try *The Great Gatsby*."

"You're serious?" Dan held his gaze. He was trying to read Jim's face. "Hated that book."

Jim smiled. "Me too."

21

MILLER SHOWED FIRST. IT was almost nine o'clock. Steven had taken Lynette to get her settled in bed for the night.

Miller tossed a folder onto the kitchen table. A Lady Fed in a black suit marched in, another agent behind her. The folder she carried was several inches thicker than Miller's.

The second suit stood by the glass door. The agent in charge. Feds seemed to move around the world according to their pecking order. Often it looked like a pack of dogs following an alpha.

They all looked very unhappy to be there, no matter where they fell on the FBI food chain. Sometimes Jim was glad his path into the FBI Academy had been blown to pieces back in college. Sometimes.

The lady agent's suit was impeccable but not highly expensive. Her shoes more serviceable than dressy. Her weapons were hard to spot at first but he noted at least two. She didn't smile as she made her way to the head of the table. She obviously assumed she would be taking the lead.

Miller stood. "I'm Detective Miller. We met..."

"On the Porter case two years ago." She gave him a curt nod.

"Right." Miller hadn't extended his hand to shake but Jim got the feeling that if Miller had put his hand out there, she'd have left him hanging.

Her gaze snapped to Jim. "You the PI Sophie Evers hired?" She opened the folder, flipped a couple of pages over, and scanned.

"Jim Bean." He said it sharply. Didn't want her to think he was intimated by the suits or the badges. He'd been in court on many occasions and had to face off with some pretty hefty characters. An FBI agent didn't faze him.

Her brow pinched as she looked back down and read a few more lines. "Okay." She glanced at him and back to the page. Obliviously it was his paper. His jacket. "Jim Bean it is then."

Jim's grip tightened, he eased his balled fists behind his back. Why would she, the FBI, have information about his history, the changing of his name? It'd been a straight legal change. His records were supposedly expunged when all the charges were dropped. But it appeared she knew something anyway. And why would they need that kind of info on this case? He was not the target of this investigation. The room got a little warmer. What the hell else did she have in that fat folder?

She slid into the chair at the head of the table. "Special Agent Ava Webb." With no foreplay she started sliding pictures of dead men toward Dan. He cringed.

Miller pulled the pics away from Dan. "Who are these men?"

The gnarled look on Miller's face said he was biting his damned lip to keep from telling this woman where to shove those photos. She should have brought this to his attention first. Discussed it before shocking a witness.

"When you put the BOLO out on Sophie Evers it triggered a case I've been working in Texas for years. These three men were drug dealers and/or pimps in South Dallas. All were killed within a three-month period. All had their throats cut. The scenes were messy. No drugs, money, or weapons left behind so we suspect the murders were a means to robbery."

She looked down. "All had had intercourse just before dying. But there were no viable DNA traces left behind. They'd been crudely cleaned with bleach spray. Likely she slept with them to get their confidence and killed them just before—"

"I'm sorry, ma'am." Danny took his dirty cowboy hat off and set it upside down on the table beside the pictures. It did a nice job of blocking the view of the mutilated bodies. "But what's this got to do with my sister?"

"Twisted trail but hang with me." She looked at Miller. "I do have a point."

"Make it." Miller's face was easing up.

She turned her attention back to Dan Hodge. Looked him straight in the eye with the authoritative gaze of a woman in charge. She held his gaze, not saying a word, until his head tilted just enough to give the impression he was asking for more info. She knew the moment he was ready to listen. Agent Webb was *good*.

She tapped the third photo in the row. "A video surveillance camera near the back on this one's apartment caught a woman leaving the building with a large duffle bag and a bad disguise. Not enough for an identification in the tape." She thumbed through the file and supplied the picture. Dan eyed it carefully.

"Two more dealers turned up about a month later. These guys weren't pimping. All they did was sell cocaine. The area was a little higher rent. And the victim's both had slit throats. This time, the wounds were much cleaner. The crime scenes were cleaner. Showed fewer signs of struggle. Each was robbed blind. One of them was reported by one of his drug runners. Dumb girl called it in because she said the guy was holding a thousand dollars of hers and she wanted it back."

Dan's face was white as the Formica tabletop. "Are you suggesting Sophie did all this?"

"This time we caught a break and a witness saw the woman in that picture"—she tossed out the BOLO—"with one of the dealers the night before making a buy."

Dan shook his head. "That's her, but, Sophie buying drugs?"

"I don't think she was using the drugs, Mr. Hodge. The most successful and hard-to-catch dealers never do. We think Sophie was treating the pimps and dealers as a means to make a living. Kill off the scum and take their cash and valuables."

She pulled out a mug shot of Sophie. "She was arrested in Arlington, Texas, with a couple ecstasy tablets. She gave a fake name. Had a fake ID. It was a misdemeanor because she only had the pills and a syringe on her and it was her first offense. She walked after giving up the name of her supplier."

Agent Webb pulled the pictures back into the folder and tucked them away. "My guess was she took the cash off these guys, sold the drugs and guns. My math says she was making a dang good living. Next I could find, she was spotted in the swanky North Dallas area. High-end dance bars selling shit to the rich and spoiled."

Webb ran her right hand over her hair to make sure it was in place. "Looked like she was reinvesting, moving up to bigger targets with bigger wallets and bigger stashes. We think Sophie has been saving all her money. I have witnesses who put this woman in those bars. Most didn't recall what name she was using. All this time we didn't know her name." She looked at Miller. "Your BOLO told us who she was."

She started to pull out two more photos, but shoved them back in the folder after glancing at Dan's white face. "There were two more bodies. Women. Young, pretty girls out behind the bars. No signs of a struggle at all. Not dealers, just girls out for a night at the clubs. Lack of a struggle indicates both were willing to let her get close. The killings were very personal."

She straightened the folder and glanced coolly around the room, making eye contact with each person ... except her silently looming partner. "Nine murders we think she's responsible for. Probably more."

"A serial killer." Miller whistled.

"Not really a classic serial because her MO has changed. She has the timing of a serial, lots of time in between, but she's all over the place. No standard method other than the slashed throats. All these men and women were killed like it was Sophie's nine-to-five job. Nothing special. She started with street scum, but then the vics got more respectable, the take larger, and the kills cleaner."

Dan's hands were shaking like he *was* a druggie in rehab.

Jim pushed back the bile threatening to make him puke. Sophie had used him. Not only to find Dan either. If she'd drugged him, why hadn't she killed him like the others? What was she playing at?

Jim eased into the seat on the far side of Dan. He tried to block the memories of her and that night from his head, pretend nothing had happened. If he ignored it long enough, he would no longer feel so violated.

Dan shook his head. "Twelve," he whispered. "Cuz I'm sure she killed two girls I was with, Beth and Amanda. And Cynthia." He looked up at the woman. A single tear rolled from his eye. "I tried to say so back then. No one would listen."

Agent Webb put her hand over his where he was picking at his thumbnail. "I'm listening."

22

JIM SAT SILENT IN the living room in the thick aftermath of the FBI bombshell. Miller, another detective, and poor Daniel Hodge had sat at the table for an hour, going over everything he could remember from Sophie in her youth. It'd not been a particularly pretty story. Dan was a decent guy and recapped it all, even admitted he'd come close to taking advantage of her once when the pair had gotten a hold of some cheap wine. He'd stopped himself despite her Herculean efforts to encourage him. Said that's when she first started acting strange.

Jim picked up a random book off the shelf. Took a hit from his flask and leaned back on the stiff leather couch to read for a minute. To think on something else.

"Ought to share with a lady." Lynette was edging down the hall. Her twig-thin legs stuck out from under her gown. Her hair was wrapped in a flowered cloth on her head like a small turban.

Jim jumped up. Her scooting around in the rolling chair was frightening enough without adding alcohol. "You should be sleeping."

"I should be dancing the night way. It's Saturday night. I'm sure there's a good band around here somewhere. It's still Vegas, isn't it?"

He eased her into the big leather recliner across from where he'd been on the couch. "Sadly, it is."

The chair seemed to swallow her whole.

"I love Vegas. Always did. Did pretty good at the poker tables. I was a psychiatric nurse. Could read people."

Jim tried to picture her young and running a table. When she blasted him with that big smile, he could see her charm.

"So, you sharing the hooch, boy?"

"Don't you think Steven will have a coronary, not to mention my ass, if I let you mix scotch with your meds?"

She huffed, leaned back, and waved him off before she crossed her hands in her lap. "Probably send me on if I had any anyway." She winked at him. "I'm not quite ready for that yet."

"Me either."

She sat with her eyes closed and face relaxed for a few minutes. Jim opened the book back up. It was a romance novel. With vampires. Not his choice, but he didn't want to move. He read the first chapter and decided it wasn't too bad.

"They think I'm too far gone to see what's what here." She leaned closer. "I'm not completely out of it, you know? I got my moments."

She twisted her head to the side, toward the stairs. "I haven't seen Danny this wound up since his daddy died. So I know something horrible has happened. And I know this isn't a motel either." She gestured to the back yard. "No hotel has a fenced yard."

"What do you think is going on, Lynette?"

"You're no reporter. My guess, you're a cop of some kind. Maybe a Fed."

She had been in the bedroom with Stephen when the Feds were there. Never got to see Agent Webb or her sidekicks. Maybe she'd heard. Either way wasn't good. Jim did not want to be the one who broke the bad news about her daughter.

"I'm not a federal agent."

"You're not Santa either, are you?" Her movements were much surer than they had been earlier. Could be her meds kicked in or she was having a good moment. Bad luck for him either way.

"No."

She scrunched up her nose at him. "Then let's not play the guessing game any longer and you tell me what in tarnation is going on around here."

Jim shook his head at her liveliness. He liked her. She kept darting her gaze to the articles on the wall.

"Is there one you want?" He stood.

"Yes. There is. It's close to the door, bottom row."

Jim made his way over. "This one?" He pointed to one that looked particularly tattered. He was careful pulling it free from its location, worried the tape would tear it.

"Read it."

He turned so the porch light shone at the paper.

"Aloud. Read it aloud, boy."

Jim sighed, not liking where this was going. Lynette Hodge was very lucid right this minute and Jim was far too tired to manage what he was sure was a sharp wit.

A 22-year-old woman who was found shot in the head in the trunk of her burning Thunderbird was remembered in an obituary Sunday as a caring, fun-loving woman who loved country western music, movies and "wearing her trademark high heels."

Nichole J. "Nicki" Thomas enjoyed spending time with her boyfriend, Kito Lisser, and their 1-year-old son, Jack.

Her greatest joy was caring for her boy, the obituary said. Thomas "lived life to the fullest," and enjoyed, "above all else, spending time with her family and friends."

"Nicki left this earth too early for us to understand, but God always has a purpose and therefore we all must believe that Nicki is still among us fulfilling hers," the obituary reads.

Thomas's memorial is next Saturday at Christ Church.

"Thank you for being part of our lives, Nicki—you will continue to live in our hearts and never be forgotten. We love you," the family wrote.

The accused is twenty-year-old Patrick Wolf, who allegedly has ties to the Hell's Angels and has been arrested for petty theft and assault in the past. He is being held in Clark County lock up.

Deputy Prosecutor Jack Driscoll said today that he expects to file charges in Superior Court this week and they will determine if death penalty charges will apply.

"We'll formally file charges in the next day or so," he said. "You'll know after that."

Court documents say Thomas was assaulted for hours and stabbed several times before she was fatally shot in the head. Her body was found in the burning Thunderbird near Forker and Bigelow Gulch roads on April 13.

A motive is so far unclear.

She nodded slowly. "Two hundred and seventy-five words."

Jim headed back to the couch, watching her face.

She gave him a weak smile as he set the article on the table.

"The number isn't the point here, is it?" Jim eased back into the stiff cushions.

At this point Jim was sure she knew about her daughter. At least she'd figured out Cynthia was the only one not at the house so she must be in trouble or dead.

"Numbers are always the point, but often not the only point."

"What *is* the point, Mrs. Hodge?"

Her eyes were slack and blank but still open enough to see what was going on. Lynette sat so still and so quiet that Jim decided she'd fallen asleep. He'd had a golden retriever in his youth who slept with her eyes half open like that. It was unnerving then and unnerving now. As Jim used to do with the freakish habit of the family dog, he considered waking the old woman just to get her to either open or close her eyes.

He refrained. Waiting.

She finally blinked and answered his question. "What it means is, who died?"

Well, shit. Usually Bean didn't mind being the guy who dealt the bad news card. But right now he didn't want the job. He kind of liked the loony lady and her articles. Providing the proof of a spouse's affair, no biggie. It was intimate, heart-breaking crap, but Jim was honest enough with himself to know their misery made *his* misery seem a little less … miserable.

"I might be confused more often than not, buddy, but I'm not stupid. At least I don't figure I am." She leaned forward. "Who died?"

Maybe he could placate her for a while, just till she wasn't as lucid. Again asshole-ish, but it was that or run like a scared cat. Cause he didn't want to hurt this woman. His eyes fell on the bookcase again. Subject changer.

"Have you read *The Great Gatsby*, Lynette?"

"I have. Fitzgerald is a long-winded piece of crap if you ask me. Most popular novelists from that time were."

"He did go on a bit." Jim chuckled and leaned back.

"And that Gatsby was a schmuck. Worked his whole life, thieving to make a fortune and then carried on, putting on all those airs and all the parties for a woman who dumped him years ago. Man wasted a fortune on the sham. And for what? A gold-digging girl." She shook her head as if she was worried over his lack of money-management skills. "If a girl won't have you then there's no sense going off all half-cocked chasing her around." She scratched her nose with her frail hand. "I mean, I was no great looker or anything, but when my husband came around, I knew he was the one and I didn't play any games. If I'd have wanted something else, I'd have told him that as well."

She shook a twisted, wrinkled finger at his nose. "Young folks these days make it harder on themselves than it needs to be. Computer dates, text messaging, whatever other crap they have going on."

"I think it was his need to be more, to be rich, that mattered to Gatsby. He felt unworthy of her."

"Schmuck." She flipped her wrist in dismissal. "Men and their pride. Buy a girl flowers, tell her you love her, and be faithful. Why is that so hard?"

"I don't know, Lynette. You make it sound easy. Never been that easy for me."

Her frown was suspicious. "Nah. *You* look like trouble. Freaky gray eyes on the outside and deep waters on the inside. Be hard to trust those eyes. But that's just going off appearances."

"Heard that before."

"Reckon you have." She waggled that finger in his direction again and her face turned as serious as a schoolteacher. "Now, before I forget it again, answer my question."

Jim looked at the floor. He needed to go wake Dan.

"Who died?" It came out as a fear-laden shriek. Lynette had thrown her body into it, causing her slight figure to lose balance and skew forward.

Jim leaned in quick and caught her shoulder in time to keep her from breaking her nose on the table.

Dan rushed down the stairs. His feet tangled but he remained upright. "Momma." He eased beside her and took her weight.

"Why is Sissy not here, young man?"

Dan hung his head and rubbed her shoulder. "You pick now to join us? Huh?"

"I didn't pick any of this, Danny."

Jim's gut felt like he'd eaten a bag of quickset concrete. He was the only one who'd made any of the choices that brought about the current circumstances.

Dan looked at him. The guy's eyes were tired, and as red as a Vegas sunset. Jim had no answers to the questions that wounded stare conveyed.

Jim would not leave Dan on the hook. He needed to be the one to tell her. To say the words out loud so Dan didn't have to. "Lynette," he said, "I'm afraid you're right."

"So something happened to Cindy?"

Dan hugged her fragile body. "She's had an accident. I'm afraid we're going to have to write her story, Momma."

Tears poured from Lynette's eyes, so fat it looked like someone had poked a hole in a bucket. They trickled off her cheeks and soaked into the fabric of her faded pink gown. Each one seemed to drain a bit of her life away. A deep burning rage Jim hadn't felt in years ignited in the back of his throat. He tried to suck in a few deep breaths to tamp it. But nothing doing. He could count to a thousand and he'd still be angry. This was why it was better to stay uninvolved. Connections were dangerous. Made you care. Dulled you. Made you weak.

"It's gonna be alright, Momma."

"How are we going to manage without our Cindy?" Her voice was almost gone.

Jim had to get up, to walk, or he was going to implode. It would be bad enough just knowing he brought this to these people and caused the unacceptable sorrow. But seeing it ...

He went out the back glass doors and circled around the front of the house. Knowing the female officer was on the porch, he came around heavy and loud. It didn't work. The jumpy cop drew on him before he had a chance to identify himself.

Jim stood still with his hands out to his sides until she recognized him and relaxed with a soft curse. "Sorry. Got an extra one of those?"

"Gun or cigarette?"

At the moment he wished he could handle a gun. But he needed to find his target before he could worry over eliminating it. "Cig."

She flipped the rumpled pack to him. A lighter was inside the half-empty box. He lit one up, coughed as he sucked in, and kept moving down the street. Instinctively, he scanned dark corners and noted lights on. Analyzing the area for possible threats. There were none apparent. The house and its location was well chosen. Probably didn't need to worry tonight. Sophie would be off licking her wounds. Re-grouping. He had this night, maybe one more, before she returned for her prey.

23

IT WAS A SHORT walk to the end of the block. After that, Jim had nowhere to go. Any farther and he wouldn't be able to put eyes on the house. He sat on the curb under the glare of a streetlight. He got out his flask. Took a long drink. Enough to drown the guilt for a moment, anyway. The anger would hang around for a good long while. Before he could take another swig, a dark Charger pulled up. The window eased down with little noise.

Jim set the flask by his side. "Miller."

"Bean." The detective looked toward the house. Lights burned in almost every room. "Everything okay up there?"

"Lynette decided to rejoin the world of the mentally competent after you all left. Cornered me about what's going on. I think she realized Cynthia was not at the party. Maybe put it together from pieces of things she'd heard today."

"Ouch." He motioned with his head for Jim to get in. "Let's go for a ride."

Jim put the cig out and followed orders. The passenger seat was tight, with the computer mounted on the console taking up a good part of the seat space allotted. His size didn't help, but he was used to the equipment in his own car and dealt by pressing his body against the door. They weren't taking a road trip.

Miller turned the radio down. "We're not having any luck tracing Sophie Evers. She's got no past or present. Feds are having the same trouble. Last we have of her was in Dallas, and the cops down there are as overworked as we are. They said they'll see if they can get someone to look into it." He shrugged. "But, when we say that on this end, the other department's shit is last priority." He stopped at a light.

"What's your point?"

"If you're really interested in helping this guy, you need to go to Dallas and pick up her trail."

Last thing he wanted to do was turn down Miller. The man had come to his rescue before and Jim considered him one of his few friends. "Surprised you're asking a civilian to help with the investigation."

Miller never took his eyes off the road as he drove, but Jim could see the determination on his face reflected in the windshield. "The sick bitch needs stopping. Finding people is what you do. Do it."

"I *need* to protect that kid and his mother."

"He's not a kid. You're better at finding people and I'm better at protection. I carry guns." The light ahead changed, the car eased to a stop.

A convertible mustang with three teenage boys pulled alongside them. The kids were sitting a little too still, all facing very forward, careful not to make eye contact with the cops.

"There's trouble," Jim chuckled.

"Not my beat." Miller reached over and gave him a small punch to the shoulder. "You know I'm right. The pair is settled in that house, getting more attention than Lynette's had in years, probably. And her son is there. I have it covered. Two of my best plainclothes twenty-four-seven. I pulled them off a big case for this. Not to mention the Feds are involved."

"Thought Agent Webb went back to Dallas?"

"For now. She left her backup *suit* to look over my shoulder." Miller turned again, driving in circles. "Do you want her to find this trail before we do?"

Jim wasn't sure. Maybe he just wanted this one over with. Maybe he didn't like the heavy responsibility he felt for Dan and Lynette. It sucked to care. "No."

"Take Double O. You should have enough of that retainer left to cover the two of you for a couple days."

Double O was a damn good choice as a wingman since he was a bounty hunter. "Why are you so interested in me doing this?"

"Because I don't like the FBI all up in my business. Cause *you* need to solve this. And if shit hits the fan again, I'd rather you be in Dallas so my Chief doesn't filet my butt cheeks for letting you so close to another case." He reached for a folder tucked between his seat and the center console, tossed it on Jim's lap. "I ... um ... tripped and the FBI file fell in the copier."

Jim barked out a laugh. "Hope that doesn't have to hold up under oath."

"You and me both, brother. You going?" He pulled back into the short cul-de-sac and stopped in the safe house drive. Dan was on the steps. He didn't get up when the two approached him.

"You shouldn't be out here. Makes you a really easy target." Jim hugged the folder as he crossed his arms, going for intimidating. Poor guy was so wiped out it wasn't going to work.

"I guess so. I'm used to being outside at night. I like to look at the stars."

"Lights from the Strip ruin that, so no use taking the risk. Don't make me kick your butt." He cut Dan some slack. "Promise me you'll stay inside from now on."

"How long is that?"

Miller patted Dan on the shoulder as he passed. "Not long if we can help it. How's she doing?"

"Not great. She's calmer. I had to wake up Steven. He gave her something to help her sleep. Said he hated to do it since he hadn't seen her that lucid in months."

The guy looked like the rooster who lost the cock fight. He was skinny, his burgeoning beard was patchy, and his hair was all over the place from being shoved under a cowboy hat.

"Maybe you can get him to give you the same thing, man. You need to rest." Jim did too. He probably looked just as bad.

"I do." Dan stood.

"I'm headed to Dallas," Jim said.

Dan stopped in the doorway, his eyes wide as he turned back to Jim.

"Trail starts there. She's got to have some of that money from the robbery-killings Agent Webb told us about. I find that, then maybe I can track her all the way here. You're in good hands. As soon as I get a clean cell phone, I'll call you."

Dan looked at his feet, then at Miller, and then started to speak. Miller was standing right there, so Jim doubted Dan would say he didn't feel safe even with cops around.

"This is the best plan of attack. I'll be more use in Texas than sitting here staring at a bunch of cops."

That was if Sophie didn't find him and drug him again. Maybe this time she would cut his throat.

24

THE DUMB DETECTIVE LED her straight to the house. He made a couple of odd turns, but he was as easy to follow as a kindergartner playing hide and seek. Even a cop wouldn't suspect a minivan of following anyone, would they? There were four billon of the oversized, ugly things on the road and most were the same nondescript silver hers was.

The house was just as obvious sitting back in the cul-de-sac, windows lit up as if they were expecting company. An undercover cop sat in a wooden swing facing the sidewall of the porch. Not much of a view of oncoming trouble or a vantage point to shoot from. They might as well have put a sign in the yard: OCCUPANT IN PROTECTIVE CUSTODY. KEEP OFF THE GRASS.

Sophie drove past the entrance to the cul-de-sac and parked three blocks away. The puppy was happy to be getting out. The thing had been in the car for hours while Sophie watched the police department waiting for Miller to leave.

Carl needed to walk and she needed to case the area. He pissed almost immediately. Squatted. Huh. She inspected his back end a little closer as he walked on. She was sure if it were a he, she'd see the evidence.

"So, Carla it is." Or maybe Carley? Nah. Carley was too girly and Carla had been the first thing out of her head. Sophie liked things simple and straightforward.

Carla led Sophie between two houses. She followed the dog's lead along a path in the stones and dried grass. That route had been carved by countless kid-sized tennis shoes making thousands of trips between houses. It wound between fenced yards but eventually led right to an excellent place to get a look at the back of the safe house.

The yard was clean and surrounded by a four-foot-high fence that encircled several mature trees. For a Vegas subdivision, a tree that could cast a shadow or make a little shade was big deal. The back porch was lit up by indirect light from the inside. And there was a sliding glass door with eighties vertical blinds closed tight yet still letting a little yellow light seep out.

She eased around the north side of the fence and studied the outdoor lights of the neighbor's house. They were on and had motion detectors. So once they were turned off for the night, they'd come on if she got too close. Not good.

She backtracked, moving slow and low so as not to be spotted by the occupants of the safe house, who were undoubtedly on full alert. Might even have someone walking around outside She'd not seen anyone yet.

She gave the leash a gentle jerk to get the mutt's attention. "No barking. You got me?"

Carla stopped and tossed her an *as if* look.

Sophie eased up to the fence behind the correct house. A shiver made its way from the roots of her hair to the tips of her toes.

He was in there. Danny was so close her body felt his energy. She inhaled, sure she could smell him in the air, almost taste his skin if she closed her eyes. She visualized her future, her plans. The house was set. The plan was laid. Very real.

The dog tugged on the leash and shook her out of her fantasy. Carla was right; not good to linger while one was on reconnaissance.

The dog was happy to continue her exploration of unfamiliar scents. Sophie let her loiter and sniff whatever she wanted as they made their way. Oddly, she was enjoying the dog's curly little tail as it wagged happily. It was a distraction from the stress. Sophie used the opportunity to memorize the landscape and the lighting while Carla tinkled again and again.

Movement grabbed her attention as she came around the far side of the house. A hairy-chested man sat on the back porch of the neighbor's house. Unfortunately, the large-bellied bastard had spotted her as well.

She dropped Carla's leash and tried to appear as if she'd not seen him. Damn her luck if he was a police officer posing as the neighbor. She tapped her fingertip on her blade to check its accessibility and then reached for an injector pen tucked in her waistband. Hidden there for emergencies and loaded for bear in the literal sense of the old saying.

"Odd place for a stroll." He stood, cigarette in hand. The bucket beside the lawn chair he'd occupied overflowed with crumpled butts. His light blue tank had a faded slogan she couldn't read on the front. Dark sweat stains outlined man-breasts above a pumpkin-sized stomach. The slob must be relegated to the backyard to smoke. His shorts were cut-off jeans, a little too short both for the current fashion and his pudgy legs. A glut of empty beer cans was scattered behind the chair.

Likely not a cop, but there was no way to be positive. Her gut told her he was more deadbeat than cop. Her guess was washed-out techie who now works at the auto parts counter.

Sophie put her hand to her chest. "You startled me." She backed up a step. "I'm really sorry to bother you. My dog got loose and I followed her this way." Carla waggled herself right up to him just as the words came out of Sophie's mouth. Good girl.

Sophie glanced over to the safe house. All the shades remained closed and still.

This guy gave her that *I'm fantasizing about you naked* smile. "Cute dog for a cute lady." He rubbed Carla's little head.

The action made Sophie angry. She didn't want this creep's hands on the pup. She did however want to cut him, badly. But she bit her lip hard enough to taste her own blood. Sometimes it was hard to refrain from killing off the bottom basal slime of the gene pool just for the sake of humanity. But he wasn't worth the attention the body would bring.

"You live around here?" He caught Carla's leash and headed toward Sophie. Moved like a man who sat around a lot, maybe watched TV all day. Maybe she was wrong on her first assessment. He didn't look smart enough for the parts counter. At least three days of smoke and body odor wafted as he approached. No. This guy was unemployed. *If* she had to guess, Sophie figured he lived off his mother or his girlfriend.

She gripped the injector. Maybe the distraction of this creature's death would be good for her. The pleasure of watching the smoky vapor of his bleeding soul as it left his ugly carcass would boost her, feed her. Might even settle her frayed nerves. The cops would shit themselves if she killed so close to Danny and his crazy mother. So it would accomplish two things: relax her and up the anxiety levels inside that house. Two birds with one shot. Three, really—she could rid society of the burden of this indigent slob.

He was making the decision easy too. His approach kept the two of them in shadow not more than seventy-five yards from safe house.

She glanced back to breath in the air from the safe house, feel for Danny one last time, and check for the best entry when the time came.

She made out two windows on the ground floor of the safe house she could breach with little effort. She blocked her disgust at the man's odor with the more pleasant thought that Danny was sitting just inside those walls. Perfect.

"We're new. My *husband* and I moved in a couple blocks over." She vaguely tilted her head.

"You buy that place on Falcon Street?"

"Yeah. That's it." Whatever you say, my dear. She reached for the leash.

He handed it over, taking an extra step, standing a little too close for polite conversation. He was trying to be large, intimidating. Oh, he was asking for it. "Cool. Nice place."

She backed up a bit. Carla happily retreated in the direction they'd come. "It is." She nodded to the leash. "Thanks."

She turned and headed off into the dark.

"See ya." The dumpy man said to her back. It was more of a question than a statement. Ridiculous. Did the fat fuck think he had a chance with a woman like her? Her pulse was thundering through her veins, rushing in her ears. She could visualize the slow surge of his blood, lazy with cholesterol, pumping through his carotid artery. She needed to hit the road but *wanted* to cut him.

Never act impulsively. You almost got yourself caught last time.

Carla tugged to go off exploring again, but Sophie reined her in.

Even that mutt's smarter than you.

She wanted to shout at the voice in her head, curse it. Her own self-deprecating critic making sure she evolved. Never good to be static. So she listened to that voice. Argued with it. No matter what drugs she took, it was impossible to ignore. Besides, she *could* ignore it. Disobey it. No matter what the voice had to say, the urges were strong. She tasted her desire like a strong shot of tequila, burning and acrid.

She turned to see the man still watching her, staring at her ass. She was next to a little shed, blocked from view from his house and the safe house. He would only take a few moments, even seconds.

She smiled at him and leaned against the shed. She crooked her hip and tossed her hair over her shoulder.

He let his cigarette fall to the ground and snubbed it out with his flip-flop-encased foot.

So easy to extinguish.

He stopped, facing her, aligning himself so his body was looming. "Forget something?"

She nodded, let the leash go, and eased in closer to him. The stench of cheap tobacco and two days' worth of Vegas sweat rolled off his skin. The idiot grinned like he'd won a prize.

She palmed the injector in her left hand, walked as if to circle around him, trailing her right fingers across his chest and over his shoulder. She brushed her breast against his back as she stepped in behind him. She wanted to give the sap the impression she was embracing him. She had to hold her breath to avoid the stink of his skin.

The slug was five-seven, roughly two hundred and fifty pounds, and she guessed most of it was in his stomach.

"You like it rough, baby?" she asked him. In her head the words echoed along with the images of others who'd answered that question with an exhilarated yes. Just as he would. Her pulse was drumming, her head cloudy with lust.

He looked over his shoulder, his lips curved in delight. A quick nod.

She tightened her grip on his neck, not enough to frighten him, just enough to make him think he was about to get the fuck of his sad, stinky life. She reached up and put her lips on his left shoulder. Made her think of salt mixed with old trash. He was moist with sweat, maybe from his arousal or it could be the miserable evening heat. She bit down. Hard.

At the same time she hammered the injector right next to her seductive bite. He jerked from the unexpected sting.

"Sorry." She kissed the spot a couple of times and he relaxed immediately. This guy wouldn't lift a finger to defend himself. "Too much?"

He shook his head, turned to her. He reached for her neck. Maybe to pull her head back. Maybe to return the bite, but his hands came to rest on her arm. Gripped. His body began to veer backward, she widened her stance to hold his weight. She wanted him upright.

He reached for her face, but missed. "I ... what ... "

She put the knife at the base of his ear. The exceptional blade encountered no drag as she drew it. The steel sliced though his skin and the platysma muscle that shaped the side of his unshaven neck like a shark slicing through a breaking wave.

Blood surged as she severed the jugular and the carotid. Once she felt the bump of her blade on the solidity of the hyoid, she yanked, speeding up the process, repeating the damage to the far side of his neck.

He bucked only once, his effort to cry out far too late. The drugs and the lack of oxygen to his lungs and brain made that impossible.

She shoved his body off to the side as he started to bleed out. She didn't want any more of his blood on her than was necessary. The clothes would have to be burned, but she still needed to hit the store, ditch the van, and head home to regroup. She cleaned the blade on a portion of his shirt that wasn't yet scarlet. He had landed on his side so most was draining on the ground.

Don't leave them bloody fingerprints for Christ's sake!

"I didn't. Shut up."

It was beautiful work. But you have to control yourself. I know five-year-olds who are better with delayed gratification than you.

Heaven forbid her inner voice give her a compliment without knocking her down at the same time.

"Can't you just let me enjoy the symphony of the moment every now and then?"

Time to go. Stroke your ego later.

She looked back at the house, the one Danny was sitting in. Maybe he was right there behind those blinds. Killing that slob left her wanting and aroused and she wanted to run right up to the door, but the inner bitch was right. Sophie needed to exercise more restraint.

The yahoos would watch this place like a hawk for days after this, but after some time, Danny would get restless and his protectors would get complacent. She could be a patient girl when she was well motivated. Dead body in her wake notwithstanding.

It was time to go home. This trip had taken longer than she'd expected as it was. She had to go to work for a while or she'd get fired. Again.

"Carla?" She half called, half whispered the pup's name. The scruffy thing trotted toward Sophie. The dog headed to the mess on the ground but Sophie caught her leash. "Don't sully your fur with that."

25

AN OIL-BURNING DELIVERY TRUCK blasted past him as he stood on the curb. The thing was puking sooty exhaust that made Jim hold his breath as he headed for the Coffee Girl across the street from his townhouse complex.

As he entered the lot, Oscar Olsen pulled in on his equally roaring—but non-oil-burning—bike. The loud pipes dared anyone to come within yards of the huge motorcycle.

Most bounty hunters and PIs made great efforts to blend into the crowd. It increased the possibility of maintaining the element of surprise until the last minute. Good for sneaking up and gaining custody of the skip tracer. Not Double O. Nope. He made his way through the world larger than life. His stature, his personality, and his appearance. He was a big boy. No changing that, so he made it work for him. Instead of sneaking up on bail skippers, he walked straight on and intimidated the shit out of them.

But as with most things hard, O had a soft side. Jim had seen O's and that made the big man much less of a threat. Oh, he could still whip Jim seven ways in seven seconds, but Jim figured he wouldn't. After O balanced his helmet on the handlebars, he stopped just shy of the door to wait for Jim.

"O! You're here," Sandy cooed as they entered. She rushed over and gave him a kiss on the cheek.

"Morning, beautiful." His voice was smooth. The kind used in life insurance and Viagra commercials. The girls melted every time O started talking. Also a good tool to have on your side. A trusting voice made people comfortable, helped them let their guard down. His size quit being so intimidating as soon as he opened his mouth. Unless he *wanted* you to shake in your boots, then that deep booming voice was only slightly less frightening than your mom screaming your full name after discovering you broke her favorite lamp while throwing the football inside the house. Again.

They slid into the usual spot, corner booth in the rear of the restaurant. Jim sat with his back to the wall. O had no fear of putting his back to the world.

Sandy trotted up with the coffeepot. "Do me a favor, O." She ignored Jim.

O gave her a look with an overdramatic brow arch.

"Say, 'Beef. It's what's for dinner.'" She poured as she made the request.

Jim laughed. She was so cute. And he'd bet the contents of his wallet she'd get the big guy to do it too.

"What?"

With a quick slosh, she poured Jim's coffee. Maybe a half cup. Her attention barely left the big bounty hunter. "You know, that commercial

Sam Elliott does? The one for the beef people. They showed a pretty steak and then you heard him say it."

O closed his eyes with a little headshake. Evidently, this was not the first time he'd heard the request. "Unfortunately, I do. And no."

"Oh, come on. Please." She looked back. The other morning-shift waitress had moved in close. She wore the same *pretty pretty please* look young girls achieved with ease.

"I told Lisa you sounded just like Sam Elliott. And she loves Sam Elliott." She clutched her hands over her heart. "Please."

O gave Jim a tepid look, as if this were all his fault. Maybe his silent chuckle wasn't helping anything. "I didn't ask you to say shit."

Sandy then pulled out the big guns, played dirty. She reached out and put her dainty little hand on O's tattooed arm. "Come on, Oscar, it's just one sentence." She'd used his first name. Like she was his little girl or baby sister. Her expectant face was more than either of them could refuse.

He growled. "If you promise not to utter that man's name around me ever again, I'll say it once. And never again."

"Yay." She set the coffeepot down and did a little dance. Lisa loomed closer.

"First *Roadhouse*, then that commercial came out, I thought I'd never get to speak again without people mentioning him or that ad." O sat up straight up. "Just once."

She nodded. Behind her Lisa mirrored the gesture. He cleared his throat. Took a long sip of the coffee. The girls were patiently waiting, but Jim thought Lisa was gonna bust if O didn't speak soon.

"Beef." He said it slow and with that Texas drawl Elliott had made a living off of. "It's what's for dinner."

Lisa clapped. Sandy squealed.

"And if you don't find me some real beef in this joint, I might just have to gnaw on you for protein."

She smacked his shoulder. "You're so sweet."

"Oh. My. God." Lisa rushed off as if to share her experience with the next person she encountered.

Jim didn't try to hide his mirth. Opened his mouth to speak, but—

"Not one fucking word from you, Bean."

"Not me."

"Now. Seriously. When is the pecker-head in the kitchen going to give up this green menu and start serving real food?"

Sandy rushed back over to retrieve her pot. "Maybe soon." She looked over her shoulder. Lisa no longer shadowed her. "Business has been really, really slow."

Jim pushed his already empty cup toward her. "So my regular business isn't enough to keep the place open?"

She gave him a little smirk and a wink. "Your tips sure aren't."

"Go on. Bring us something resembling breakfast," O said.

She sashayed off.

O looked at Jim. "I bet *your* tips are the only reason she can feed herself."

Jim shrugged. Sandy was one of the few women he did trust. Not that there was any kind of relationship there. She was a hardworking girl trying to make a living. That could be difficult in Vegas, and he couldn't bear to see the girl hit the streets to make her bills. He was known to leave a twenty or two on the table at times.

"She puts up with me almost every morning. Should get more than a couple bucks."

They sat quietly for a minute. O looked out the window at the passing traffic. It was a comfortable silence that comes from spending time with a guy. Time and danger made men comfortable with one another. And they'd shared both.

O took another drink. The action brought them back into conversation position. "You lookin' for some work?"

O often let Jim pick up some skips in his bounty hunter business for extra cash when things got slim in Jim's world. The offer usually came with the suggestion that if Jim advertised and had a better website, he might get more clients, or better-paying ones. But that was for a later conversation. Today Jim was the one with the offer.

"Nope. I want to hire you this time."

O's brows rose. "As in a bondsman? You get arrested and I didn't hear about it?"

"No." *I got drugged and screwed by a serial killer and need your help finding the bitch.* "My last client hired me to find her brother. Said he'd been into drugs."

"Sounds about normal for you."

"Well, that's where the normal ended. Turns out my client was only pretending to be the target's sister. She killed the target's sister and stole her identity."

"Oh?"

"I need the backup." Jim liked to work alone. But heading into unknown territory without backup was risky. And he might be lazy, but never intentionally stupid.

This was his burden. His problem. And sooner or later his night with Sophie might become pertinent to the investigation. But if he was going to tell anyone, O would be the guy. Still, he'd wait until that info was need-to-know. Sophie Evers was a grade-A whack job who made his usual list of clients seem like church ladies. Miller had been right. Having some backup with this bitch out there would be smart.

"With your help I'll find her faster. I got a young man and his elderly mother stashed in a safe house, along with her care worker."

"And a couple badges, I'd guess."

"Yep. Not ideal."

"Sounds interesting."

"We'd need to head to Dallas, today. I have a couple leads to work and a copy of an FBI file to decipher."

"How'd *you* get an FBI file?"

Jim shrugged.

O took a sip of his coffee. "Get to fight with the Feds too, then?"

"More than likely. Pretty female Fed."

"I'll be. This day is getting better."

"I can even pay you."

"Now you're just pulling my leg." He winked but sadly it wasn't too far a stretch.

Jim took a deep breath, unsure why telling O this seemed embarrassing. Probably because Sophie had shown him she could get to him. That he'd been stupid. He rarely repeated stupid.

"We're thinking this chick's killed around ten people, O. Some of the corpses have been scumbags and some are just regular civies. I'm invested in this. I fell for her lies, found her ultimate target, and served him right up to her. Almost left him to her too. I'm responsible. I've spent time with her. She's very good at being bad."

"Dang. You have the strangest shit come across your desk."

"Tell me about it. You in? I know you have a business to run here."

"I got people who can do my job while I'm gone. You could use someone working for you too. Then you wouldn't have to pull me away from picking up strays every time you need help."

"Build my business and hire someone reliable?" He mimicked the advice that O tossed his way every time they talked.

O rolled his eyes at Jim's sarcastic tone.

"That means I'd have to deal with that someone. I hate that someone already and I haven't even hired him yet."

"Why do you hate everyone?"

"I don't hate you."

O smiled. "Yet." He pointed a long, ringed finger at Jim. His late wife's name was tattooed along his knuckles. He'd lost her here, in Vegas, on their honeymoon. Traffickers grabbed her in a club, right under O's nose. He'd stayed to find the creeps, but only found a trail to a dead body.

"I'll be your Huckleberry ... on one condition." O leaned back in the booth, his body language suddenly cocky. "Gun range."

Jim let his head hit the back of the booth. "I don't want a gun." He sounded like a whiney teenage boy being assigned chores.

"You need one. I'll help you."

Not the range. Anything but the range. It was bad enough he was feeling like a weak-ass punk after letting Sophie get him by the balls, now he had to prove to O he couldn't shoot for shit.

"I'll hire someone else."

"You really that afraid to shoot, man?"

"Not fear. I told you, I suck with a gun. You want me to carry a gun, give me a sawed-off shotgun. Hell, a grenade. Cuz anything that takes more skill than that, I'm useless."

"Grenades? That's subtle." O pulled a ten out of a beat-up leather wallet and tossed it onto the table. "Two hours. Scruffies."

Jim knew it. The outdoor range on the west side. "The food's not even here yet."

"No *real* food is ever gonna show up here." O stood and tapped the table. "Two hours."

26

SHRILL LYRICS REVERBERATED AROUND the car. Not that Sophie could understand the words to any of the tracks. It was in Italian. She knew the story the opera told without the actual words. A count kills his countess after an affair in the afternoon. Classical opera, full of death and tragedy. It had taken years to understand why it spoke to her at such an early age. The death, the tragedy, it all mimicked her childhood, her life.

The crap audio system in the late-model minivan was not designed for the tonal depth of the piece. Not many speakers were. But the intense harmonics and the riot of sharp voices battling deep emotion worked to calm her scattered thoughts.

That the pup slept through it amazed her. It was loud and obnoxious and she loved it. That affinity had started in high school. The music had made her foster parents insane. Anything to annoy them had become a fast favorite.

In the process, she'd acquired the taste for the bloodlust themes and desperation in what little of the lyrics she understood. The passion of the music always made her blood run hot.

Music was one of the few things Sophie felt a passion for. The rest of the entitled and commercialistic culture could cease to exist and she'd miss little of it. Everyone on the planet could dissolve and she'd miss no one. Well, no one but Daniel Kent Hodge. A therapist once told her those weren't real feelings, just a mere obsession. Fuck him. She felt them. Danny would too. Either way, the music fueled it and her.

After graduation, when she'd held a series of meaningless small jobs, classical music had helped her move up in the world. Escaping to it helped curtail her anger. She could disappear and the stress of working with the inane idiots at the Taco Hut would slip away.

In a way, it pushed her and was part of the plan on how to get out of the lifestyle she was doomed to live because her dumb whore of a mother had dumped her. It had been while lost in the frenzied notes and octaves that she decided she could use her body and her anger to rise above the carnage of her existence. She could work herself into a musical trance and think through her issues. It had helped her decide that taking out pimps and drug-dealing scum would be far more lucrative than selling pretzels or burritos at the mall.

A flash of blue caught her eye, followed by another, blaring for her acknowledgement. Fuck. She did not need this now. How long had the annoying cop been back there with his lights flashing at her? She glanced down. Apparently the music had worked its way from her brain to her right foot.

She turned down the music and considered just driving on. Her tool bag was in the floorboard on the passenger side. Close enough to reach out and snag her blade sitting snug in its sheath.

She slowed to pull over. Carla raised her little head from the seat next to her.

"Don't worry, sweet pea, it's just the stupid cops."

She fished for her current set of documents as the officer took his time to run the plates. She made sure the name was the one she wanted to present at the moment. No worries there. The van was registered to Eloise Fowler, Noblesville, Indiana.

She waited.

The cop stayed in the car.

Checking her plates shouldn't take that long.

Time passed, but Sophie didn't worry, nor would the ice job intimidate her. She glanced at the clock on the dash. Five minutes since she'd come to a halt. If he was looking for any sign of criminal activity, he'd find none. She was getting peeved.

Finally the silver door on the squad car opened. Sophie let the window down as a young officer stood. A small, round female approached. The woman tugged her black slacks up by the utility belt. Different to see a female officer alone at night. Sophie assumed another cruiser was close by in case of trouble.

"License and registration, ma'am."

Sophie shoved the required documents toward the window, sighing loud enough to show her displeasure at the interruption of her travels. And the bitch cop had the nerve to closely examine the license as if she suspected a forgery. There was nothing to suspect. The minivan was bought and paid for with cash at Herb's Used Cars last month by Eloise Fowler. Registered in the same name. Insurance carried by Eloise Fowler. Driver's license with Sophie's picture read Eloise Fowler.

And her van wasn't suspicious either. They were near the Yosemite National Park. Several duffle bags and a cooler occupied the back, and a puppy happily riding by her side made for a great cover. A camping adventure. Nothing out of sorts, nothing to see here.

"You realize you were going twenty miles per hour over the limit, Ms. Fowler?"

"Of course I do. The speedometer is directly in front of my face. Any moron who tries to tell you they don't know they're speeding is lying."

Sophie didn't look away from Carla to see the cop's reaction to the frank comment. She was in a hurry and wanted to get the ticket and move on. She didn't care. Nothing would be on her record, no need to pay whatever fine might come along with such a grievous disrespect for California speed laws.

She glanced at the out-of-shape woman. Her collar rode high on a squat neck. No sign of an Adam's apple moving as she preached the cops' sermon.

"That's considered reckless driving. I can't let this one go. That far over, you're facing a loss of driving privileges. Probably going to lose this license for at least six months."

Sophie sat silent as the policewoman waited for an elaborate lie. The plea for a warning ticket. Sophie checked her nails.

"But hey, no excuses, no argument. I like that."

"I don't give a shit what you like. I have places to be. Can you cut the chit-chat and let's get this over with?" She shooed her with a wiggle of the fingers.

"Don't antagonize me, Ms. Fowler." The cop hitched up her belt again and Sophie caught her checking to see that her weapon was at the ready.

For an instant Sophie's fingers itched to take the challenge. Who could kill faster on this deserted bit of highway? She was at a distinct disadvantage sitting in the van. But the cop was fat and several years older than when she'd passed the physical requirements of the training academy. Sophie was fit. Strong. And smart.

If she irritated the bitch cop enough, the officer would have Sophie *step out of the car.* Advantage was definitely on Sophie's side then. She would have the upper hand in close combat. The element of surprise alone was a winning factor. The completely unexpected ability to turn from belligerent speeder to killer in an instant. This cop would never see it coming. Sophie could disarm her, and then kill her with ease. Who did she think she was dealing with anyway?

"There's no law that says I have to be nice to you, is there?" She didn't give the officer a chance to respond because she knew very well she was right. "Are we done?"

She looked the cop directly in the eye, showing no fear, no intimidation.

The officer shoved her citation through the window. "I'll see you in court. There is a law that says that."

Sophie smiled at the woman, genuinely pleased, knowing she would not be going to court. "Thank you very much."

"Slow down." The cop handed her the license before walking back toward her cruiser. Sophie could go after her and slit that short little neck in an instant. But she had other, more pressing things to attend to.

27

THE DOOR TO SCRUFFIES looked more like the entrance to a strip club than a firing range. Screaming red neon confirmed the establishment was, in fact, open. There were fliers and posters plastered over the entire surface of the glass door, blocking any view of the interior. He'd not been here before. Jim had not stepped into a range since college, when he was getting ready to join the cadets at Quantico.

He'd sucked. Not in the *missing the center mass of the body-shaped target by a few inches* kind of sucked. No. He missed the entire body-shaped target almost every time he pulled that trigger. Not long into training, he got frustrated. He'd stood in that booth and looked down the range with his ego in full control. No way he was going to be the worst shot in the class. Not him. He'd mastered so many other things in life with ease. The fact that weaponry hadn't come naturally worked his nerves like a dull knife on a thick rope, slow and fraying.

Instead of reasoning out the bad aim, his move was to use a gorilla grip on the gun, the idea being he could manhandle the weapon into improved targeting. Sounded good at the time. The instructor had given Jim nothing but disapproving looks, which only fueled Jim's overreaction to the situation. Arrogant and mean, the retired trooper was probably doing these classes to pay for alimony. For at least two ex-wives.

The last straw came on a Friday. He remembered it like a bad dream. Jim had fired. His tight grip pushed his aim so low, he shot the *inside* of the range booth.

The slug ricocheted backward at an angle, which took it dangerously close to the thigh of the asshat instructor. The man had to jump out of the way of a .40-caliber slug. It wasn't *really* that close. Given the mouth breather's goal was to make everyone around him feel small and stupid, he used the accident as expected.

He'd roughly extracted the weapon from Jim's shocked, shaking grip, followed by a teardown fit for a teenager who'd taken his father's car keys. Then to make the scene complete, the instructor had tossed the gun dramatically into a case and told Jim a five-year-old could outshoot him. Although true, the public slur pulled at his ego. Insult to injury. The rest of the class was looking on, most trying to stifle their amusement. Not to save Jim any embarrassment, but to keep the instructor's attention away from their own shortcomings.

Mortified, Jim went straight to the karate studio and signed up for classes. He'd taken them as a kid and figured accidentally killing a man with your bare hands was a little less likely than with a gun. Intentionally … well, that was another story.

With a deep breath to suck down his memories and his ego, Jim stepped inside Scruffies. O stood at the counter. He'd signed them in. Jim gave over his license for their records. Muted gunfire echoed throughout the building. Through the thick glass behind the counter he saw a couple of guys and women were already on the range. He'd hoped for a more private lesson.

O turned and headed back for the door.

"You forget something?"

"Nope. We're shooting on the outdoor range. It's around the far side of the property." O used his body to push the door open but didn't wait for Jim to follow. He had to rush to catch up as O started up his Tahoe. Jim hopped in the passenger seat. "I thought we'd be less claustrophobic out here."

O was right. The outside range was a picnic table under a carport shelter with a long, waist-high bench along one side to hold the weapons. Their shooting alley was far enough away from two other shooters that he didn't need to worry about anyone but O seeing the fiasco to come.

O pulled out four twenty-five-round boxes.

"Don't need too much ammo. If I haven't sent you running for cover by the time we finish one box of that, I'm buying lunch."

"You're buying lunch anyway. What time do you want to head to the airport?" O shoved a magazine into the gun and pulled the slide to load the chamber.

"Three."

The big man held the gun in his palm. "You get any real instruction?"

"Does an old trooper yelling at me for two days count?"

"Yeah. Here. Loaded five. Keep it pointed downrange, please."

Jim took it. "So you *have* seen me shoot." Cool metal was slippery in his sweating hand.

"It's just good practice. Finger off the trigger too. Keep it that way till you have the legal right to shoot and the intention to do so. No walking around dark houses with your damned finger on the trigger.

Cat might jump out at you and you shoot your partner in the ass." O demonstrated, keeping his finger pointed up the barrel but very close to the trigger.

Jim mimicked the finger position. It was comfortable.

"Now shoot."

Jim turned his attention to the targets. They weren't the paper silhouettes that he'd used in the indoor range. Still body-shaped, these were metal and dangled from posts like hammered steel hangmen.

Jim took a deep breath. "This won't be pretty." He held the gun up with both hands in the grip he was taught. His finger slid to the trigger. He squeezed slow. He didn't want to hear it. His jaw hurt from his clenched teeth. After what seemed like a day too long, the gun went off. No sound of metal. He looked at O.

"Try again."

Jim repeated the same action. Still no sound of metal on metal. Hopeless.

"You shoot like a girl."

"Fuck you."

O moved close and shadowed Jim's stance. "You were all leaned back with your hips forward. Looks like a pregnant woman, all belly out. And you anticipated the bang, making you lean even farther back."

"Did I?"

"Yeah. Could you even see the target when you pulled the trigger?"

Jim thought about it. No. Crap, that was embarrassing.

Never told the old trooper he'd lost sight of the target. But he now realized what he was doing. Same thing with the baseball as a boy. The pitcher would let go of that hard ball and Jim's eyes snapped shut knowing it was flying uncontrolled at his head. Not to mention he was trying to force as much power to the bat as possible. No need to cover his inadequacies with O, the man had already seen many of them.

"I think I closed my eyes."

"Hell yeah, you did. And to compensate for that you're gonna automatically point that gun almost straight down." O demonstrated, his hips pushed forward, his gun arm pointed down and his eyes closed.

"Fucking does look like a pregnant girl."

"Don't say that too loud. There's plenty of girls around here who shoot better than the both of us. Now, try again. Lean those shoulders forward. Relax. Point the dangerous part forward and aim. Use that finger pointing forward as a guide. Forget the sights. Point at what you want to hit. Take a smooth breath and pull that trigger. Keep your eyes open and on the target."

Jim changed his stance. It felt better. He pulled the trigger. Felt the sweet spot, concentrated on keeping his eyes on the center of the human-shaped metal plate he was pointing at. The blast made his ears ring even through the earplugs, but he managed to keep his eyes open.

Clank. Metal. Hit.

He looked at O. "You look more surprised than me."

O chuckled and fired off five quick rounds. Each hit. Center mass.

Jim lifted the gun, sighted, and fired the remaining two rounds in his magazine.

"Still low and to the left, but that's just a problem with anticipating. You'll get past that." O handed him a box of fifty rounds. "Five at a time. Reassess. I'll make comments."

O leaned back on the picnic table and lit a huge cigar.

Jim slapped in the reloaded magazine. Checked his stance. Took a smooth breath and squeezed as he let the breath out. Very zen. Clank! Clank! Miss. Clank! Clank!

"Not bad for a guy who said he can't shoot. All you needed was an instructor with half a brain."

"Good thing I have one of those." Jim looked up from reloading. "You're lucky to have half a brain."

"Shut up and shoot. Need to be at Ely's in an hour. He says he's got something on our whack job."

"Oh?"

"Yeah. And he's got us some toys for the trip."

28

ANNIE CIRCLED JIM'S LEGS as he sat at Ely's table. The cat was desperate for his attention. So much so that she jumped up and perched contently in his lap. He ran his fingers though her long, silky fur. Not a luxury he experienced very often. The cat loved to be close, but touching was usually a deal breaker. She doled out that kind of intimacy in small sweet moments. Jim needed to spend some time at home.

When Ely tossed the blue folder in front of Jim, Annie fled the area and returned to watching them from her normal spot on the top level of the countertop.

"How'd you get a copy of this?" the techie asked.

Jim shrugged. "Contacts."

"But this is actual FBI paperwork."

"It's a copy."

"No, dude. This is original sin, right here." Ely bit his lower lip.

Crap. "Evidently it got mixed up with the copy."

Ely tapped the folder. His thin frame was made thinner by black fatigues and a black tank. When he turned around, the back arm openings let some of his scars show. Scars from months of being a POW. Remnants of horror stories that must come to him in the night.

His right forearm was tatted up with an odd pattern of old and new ink. Each little thing meant something to the wiry vet. Jim never presumed to ask about any of it, but sometimes when Ely was stoned, and they were alone, he told some stories. Jim always listened. Never asked for elaboration. He'd let the guy go into heavy details, even when they made Jim thank whatever lucky stars there were that his own misery and pain was not what Ely had lived through.

Jim feared he wouldn't have made it through something like being beat with bamboo until blood ran down the backs of his legs, staining the dirt floor under numb knees. And Ely still cared about people. Jim rarely did. Didn't trust. Even getting close to O and Ely had been hard.

"Hope your source can cover his or her ass, man."

"He can." Jim hoped. He'd call to give Miller a heads up. If they needed to make a trade, he'd make it happen before leaving for Dallas.

O lit up. With all the pot smoke in the house a little bit of cigar smoke wouldn't hurt anything.

"That secondhand is going to shorten my life, you know?" Jim waved his hand to usher cigar smoke out of his face.

O puffed out. "You smoke sometimes. Anyhow, that's not going to be your downfall, Bean."

"No?"

"Nope. Your solitude."

"I'm dying of solitude?" That was prime.

"Yep. You care about nothing. No one. You got nothing to lose. It makes you a good investigator, would have made you a great soldier, but it's gonna get you killed. Last time we were in on something together, you jumped off the roof of a two-story building."

"And?"

Ely nodded. Not like he had any more personal connections than Jim did.

"Moving so fast, you're gonna breeze past that line in the sand one day. The one you shouldn't cross. You'll go too far. And you'll do it without thinking twice. Why? Cuz you got no one to worry over you." O sucked in a draw, closed his mouth, his cheeks puffed from holding it.

O was mostly right. But Jim figured even if he had someone these days, he'd still call all the shots the same. "I got you guys. And Annie."

Ely nodded, his whole upper body moving with his head as if grooving to some beat Jim and O would never be able to hear.

"Just consider going on a date."

"A date?" With flowers and good night kiss pressure? No thanks. He'd stick to the strippers and one-night stands.

Like in Texas with Sophie. That was how he would have to file that event in his head. Just a drunken misadventure. An image of her straddled over him made his stomach turn. "We got a case here or we gonna continue with this joke of a love life intervention?"

"Have to have a love life to intervene in it." O took another puff and leaned his head back so the exhale billowed straight overhead.

The smoke danced around the weird Circus-Circus act sculptures hung above.

"What do you think, Ely?" Jim asked.

"Of the folder? Bitch don't like anyone and has no conscience."

O laughed. "No shit." He leaned forward. "What's her plan, though? It can't be to kill Hodge. Too much drama for that. She's clearing a path of bodies to get to him. There's got to be a motive here we're not seeing."

"Agreed." Jim stood and paced toward the front door. "She could have killed Dan back when she slashed his old girlfriend. And again when she got his buckle bunny."

"They ever have a real relationship?"

Jim turned back to the guys. "Nah. He said she was too young. He was in high school, she was in middle. I'm guessing the attraction was probably all in her head, even back then."

O shrugged. "So she loved him and he didn't return the favor. Since she's diced up pimps for money, I'd think unrequited love would be a killing offense."

Ely opened the file. Pointed at the pics of dead men and women staring up at him. "If these are all hers, she's changed her technique as time has passed."

"If?"

"Yeah. I mean other than the girlfriends, the first two crimes were pimps. In those days not a lot of care was taken if a dirt bag, drug-dealing pimp with a two-foot rap sheet got offed. Clumsy evidence collection at best. Couldn't pin those on her without a confession, is my guess. The next two or three aren't much better. Wasn't until she moved uptown that her vics got middle class enough to have the crime scenes well documented and collected."

"We have to get moving." O mashed his cigar into a tray. He looked remiss at leaving a good half of it behind. "Flight's in a couple hours. Can you keep looking for something in that file, Ely, something we're not seeing?"

"Yep. Have just the tool for opening the mind."

O snorted. "I bet you do. Maybe you can give us a good place to start?"

"Of course. Get that file back to Miller," Ely said.

"Why'd you ask where I got it if you knew?" Jim asked.

"Two ways that could have gone down—Miller or maybe you seduced it off Lady Fed." Ely's grin was lopsided. Suspicious.

No way. She was smart, successful, and beautiful. Everything he would love in a chick, but he'd never get past the fact she was an agent and Jim was a slob with a drinking habit. "Hardly."

They both eyed him.

"How'd you two know about Lady Fed anyway?"

The pair shrugged, neither doing a particularly good job of faking their innocence. Fucking Miller. Maybe Jim should keep that blue folder and let Miller deal with the consequences.

"See, I knew there was a woman for you." O winked. "Classy agent lady?"

Not a chance. No Feds for him.

Ely slid a yellow folder to Jim. "Made extra copies." He met Jim's eyes. No humor. Then glanced to the folder and back. It took all of two seconds to know what Ely was thinking about. Jim had forgotten to take his own rap sheet out of the file. Lady Fed had pulled his records. Records that should have been sealed.

His palms itched to hit someone. Not that he was hiding his past from Ely, but few knew he'd faced all those inflammatory charges and had changed his name. Seemed that number was growing. Miller, O, Lady Fed, and now Ely. If Ely gave him the pity face, Jim was gonna punch it.

"I think you need a woman who don't keep the clock running, Bean," Ely said. So it was the hookers and not Jim's history he was all bashful over. Surprising.

"The day you can keep a girl, call me. I'll consider it. Until then … "

"I have a girlfriend." Ely gave them a smug look and headed to the back end of the building. He stopped to twist the tumbler of the combo lock on his closet.

Jim called it the Toy Room. He'd only seen it a couple times, but he knew there was shit in there from both world wars. Real stuff. Fun stuff. He had the latest state-of-the-art techno-warfare munitions as well. Things Jim was sure Lady Fed would love to know were residing with a stoned, batty ex-Marine. Jim loved looking at the old shit.

"New girlfriend? Do tell." O followed him in.

Jim trailed. He sucked in a deep breath, loving the smell of gun oil and black powder. Now that he had figured out the basics of his shooting problems, maybe he should consider getting his own handgun.

He picked up a good-sized one, maybe a 9mm. Could have been a 40-cal. He had no real clue.

"She works at the Mellow Man pizza place downtown. Old hippy. Skinny. Pretty eyes."

Sounded about right for Ely. Someone from his era was a good thing. Might understand the PTSD and all the scars. Jim checked the gun to feel its weight in his palm. Felt light.

"Don't get ahead of yourself, Bean," O warned. "You need a lot more practice before you start waving those things around. A few plinks at a target does not a marksman make."

Jim turned the gun over. Inspected the other side. "Thinking about it doesn't hurt anyone."

O pushed the muzzle away from the open room. "Unless you let loose a panic round or something and put a hole in good old Ely here. Whatever would his girlfriend do?"

Ely snickered. "She'd likely move on to the next guy with a big... bag."

"Is that the kind of relationship you want?" Jim wasn't sure why he asked that. Ely was a grown man. And shit if he wasn't experienced, but Jim still worried someone might take advantage of his generous nature. Last thing the vet needed was some chick cleaning him out.

"She's all yours when you want it, dude."

Jim put the gun down. "Only kind of bag I have carries groceries. Your girl probably won't like that."

Ely laughed and bobbed his head towards the gun. "The *piece*, I meant, not *my* piece." Ely dug in a box filled with shipping peanuts. He pulled out a smaller black plastic case. "New tracking device. Comes with a phone app. If you can get it in a purse or briefcase, you can track right to the object."

Problem with that was purses and briefcases got left behind. But it was better than the big magnet trackers Jim stuck on car undercarriages.

Ely took a couple small boxes off a shelf. "Earwigs. Set of four. I got a few more flash-bangs if you want them, but not sure the airline will let you carry them on. More than three ounces."

"No shit." O took the electronics. "I'll hook up with a bounty hunter I shared some info with in Mesquite. He'll take care of anything we need beyond my sidearm."

"Don't think we'll need too many toys, O. It's like we're hunting a ghost. We don't find her, there's nothing to shoot at. It's unlikely she's back in Texas."

"She could be anywhere."

"Girl's gotta have a home base." Ely led them out of the closet, making sure the thing was locked up tight before he stopped and put his hands on his hips, staring up at the eagle hanging over the upstairs railing like a gargoyle on steroids. "She has a plan, she wants that Hodge boy. She's got somewhere ready to accommodate the dude. Whether it's for loving or killing, that's your worry—the nest."

29

"HOPE YOU GOT THE insurance." O got out of the car and stretched his legs. The trip from the airport had taken near forty-five minutes.

Jim pushed the button on the fob but also double-checked the handle to ensure that it wasn't opening. Not that any door locks made were going to help. This was the kind of neighborhood where if a person found themselves there accidentally, by wrong turn or bad GPS, they snapped the locks shut as they drove. They prayed to whatever god they pleased that they hit all the lights green until they could get back on the freeway. When they had to stop, they kept their eyes forward, wondering if the kids on the corner were going to hijack the car. Even the streetlights sagged in depression as they hung over dirty, narrow streets.

"I did. Good thing you wanted to leave most of the equipment in the hotel room."

Jim turned back down the street they'd driven up. They'd passed the address.

It looked vacant. Graffiti-painted plywood covered the only window on the first floor. As they approached the smoky glass door, a small boy ducked through the opening. He glanced at the pair with a surprised look but kept to his intended path without much change in pace. He must have figured them for cops. Or thugs. Either way, he wanted no part of them.

The door was perpetually a foot and half open. Jammed. Jim found it incredibly hard to pull it the rest of the way. It creaked as if the metal would snap.

Inside the dusty stone foyer was a bank of mailboxes and an intercom system. Some names were still taped beside dingy red buttons. But the case holding the intercom system had long since been pried from the wall and twisted wiring hung exposed and dead. "We need 4B."

Neither even tried for the elevator.

Only four flights. Shouldn't be too bad, Jim figured. Wrong. The urine stench was only slightly overpowered by the smell of molded ceiling tiles. Random clothing, paper, and a few broken needles littered each of the landings. They moved at a steady pace. O had not unholstered his gun, but his hand rode on the grip as he eased up the steps, keeping to the outside wall. His attention stayed a flight higher than his feet.

Jim ducked close behind. Military formation for two guys who'd never worn a uniform. Different kind of training for their type.

The door to the fourth floor was closed. Jim wasn't exactly afraid as O pushed it open, but he'd sure rather be sneaking through a cheap Vegas hotel over this rundown housing project any day.

"Feels dead in here," O whispered. He seemed just as spooked. Not scared. Hyper alert.

The matted hallway carpet felt lumpy under Jim's feet. Maybe it had been green at one point, but it was now so dust-coated it looked gray in most areas. The first door they passed had a tin letter *H* hanging crooked under the peephole.

"B's at the other end of the hall," O said over his shoulder.

"Of course."

The next door stood open. Jim glanced in. Empty. Single abandoned chair sat under the far window.

Jim could hear a TV. Game show. *Family Feud* maybe. It was coming from another open door, third to the right. The next door they passed was broken and hanging crooked on the bottom hinge. O scanned the inside before passing.

He pictured a tiptoeing cartoon character stopping and bobbing his head around every corner just waiting for the bandit to jump out. "This place must have been condemned years ago."

O was still whispering. "If there's a TV, there's power here."

They made it to 4B. The door was closed. Jim tried the handle. "My bet... No one's been here in years."

Before O could reply, the door swung open. An elderly black woman in a bright yellow floor-length evening gown stood before them as if she were expecting them. Her face was made up like a teenager ready for a prom date, her long gray hair twisted in a sloppy braid on the top of her head.

"Well. Early. I like it." She motioned for them to enter.

"I'm Jim Bean. A private investigator from Las Vegas—"

"Vegas!" She spun in place. The dress flared at the bottom, making her look like a flower. Her big feet were covered by tattered gold sneakers. "I danced on the main stage at the Flamingo in '62. Eight straight weeks."

"We're looking to see if anyone here remembers a Kiko Henry," O said as she sashayed up to him.

"You are a big one, aren't you? In my day, young man, I would be inclined to explore all that creamy white skin of yours." She motioned up and down his torso and tilted her head.

"Kiko?"

"Hmm ... " She turned and glanced at two pictures on the wall. Both family portraits. Could be hers, could have been there before she decided to squat in this apartment.

"That the boy that got himself sliced up about ten years back?"

"I think it was seven."

"Bah," she scoffed. "If memory serves, he was one of the hustlers. Selling smack to the kids 'round here and the boy had the girls coming and going. Got cut up one night. Died in his skivvies." She looked out the dirty window. The TV was plugged into a big extension cord that was affixed to the wall and ran out the window.

Jim glanced out. Smiled.

The cord stretched to the building next door and connected to another extension that ran to the roof. Four or five other cords zigzagged back and forth across the alley. That was the power. He almost asked her how she managed to get water but decided he didn't want to know. She was living on three outlets on an extension cord.

Instead he asked, "You ever know any of his girls?"

"Me?" She clutched the rhinestones at her chest. "No, sir. I been keeping my mouth shut and my eyes on my own business for a long time. Keeps me alive, it does." Her nose scrunched up. "Why the cops digging into Kiko's mess anyway? Dead black man in this neighborhood is no big deal today, much less a dead pimp from seven years ago."

"We're not cops." O almost stiffened at the accusation.

"You said you was an investigator."

"*Private* investigators," Jim said. " We're looking for one of his old girls. Her family is wanting her back." Lie.

161

"Well. You have a rough row to hoe, brother." She patted O on the tummy, leaving her bony hand there. "Ooh. You want to hang around and see what an old lady can still do?"

"You still got that in you?" O winked. His charm worked even on the old and insane.

"Not sure. That's why I asked. But I'll give it my best." She cackled. Her eyes sparked with life. She seemed content with her place in this run-down, empty building.

Jim backed toward the door. "You okay in this apartment, ma'am?"

"Been okay in this building for twenty-six years. I moved over here to this side of the hall after the power died."

"So you were across the hall when Kiko lived in this apartment?"

"Yeah. They cleaned the blood up good and then another couple tenants come and gone before I slipped in."

Jim fished the picture of Dan and Sophie out and held it for her to see. "This girl." He tapped the picture. "You remember her?"

She strained to look at it. "If I seen her, I don't recall."

It'd been worth a try.

"Most of his girls were white and young. Boy was bad news. Lord forgive me for saying it out loud, but I shed no tears when he got cut."

"Not sure anyone did, ma'am." O bowed a bit. "We'll be on our way then. Lovely to have met you, my flower."

She curtsied, holding out the ratty old gown as if in royal court.

They closed the door behind them and left her humming to herself.

"Her smile was ruined by those rotted teeth, but it still put off the warmth of the sun."

Jim stopped to look at O, confused. That poor woman was living off the grid and barely making it day to day. She was clearly broke. Somehow, O had been lightened by her.

A slamming door echoed in the corridor. Jim jumped. Good thing O hadn't noticed.

"Quit your grinning, lover boy, and put your hand back on your sidearm. Besides an aging showgirl, we have no idea what other surprises lurk in places like this."

30

CARLA TROTTED OFF THE porch as fast as her little legs would carry her.

"Don't go off too far. That drive wore me out. I don't want to be chasing you."

Sophie went in and rummaged through her quaint kitchen cabinets with the carved wood trim and found an odd glass bowl that didn't match the rest of the set. All the furniture and the kitchen trappings had come with the purchase of the cabin. The woman who'd designed the look had done a nice job. Some kitschy mountain cabin decor graced the place, but not so much it was cliché.

She ran the water for a moment before filling the bowl. She'd been gone for a while and didn't want crud from the old pipes in the bowl. Carla barked at something and Sophie headed out to see what the pup had found. She sat down on the top of the few steps leading down from the porch and looked out to the lake.

It was a perfect house. The secluded little log cabin had been a jewel to find. Foreclosure, so she got it cheap. Maybe that isolation had added to the reason it was on the market so long. Too far off the beaten path for most, but it was tailor-made for her. Quiet.

"Carla."

The dog looked up from whatever she was sniffing at the edge of the lake.

"Come here."

As if she'd been responding to Sophie all her little life, the creature turned and pranced right to her.

"Good girl."

Happily, Carla took the attention for a moment, but her desire to explore took over soon enough. Sophie understood. Her first time here, she'd walked every inch of the area, memorizing the downed trees, the masses of dense bushes tucked here and there, and exactly how far it was before she could see another cabin. More than far enough for what she needed.

She kicked her shoes off and walked barefoot to the bench through the tall grass below. Her cell rang. Her work cell. She'd only turned it back on once she'd entered California.

"Successful trip, I trust?" Dave wanted numbers right off the bat. She had to physically shake her head to remember what little sales work she had done on this trip. She'd been gone five weeks. Dave gave her the perfect amount of freedom, but he would want something to show for her time. She worked on commission, so he didn't care how long it took to woo the hospital administrators to buy their system. But, it'd been a week since she'd even checked in.

"How's three out of five sound?" Along with two dead bodies. Brings me to a grand total of fourteen, but Dave wasn't interested in *those* stats. The schitzoid swing from sales professional to dirty cabbie was harsh, but the sales calls had paid off. So had the cabbie job, for that matter.

"You are the man. Umm … woman. Which three?" Dave's excitement was really cute.

"Desert Springs, Sunrise, and Valley."

He'd hired her to sell software systems to hospitals without much of a background check. Changing your identity was hell on the resume. But the car salesmen turned software marketing VP had said his gut told him she was a beast.

She'd laughed at how right he really was. After several horrid interviews, she'd taken his confidence as a motivator. What's it hurt him? Job was pure commission. If she failed it would only cost him a little training time. He'd made his money back in spades. In less than a year she was getting all the big leads and was assigned the best territories.

There was one more thing Dave wanted to hear. "Duke left a message today too."

"And? You're killing me, Maria."

"It's a go. Two point five, Dave. The entire network—hospital, outpatient, heart center, and medical facilities. Tech guys will be busy until next Halloween. I'll send you the specs and orders soon."

Carla came back up and jumped on her. Sophie didn't feel like being Maria at the moment, but that was the price she paid. A few minutes on this call and a full day's work tomorrow and she'd be set for a while.

"Damn. I'll need another project manager for that one. Nice work. You beat everyone's numbers again. One more and you'll have the record. Your bonus should be enough to buy a house."

"Already did." She laughed. "Gotta walk the dog. I'll email you tomorrow." She paced into the house and down the little hall.

"When did you get a dog?"

Carla had followed.

"Found her in Vegas and decided to keep her."

"Cute. Bring her when you come in. And when might that be?"

She stopped in front of a closed door and placed her palm on the wood. "Think I'm off to Dallas in a day or two. Want to follow up with Baylor. That COO is not happy with the system they have at all, but he's hesitating because it's only a year old and he dumped a wad into it. I think I can talk him over the hurdles if I keep at him."

"Great. You need anything from me?"

She patted the wood. "Not a thing. I'm all good."

"You sound … cheerful."

Sophie chuckled. "I guess I had better stop that, hadn't I?"

"No. That's not what I meant. I mean it's good to hear you sound so cheerful."

"Bye, Dave."

He huffed. "Later."

She disconnected the call and pushed open the door. Carla stood in the doorway.

"This is Danny's room."

There was a bed with hand and leg shackles like the hospitals use, several blankets folded neatly at the foot. A small beside table sat alongside it. The lighting was wall mounted so it couldn't be used as a weapon. She'd put two chairs in the room. One was a small plastic one for her to sit next to him and help him though his illness and she'd bought a more comfortable rocker so she could watch him as he slept.

Carla rushed to the bed and jumped on it.

"We must be patient, it may take him a while to come to love us again. Well, me. To love me again. But we will be a happy family."

You're gonna fuck this up.

The condescending tone grated Sophie's ears.

She was not. And this time she would ignore that voice and not play into her hate. Maybe she actually was cheerful. She was only a few days away from being with Danny, it didn't matter.

You better not wait too long. What if they move him?

Taunting.

What if that crappy van you picked out breaks down?

Criticizing.

What if you run out of drugs?

Undermining.

Sophie slammed open the closet door as the volume in her head reached a screeching crescendo. She ran her finger over boxes and tubes, checked the supplies off the mental list she'd memorized over a year ago. It was all in order. Drugs, bandages, plastic sheeting, bottled water, and men's necessities, all purchased months before. She had thought of everything. It would be fine, if she didn't fuck it up. How long should she wait for the cops on protection duty to get complacent? "Two days? Three?"

Carla yapped.

"Three days."

31

"**IT'S PAST MY DINNER** time." O rubbed the back of his neck with a white bandana and then shoved it back in his pocket.

Even after dark it was over 80 out and the humidity levels had to be topping out over 90 percent. They'd been walking around the known hangouts of the local working girls for a couple hours. It was close to ten and Jim's stomach was churning too. But that came with the territory. You kept at it until your leads were all gone. And there were still girls out there.

"You really think one of these girls is going to have been on the street that long? Long life for a pro." O looked over another girl they were approaching.

Most looked closer to twelve than thirty. "You're probably right, but we don't have much more to go on."

"There was a Mexican joint a couple blocks back. I say we get some enchiladas and a margarita. I think better on a full stomach." O turned without waiting for Jim's reply. Guess that was an order and not a request.

"Don't we all?" Jim followed.

He'd asked at least fifteen girls about Sophie. Shoved her picture under their noses telling them her mother wanted her home. Most could have cared less whose face was printed on that paper. They had their own sob story and no one was looking for them. No progress. Didn't even get a hunch one of them was lying to him. It had been too long since Sophie walked this dirty mile of concrete.

Tomorrow, come daylight, they'd visit the next crime scene in the file. Ely said it was in an abandoned warehouse. No electricity. Known area for gang activity. Jim was beginning to doubt any of the old crime scenes were going to give them much on where Sophie might be now. But all they had was the FBI file. He needed to retrace Sophie's steps.

The waitress seated them and handed them menus. O ordered two margaritas, on the rocks, with salt. She went on her way. The menu was similar to every little Mexican joint in the world. Jim knew what to order without looking. He studied the picture instead. Sophie looked happy. Dan was smiling too, but his eyes didn't reflect her joy. He was a teenage boy with a kid stuck to him like a shadow.

The waitress put down the drinks. O ordered his chicken enchiladas. Jim dropped the picture. "Speedy with beans."

"Chicken or beef, sir?"

"Beef."

"Is that Beth?" She pointed at the picture of Sophie and Dan.

"You know her?" Jim held the picture out for the woman to take. She was in her late thirties, maybe early forties. Old enough to have been around.

"Yeah. She comes in a lot. Well, she used to. I haven't seen her in years." She shrugged. "She got a big-time job and moved outta the ghetto."

"We're trying to find her for her mother." Jim made sure he made eye contact with the woman. Softened his face. "Do you know where she went to work?"

"Not sure. It's been a while."

He nodded, not wanting to pressure her. The memory could be a temperamental thing. He was in no hurry, he had tacos and margaritas to enjoy while she thought on it.

O spoke up. "We think she changed her name too. You know what last name she was using back then?"

"Girls do that around here." She looked down. "You know she was working the streets then. Getting a real job was a big deal. She was so excited." The waitress tapped her pencil to her lip. "Stratford ... or maybe Stafford."

Nice. Something to go on. A good lead from an unexpected source. He loved his job. Not that this case was really his job, was it? His job here was to make amends for his colossal fuckup of bringing Sophie to Dan's doorstep.

"I'll get you waters too." She left.

"You are a lucky bastard."

Jim half laughed. "Not me, bro. My luck is all bad. Remember, it was my luck that got me into this."

She rushed back over. "Stanton. Elizabeth Stanton." She looked quite pleased with herself. "I remember her pretty good. She would come here before going out for the night. She'd buy extra food. We thought she was feeding some of the homeless folks that lived under the overpass. Or maybe some of the other girls. I talked to her a lot. So did the old manager. But he's long gone."

Jim did not to think of Sophie as a saint delivering food to the helpless. She was a bat-shit crazy killer. Psycho. Maybe she was nice to people to get what she wanted. Stands to reason she was helping these people to get something from them.

"That's great"—O looked at her nametag—"Alejandra." He, of course, used the perfect accent to make her name sing.

She beamed at him. "I'll put in the order for your food. It won't take too long."

"Thanks, love," O said to her as she departed, garnering a quick smile over her shoulder.

Jim was already texting Ely the name Elizabeth Stanton. "Do you get laid? I mean does that shit work?"

"I don't do it to get laid." O smirked. "But that is sometimes a side effect of being nice to women. You should try it." O tilted his head. "Maybe just being nice to anyone you're not in the process of trying to get information out of."

Wow. That was the same thought he'd just had about Sophie Evers. "Tried it once. Didn't suit me."

Jim saw her as soon as the door opened. Suit wearing, not sweating in the heat Special Agent Ava Webb. She made short work of scanning the room and finding his face. There was no hiding from her. He tucked the picture, which he'd left out to help with Alejandra's memories, into his pocket.

"Mr. Bean." She glanced at O and gave him a small head nod. Very professional. She dragged over a chair, positioned it at the end of the booth, and plopped down in it. Her legs crossed with grace. Her shoes were sexy, but very sensible.

"Join us," Jim said, none too friendly.

"Hello." O leaned toward her. "And who do we have here, Jim?" O stuck out his hand. "Oscar Olsen."

"Hello, Mr. Olsen. Or should I say Double O?" She let her gaze swing back to Jim for an instant before she took O's hand. "You have an interesting history."

She thinks she's so smart for knowing everything. Well, it was her job. It was also fucking irritating.

O didn't flinch. His background was a tragic, painful mess and he wasn't the slightest bit ticked off this lady Fee Bee knew his deets. "And you have beautiful eyes."

Jim, meanwhile, needed to make a visit to his anger-management class over the fact that his records were still available to her. He'd seen his sheet in that file. He wondered if Miss Know-It-All understood the ramifications of his arrest and exoneration. That he'd be in her shoes right now if that night, that lie, had never happened.

"I seem to be the only one without the pleasure of your acquaintance, Ms. ... "

"Special Agent Ava Webb."

"Ahh. Lady Fed. Very nice to meet you." O exchanged an approving look with Jim. As if he had anything to do with her appearance or her presence at the table.

Jim had no worry that O would give her the information they'd just received, but little Miss Alejandra might just do so when she brought the food. Jim was not ready to share his boon with the FBI just yet. First on the scene gets the best info.

Webb leveled her steely gaze back on Jim. "I assume you're here investigating Sophie Evers?"

He glanced around the tacky restaurant with its dime store sombreros and brightly painted mural. "Just visiting Dallas. Lovely city." Most of it was. This particular area, not so much.

Damn, her eyes were green. Really green. Like his cat, Annie's, eyes. Green and deep and mischievous. Her hair was a normal brown but it seemed to be vibrant even pulled back in that tight-assed ponytail.

"I suggest you find a better area for your vacation needs, Mr. Bean. We have an active investigation to run and we don't need you muddying up the waters. We're recanvassing; you don't have to."

We. Her quiet suit of a partner must be around. Made sense.

Alejandra was coming with the food. O slid out of his side of the booth and excused himself with a brief word in the waitress's ear.

She set the plates out. "Would you like a menu, señora?"

"No, thank you." Agent Webb only gave the girl a fleeting glance before turning back to Jim.

He gave her his best surprised expression. "You ordering me out of city limits, Sheriff?"

She cracked a tiny smile. "I'm asking you to go back to Vegas and wait for word from us. We have this under control. Go play bodyguard there."

Ouch. "I think I like it around here. Considering moving down south."

"It's hot and humid and you won't like the locals." She stood. "I know your cop buddy must have shared something, or everything, from our file, Mr. Bean."

O folded himself back into the booth. "Call him Jim. He's not as bad as you think when you get to know him."

She didn't reply to O. "If you fuck this up, Detective Miller's ass is in hotter water than yours. This is our jurisdiction, and our investigation. Go home."

But it's my responsibility.

"You can't make me leave." Jim raised his brows, knowing the Feds could well make trouble for him, O, and Miller if they wanted to. But she couldn't make him go. She had no authority over him.

"I can have your investigator's license pulled. Stealing federal files is a serious offense."

He smiled at her. Well, she could probably do that. But it would take time. And if he solved this case before she got his license, what would she have to gain? "Do your worst, Agent Webb."

She marched away. Jim tried not to watch her go. He failed.

He turned back to O. "No way she can send us packing." But Jim did worry about her pressing charges on Miller for something like mishandling federal evidence.

"You have to go the hard way all the time, don't you?"

"What are you talking about?"

"That one? Out of all the women in Vegas, *that's* the one who heats up your tamale?" O took a big bite of enchilada.

"What are you talking about?"

He chuckled and dipped a chip. "You got the hots for her. Might as well take out a banner and fly it over the neighborhood, bro. It's written all over your body."

"Is not." Jim felt the lie on his lips. His luck sucked.

32

THE MARGARITA WAS HARSH. Probably the cheap tequila. But it was cold and it contained a good amount of alcohol. Basic survival needs.

The food far surpassed his expectations. The hole in the wall in Dallas was as close to authentic Mexican as he could get without a passport. No sour cream, no corny uniforms or giant blow-up beer bottles. He was about to happily bite into his second taco when Special Agent Ava Webb marched right back in the restaurant. Toward him. She still looked good, but she didn't look happy.

"Miss me already?"

"Apparently." Webb kept her gaze steady. "I'm not exactly in a sharing mood. But I get why you're interested in helping Dan. And I get that there's no way you two are going to back off ... Is there?"

Jim gave her a shrug. She only knew the half of his desire to get Sophie Evers. He wouldn't be enlightening her on the rest.

Her face briefly twisted into disgust before she spoke. "I just got a call from Vegas."

She didn't immediately elaborate. Jim's heart pounded. Her stern face was not helping. She'd make a great poker player.

"Cops found a body in the backyard behind the safe house, just outside the fence. The guy's throat was slit. My agent said it was messy. Probably unplanned and happened fast. ME just picked him up. Early guess on time of death was late last night. Dan and his mother are fine."

Jim's world tilted. "How'd she find them?"

Webb took the question as an invitation to sit. "Who knows?" She took a chip from the basket and bit off a tiny part of the triangle.

O pushed the salsa in her direction. "Miller moving them?"

Another safe house would be best. Unless she was hanging around to follow them to the new one. But why kill right there? Why not go on in and get Dan?

She took another chip and loaded it up. Jim should warn her he'd ordered the extra hot. He didn't. Let her play rough and tough.

She didn't pause to question the dip. Whatever. She bit down on the chip. No flinch. Didn't reach for water. O pushed his over just in case. Jim had thought about it but decided to make her sweat it out. Problem was, she wasn't. Can't fake that shit either. When a normal guy's mouth is on fire he sweats, turns red, eyes water.

"You read the file, right?" Still no signs of stress from her. *Nada.* Assumption: Jim and Miller had broken her rules and had the FBI file. There was no reading this chick. He couldn't tell if she was fishing for something to nail him on or what.

He shrugged. Wouldn't directly incriminate Miller.

"I'm thinking you know Sophie's killed in spurts. The first two in Stephenville, Texas, were anger-motivated. She saw the girls with her man and that's that. Blatant disrespect. Obviously doesn't value human life and she's got the drive to continue to kill like a serial."

She looked at O. "Then here in Dallas. It was a hodgepodge—some look revenge-motivated, some for profit, and a couple could be spite or practice with a new technique. With each one, though, she got smarter, stronger. The girl lives like a shadow. Selling drugs right under our noses, turning tricks. Then she goes silent for years."

Agent Webb finally took a sip from the water glass. But it wasn't in desperation or pain. She could take the hot stuff. She continued, now looking past O more than at him. "Since it seems your Danny boy is her final target, I'm thinking the closer she comes to fulfilling that long-term goal, the hastier the killing, the more her mental state is deteriorating. Her perception is getting more and more shattered. That plan, it's been her driving goal for years and *now* it's time to act. It's do or die. The guy behind the house looks like a slip in her control."

"You one of those profilers?"

Her gaze snapped to O. "Took a couple classes, but it's not my job description. My guess is she just lost it when the neighbor came up on her. She was snooping around and got spooked. Why else would she kill right there? It's dangerous. Very bold, more like stupid. She'd have to have known we'd yank them out of that house and place them somewhere under deeper cover."

"She's done more than one stupid thing." Jim almost wished the words back in his mouth. But Agent Webb was sharing; he should too. She may give him even more. She could drag him in and question him even though he had already shared most of his exchanges with Sophie. She had the report from Miller.

"Hiring me wasn't all that bright. She asked me not to confront Dan after finding him. That's all well and good. And if this had been an adultery case, I would have followed that request to the letter. Nothing but a photo and video confirmation. But her backstory on

Dan was too far off. It didn't match the guy I found. Dan didn't remotely look like a lost junkie. I followed my gut."

"Good thing for him." She took another swig. Still no sign of sweating the hot sauce. "Sophie's good at hiding her identity. She's done an inordinate amount of prep work. So much so that she's lived several separate lives at once. She's not dumb. Why hire you to track him down in the first place?"

"Hiding and finding are two different things, Agent Webb." O took an enormous bite of his enchilada.

Webb watched him chew. Big guy with a big bite was quite the sight. She stayed silent as he took a rather large swig of his 'rita before continuing. How did people get so comfortable with this man so fast?

"Finding takes connections and legal avenues. Hard to use legal avenues when you're trying to stay off grid as much as she is."

She tapped the table. "You got a line on anything I need to know, Bean? You can stay and share, or go home and follow up that death in Vegas. But I'm lead. I cannot have you interrupting my investigations."

She was right. It would slow things down if she was interviewing the same people Jim was. They did have a little something Ava Webb did not: a name. He wasn't sure he wanted to give it up. She might take it and go off and leave him out of the loop. She could. She should.

He would.

Alejandra refilled their waters. "You sure you don't want nothing?"

"Am I staying or going, boys?"

Jim *wanted* to be around the hot sauce–eating Special Agent Ava Webb, even if his gut told him she was trouble. As in girl trouble. The feeling made him want to tell her to shove off. "Let me in on a part of it."

She balked, leaning back in her chair. "Not a chance."

"I can help. I'll be quiet. All input *after* your interviews. I need to be doing something here, Agent Webb."

She huffed. Considered. Jim, O, and Alejandra were all staring at her.

"I'm a dammed good PI."

Webb stood, paused at the edge of the table for a moment, silent. Maybe trying to talk herself into a sharing mood. Maybe trying to talk herself out of it. He wasn't going to say anything and make her decision fall against his favor. He wasn't fond of working with the Fee Bees, but they had fucking good resources. And in this case, the end goal was the same for both of them.

"This is against protocol," she said finally.

O looked at the waitress. "Staying."

She sat back down. "No menu, I'll have the Speedy with beans."

O barked out a laugh over the food order coincidence and winked at Jim. He got a frown in return. O just kept grinning. Dear god, the man was going to try and play matchmaker. Jim would put a stop to that easily enough. For now, business.

"Waitress recognized a picture of Sophie. Said she was a pro until she got a good job and moved on. Said she went by the name Elizabeth Stanton."

Webb stopped with a chip almost to her lips. "Like the social activist?"

"You know the name?" O asked.

She rolled her eyes. "Elizabeth Cady Stanton was one of the early advocates of women's rights. Basically started the suffrage movement. You know, equal rights? Women get to vote?"

"Oh." O dabbed at some melted cheese that had found its way onto his shirt. "*That* Elizabeth Stanton. Out of context. I wasn't thinking in historical terms."

She tapped out a text. "I'll see what we find on Elizabeth."

He wondered if Ely would find something as fast or as good as the FBI.

33

JIM WAS DRYING OFF when he heard the knock at the door. He'd jumped in the shower right after leaving the restaurant. Wanted the grime and sweat of the dying neighborhood and the steamy Texas heat off his skin before he went to sleep.

"Yeah?" He never put his eye to a peep hole.

"Pizza delivery." O's rumbly voice was easily recognizable.

Jim swung open the door. To his great and unpleasant surprise, Agent Webb walked in ... followed by Oscar *you're getting your ass kicked* Olsen. Jim tightened the towel wrapped around his waist. Did she give him a good once-over before she turned away? Probably not. He needed some sleep.

"Sorry, bro. Didn't know you were ... um ... naked."

"I'm not naked." Jim headed to the bathroom to grab his jeans. If O was matchmaking at this time of night, Jim was going to find a good payback.

"Mostly naked," O allowed. "Nice abs. Been lifting again, I see."

Through the mirror Jim saw her give an eye roll. She didn't find his nakedness quite as amusing as O. Could be a good thing. Could be bad. And his gym time was to burn off steam. Properly release his anger. Or so the court order had read. Didn't hurt to be in shape in his business either and O knew it.

"Why are you two here, O?"

"Ran into Lady Fed in the hall. She was on her way."

Jim popped his head out of the bath as he buttoned his jeans. She didn't correct O's comment.

"I got something on Elizabeth Stanton."

As if on cue, his phone started blaring "Smoke on the Water." Ely. The phone was by the bed, across the room. She was a Fed, worked around men. His walking around shirtless shouldn't offend her sensitivity. And if it did, he wasn't sure he cared. He picked up the phone. "You have good stuff for me?"

"I do, my fine friend." Ely was always on target. He'd get the chance to one-up the woman. "I do. How's Lady Fed?"

What? "How do you know about..." Jim was going to say her name, but that would give her reason to believe they were taking about her. She was smart enough to see they were all plotting to put them together as a couple. Probably already picked up on it. That pissed him off too. He had no intention of adding to the farce. He glared at O as Webb looked out the window. Not that the view was exciting. His room overlooked the parking area.

"Good news travels fast," Ely said.

Jim gritted his teeth. "There is no good news. Unless, of course, you have some for me."

"Bummer. And I do."

"Well?"

"So you want the Stanton stuff or the mother stuff first?"

Jim looked at the Fed. "You coming up here to share info on Stanton?"

"Who is that?" she asked.

At the same time, Ely asked, "Is that Lady Fed? You in her room?"

"Special Agent Ava Webb, meet Ely. Go on with the Stanton info." Jim hit speaker button. "This is my research guru, Ely."

"Hello, Miss Ava Webb, Lady Fed." Ely was stoned. He all but sang out her name.

Her brows drew at Ely's tone. "He together enough to be reliable?"

Jim sighed. "Would I have put him on speaker if I didn't think he was okay?"

She frowned and stepped a little closer. Her eyes scanned his chest again. That time he was sure of it. Jim inwardly smiled.

Ely started, "Elizabeth Stanton. Born in Sweetwater, no real records until '89. Graduated University of North Texas in Dallas with a logistical something or other degree. Social Security records show two jobs in her career. One short term at a car rental company, the other with a warehouse distribution firm. You know, trucking and logistics and shit. She was there at least six years. Then she drops off the face of the earth. No money trail. Nothing."

Jim rubbed his chin. "That time period. The seven years or so she was employed. That the quiet time in the killing spree?"

Agent Webb nodded.

Ely said, "You got it."

So they had the same information. Where was her partner from the Vegas office, anyway?

"All lines up." O oozed into the chair at the tiny desk in the room. He'd been drinking all evening. Jim had a stash of scotch he'd been about ready to crack open. He wanted it now.

"But it tells us nothing." Jim shook his head. "So she had a job. Killing pimps seemed to be her job for a while before that. Pays her way through school with the drug sales? Then she goes all respectable? That would mean she was in school, turning tricks, *and* selling drugs. Busy young lady."

"Makes her smart and hard working. But fragile and easily thrown off kilter," Ava added. Jim shook his head at himself for thinking of the agent by her first name. He'd intentionally kept her at a distance by reminding himself she was an FBI agent and Jim was not. It would be like dating a really rich chick. You'd never be on her level. Not really.

"No shit," Ely said. "But I got another bone for you."

He paused. He always did. Jim could see him sitting at his wall of computers and grinning like a kid with a new Xbox.

"Don't keep us hanging too long," O shouted so he'd be heard from across the small hotel room. "We're all here looking at Jimbo's throbbing pecs while you shoot for the dramatic pause. It's taking away from the effect."

Jim grabbed a tee from his bag and pulled it over his head.

"Stealing my thunder, Bean?" Ely drawled.

"Ely."

"I found her real mom, bro."

"Sophie's real mom, not the foster mom?" Jim had talked to that family. They'd said terrible things about the girl. Not surprising, given what Dan had said about the way the fosters had treated her. Nothing to really consider there, since he was sure the foster father had abused Sophie.

"Exactly." Ely cleared his throat. "Her name is Mary Callas. Looks like she gave up three kids to the system over about seven years. Get this. All three were named 'Something' Ryan Evers. Oldest, Samantha

Ryan Evers, died in a car wreck in 2001. Middle, Sarah Ryan, moved to Idaho and got married real young. You Feds find that shit out?"

Ava frowned. "Not yet. We didn't have a lead to make us think tracking down the birth mother would be of importance."

"You were not adopted then, Miss Lady Fed. My girlfriend was. She's looking for her mom right now. Probably dead, but I think maybe all abandoned kids feel the desire to seek out mom."

She nodded to the phone. "You got me there, Ely."

Ha! His guy had one-upped the Feds. Take that. "Nice job, anything else?"

"No. Annie misses you. You want to talk to her?"

Ava raised an eyebrow.

"Miss her too, but I can't talk now. Work to do." Interesting. Maybe Agent Ava was a little bit jealous.

O butted in. "Give her some tuna."

Ava looked appropriately confused at O's order.

"Cats love tuna, don't they?" His tone dripped amusement.

So much for making the Fed think there was a little woman named Annie at home waiting for him.

"They do," Ely agreed.

"Goodbye, Ely."

"Later, Jim. See you in the a.m., O."

Jim looked at Oscar.

Ely sang over the phone, "Goodbye, Lady Fed."

Jim ended the call. "Heading home?"

O shrugged and put his arms up, locking fingers behind his head. "I figured you and Agent Webb here have things firmly in hand. No need for me to be tagging along. I got a business to run."

His leaving Jim alone with Agent Webb was definitely playing matchmaker, but O's reasoning made perfect sense. No way to argue

185

it. Jim was the one emotionally invested in the case, not O. He'd be available if Jim needed him, no question about that, but talking him into staying was impossible.

"I'll check in on Dan as soon as I get there and often. Is he in the same place?" O asked.

"We haven't made the move yet. But I'll clear you when we do. Probably tomorrow."

"Why so long?" Jim would have figured for a quick move.

"Sometimes we do a fake-out move. Let the bad element believe the subjects have been moved. His mother is old. Taking her a long way off would be hard on her. My partner is there, coordinating with the locals. Dan's being consulted today, we're getting his opinions."

"Wow. Considering the subject's opinion." Not what Jim expected to hear. "Kinder, gentler FBI?"

She smiled. "Not exactly. People in protective custody tend to stay in custody longer and stay safer when they have some say. Likely, we'll move your boy and his mom to another local spot. She's really frail. Don't want it to be too hard."

O piped up. "So I'm out for the night. On a jet plane in the a.m. Call me if you need." He gave a pathetic salute and left Jim standing in his hotel room with Special Agent Ava Webb.

"Tomorrow. Distribution company and the mom's house?"

Jim nodded.

"Eight. In the restaurant?" She was looking at the carpet. Or was it his bare feet? He hadn't answered, so she looked back up. Damn, her eyes were green.

"Got it. Breakfast at eight."

"No. Ready to go at eight."

Not a breakfast invitation then. He needed that scotch.

34

IT WAS DEFINITELY NOT a breakfast date. She met him in the dining room precisely at eight a.m. He was finishing up his steak and eggs, which was better than the paleo-vegan mush at the Coffee Girl, but the place lacked a certain charm—that charm being Sandy. He hoped that girl stayed in school for a long time, otherwise he'd need to go farther afield for his normal breakfast.

No surprise, Agent Webb seemed miffed that he wasn't ready to leave. She slid into the booth with a snippy greeting. They ran over what facts they had.

He paid the bill. They headed to Hickville, north of Dallas somewhere. No trees. Lots of dust. Ninety-three degrees at 9 a.m. Breathing was as laborious as sucking air through a swimming pool.

Heffelmire Distribution and Trucking was not the small, tired business on the verge of ruin Jim had expected. Not really sure why he'd thought that anyway, other than it was in a small town outside a huge metro area. He'd been dead wrong.

Instead of a shack, Heffelmire was a complex, thriving enterprise. Two office buildings and several huge warehouses sat safe inside an eight-foot fence topped with shiny new razor wire. No one was coming into this place without cutting up his ass cheeks. If Jim had bothered to spend the time counting, he was sure he'd find at least fifty tractor-trailers and half that many box trucks in and around the warehouses. Alejandra was right. Sophie had gotten a real job.

"Someone from HR is meeting us at the main building."

"You called ahead?"

Agent Webb let the window down to show her ID to the man working the gate. He jotted her name and the plate number in a log. "Yes. It's best to have an appointment."

"First building on your right, ma'am." The security guard waved her on with a sleazy grin.

"I never give people a heads up. That's opportunity for a guy to decide what you want and how he wants to handle you. If he's got something to hide, he's ready to talk. Lying's easier if you're prepared. I like to take them off guard."

"And if the person you want happens to be out to lunch?"

"You get what you can from the secretary or a co-worker. They'll be back."

She got out and leaned on the roof of the car. "Seven-year-old employment records? You really think anyone here has old information like that off the top of their heads that they want to protect?"

Anything was possible. He shrugged. No way he'd admit she might be right about that, and followed her into the building. She was still wearing a dark suit—possibly the same one, but it looked clean and pressed. Did she take the time to press it this morning? Jim checked his jeans to make sure they weren't stained.

Webb took the lead. She was the Federal agent in charge at the moment. Why would she let a lowly PI take point? Made for a great opportunity to see how people reacted to her. How she did her job.

She flipped out the badge. "Agent Webb, here to see a Millie Stubbs. I have an appointment."

The receptionist smiled. "I'll call her right away." She motioned to a clipboard with a sign-in sheet. "If you could, please."

She called and chatted with Millie in a hushed tone as Jim and Webb left their full names, the name of the party they were visiting, and the time of arrival. The woman took the board and handed them each a visitor badge as she logged the badge number beside their printed names.

Jim eased over to the large windows overlooking the complex. A security guard walked the front of the building. Probably cameras in the parking lot too. Lots of security. With a small turn, Jim scanned the reception area. Inside, two surveillance cameras scanned the reception area.

"What kind of distribution do you do around here?" he asked.

"All kinds. Domestic. International. Land, sea, air. You need it moved, we're your logistics experts." The phone rang. The receptionist grabbed it as she pointed to a small seating area and mouthed *Have a seat* before rattling off her canned greeting.

"Bet this is the biggest employer for miles around."

"Looks like it." Webb was also scanning. Checking the environment. Her cool eyes assessing. "Why take off? I mean, this is a real job. One she got from an education she earned under an assumed name, as if this was going to be her long-term life. But then she abandoned it," Webb pondered aloud.

Heels clicked sharp and snappy on the floor. Efficient. Millie Stubbs rounded a corner, but she wasn't what he'd expected either. A

Millie should be older, grayer, probably a little chunky. But this Millie was in her mid-twenties, dark blond hair with a pert nose and stick-thin figure. Her beige pinstripe suit made her look like a walking ruler. She was not smiling.

Webb stood. Extended her hand. "Special Agent Webb, FBI. Thanks for seeing us on such short notice."

"Not sure how much I can help. I pulled Elizabeth Stanton's file. She did work here on the dates you gave me. Almost exactly."

"And she left why?" Jim stood. Millie looked down her nose at him. Could be his unshaved face, could be his causal attire. Either way, Millie was not impressed.

Millie put her hands behind her back, making her look even more like a talking ruler. "Afraid that's confidential. I can't release the circumstances around someone's termination. It's against privacy laws." She tilted her head down but looked up at Agent Webb, as if she were looking over glasses. "I would think you would know that, Special Agent Webb."

This chick was a barrel of laughs.

"Would you hire her again?" he asked.

Millie's sour look made Jim want to smile. He knew the laws. But he didn't want to push any more of her buttons than necessary. Yet.

"I'm afraid not."

"So, she was canned?"

She said nothing. Just stood there looking straight and smug.

Webb let out a heavy sigh and cocked her hip slightly to the side. She clasped her hands at the fingers and impatiently tapped her thumbs together. Quick as a snake strike, her face contorted. Millie took a very small step back. Jim loved it. Special Agent Webb turned bulldog in a heartbeat.

"You can be as smug as you like, Ms. Stubbs. But I'm investigating murder cases and the body count is now over double digits. Do you think you might have *something* you can share from your files that could help us?"

Millie's face paled. Her hand went to her chest. "Wow. Murders?" The word *murder* usually takes the starch out of the smug one's britches. "And one of our ex-employees is involved?"

Jim decided to speak. "We're trying to track Stanton down, follow her history. It could help us solve a series of murders and prevent any further violence. Any help you can provide would be beneficial." He'd play the nice guy. It wouldn't kill him this once.

"Umm. Legally, I can't say too much." She glanced back toward the hall she'd come down. "I looked at the file when you called. I, of course, was not here at the time. But the termination was robustly documented. Without a warrant, I'm afraid I'm only willing to say she had a rather heated personality conflict with another employee."

"Can you tell us the employee's name?"

Millie hesitated and glanced back again to make sure the receptionist was not listening. "No." She bit her lip. Her little pointy-toed shoe tapped the tile. "I *can* suggest you stop in at Woody's Place to have a drink. The 'bartender' is a great guy. He's been around and may have stories about local history." She actually used air quotes for the word *bartender*, as if they were stupid.

Agent Webb pulled out a card.

Millie took it. "Hope that helps."

"Me too. Thanks."

"Tell Max I said hi." Millie turned and strolled down the hall, seemingly satisfied that she'd helped the FBI and not broken her rules.

Max the bartender was either the ex-supervisor or someone who would know what had happened. Hopefully he had something pertinent, if not...

"How long does it take the FBI to get a warrant?"

"Too long. My hope is Ms. Millie just made that unnecessary."

35

"STOP BY AND SEE Max on our way to Mary Callas, the mom?" Jim closed the car door.

FBI car. Big and dark and with state-registered plates. About as stealth as the Empire State Building rolling down the Strip. She drove. He'd never be caught in a dark blue or black sedan of any type. Cop car, cop engine. In his line of work, the car should say nothing about the man or his mission. Special Agent Ava Webb, however, had a cop car. Rolling authority.

"Logical progression." She punched Woody's Place into the GPS. "Only ten minutes in the wrong direction. Back towards town."

They had to have driven right past it on the way out here. Jim hadn't noticed. What had he been paying attention to? Not like him to miss something like that.

The gravel parking lot had only three vehicles. An old Chevy and two compacts. It was ten a.m. Probably just the owner and the cooks prepping for the day. The front door was unlocked. Webb pushed the door in and eased through without waiting for him to open it for her. Jim followed. Scanning.

He was right. Not one customer in the wood-paneled place but behind the counter was a graying man in a T-shirt with an outline of Texas on it. Inside the state lines was a cowboy pointing a gun straight ahead. The caption read: *We don't call 911.*

Nice.

"You must be Max," Webb said as they approached.

His face was tan, like a guy who spent too much time outside. Maybe enjoying fishing now that bartending was his gig and days were free. He had more gray hair then brown. Max put his knife down and wiped his hands, carefully returning them, palms down, to the bar, where they could be seen. This wasn't his first rodeo.

"Not if you're the law." His face was easy. Calm. Not a twitch. This man was guilty of little.

Jim wished he was the one talking to this guy. Figured PIs might do better with guys who don't like cops than a Fed in a suit with a shiny badge. He was less coppish than her by a mile.

But she had to flash the badge. Protocol.

Max straightened. Pulled away from them. "What's the FBI want with me?"

She eased onto a barstool. Unbuttoned her jacket. Nonthreatening. "We were wondering if you ever worked for Heffelmire."

"I did." Crossed his arms eased back a step. More standoffish. He was ready to clam up completely.

"You ever work with an Elizabeth Stanton?"

He leaned back against the beer cooler. If he could have oozed his body thought the wall of liquor bottles behind him, he would have. His body language couldn't be any more closed. "Eliza. Yeah."

"You two have issues?"

His expression went flat, his body stiff. Even his eyes didn't blink. Jim felt the anger from six feet away. "What's this about?"

"We're looking for her."

He huffed, unfolded his arms. His shoulders dropped. A big relief. But why?

"You ain't gonna find her here!" He snickered and started cutting limes again.

"Don't suppose you know where…"

"Nope. And don't want to. If you find her, keep her the hell away from me." Lime juice shot in Webb's general direction. "Sorry. Can't help you."

Jim sat too. Why had the man relaxed so suddenly? "What happened with you two, anyway?"

Max looked down at his work. Hesitated. "Nothing I feel like reliving." His glance was down and his eyes avoided both of them. "Why are you looking for her?"

"We need to ask her some questions. Having a little trouble finding her," said Webb.

Max studied Webb and glanced back at Jim. Maybe he did know something. His face lit up as he stopped the cutting again. He leaned forward on the bar. "Feds only show up when something *real* bad happens." His accent thickened as he leaned forward, his arms on the counter like he was ready to come over the bar in a big leap. "Crazy bitch done killed someone, didn't she? "

Webb glanced to Jim. Nodded. She was going to let Jim go with this one. Fine. "Actually, a bunch of someones," said Jim.

Max's meaty fist smacked the bar hard enough to make the cutting board jump. "Told everyone she was a certified psycho." He rested the knife on the counter. "How?"

"Stabbings."

Eyes closed as if to ward away some reality Jim and Ava didn't understand. "She use drugs first? You know, to knock 'em out?"

"We think she sold drugs for a while in Dallas under another name, before she came to—"

"No." Max's head shook and his gaze found Webb. "Did she use drugs in the killings? Like date-rape drugs?"

Ava tapped the counter, thinking. "Not that I'm aware of."

Jim's heart, meanwhile, thudded in his chest. Each beat heavy, sluggish. He knew what Max was asking. "What do you mean?"

Maybe Jim wanted to know the answer to that question. Maybe he didn't. Memories of his experience with Sophie assaulted his own head space. Her voice, drug-garbled and vacant, echoed in his ear, ran like a bad music clip. The vague feeling of violation crystallized with every word Max uttered.

Max looked around as if someone might have invaded the space as they had been talking. If he was going to tell a secret, he didn't want the world to hear. "Eliza invited me for drinks after work one night." Aimlessly, Max stroked the tattered bar top with his towel. "I thought it would be a crowd. Usually was. Turned out to be just her and me. No big deal at the time. We were co-workers. No reason to not have a drink with a co-worker, you know?"

He looked at Jim to confirm his feelings. Jim gave him a short head tilt to agree. Max concentrated on the wood surface to avoid looking at Ava.

"Well, it got out of hand fast. I was drunk, real drunk, after just two beers."

Jim knew where this was going. Wondered if the sweat he felt beading on his forehead was noticeable.

"She offered to run me home. I remember *that* part. Then I remember a little bit of a hotel room. And her naked. And ... "

"We get the gist, Max." Jim said it to keep him talking. His own demons were twisting in his gut with each word. It would have been so easy to vomit right there at the bar. Jim swallowed down his own anxiety like dry bread. Didn't really want to know the rest. But they needed to hear this guy out. "Go on. You can leave out the details."

"I told this story enough. Hell, the whole town knows about it. I been bartending on the side for years. Everyone knows me. Small place like this, the bigger the secret, the faster it spreads."

Damn. Jim knew that. "Go on."

"Woke up in the hotel. I was … well. I knew I had … been … " He rubbed his fat finger under his nose and exhaled. "Raped." He stared at the bar for a moment.

Jim didn't like the word. It was like acid pouring into ears. He accepted that he'd been taken advantage of, even duped over the investigation. But rape?

Ava gave him time before pressing for more. "You confront her? After the incident? Report it to the authorities?"

Max finally looked at her. "I most certainly did. The next day at work." He shook his head. "I went right to her office and told her what I thought of her little escapade." He waved his hand. "But that didn't work out like I expected it to, either."

"No?"

"She took offense to the accusations. Got all mad. Started yelling. Standing as far from me as she could. Saying I was harassing her. Turns out, the night before she'd filed a sexual harassment complaint *against me*! Took me hours to get over the drugs. She made her complaint before I could do anything, say anything." He rubbed the towel across his brow. He was sweating more that Jim, but not by much. "You can imagine my reaction to that. I felt like shit. I'd been taken advantage of. Was worried what the wife was going to think."

He leaned against the coolers again. All the color was gone from Max's face. "We got into one hell of a shouting match. The whole office tuned in. Then she came over the desk after me. Looked like a cheetah on attack. Screaming like *I* was the rapist. The cops came. Then they didn't know who to believe."

Jim's vision went a little blurry with anger. Not only was this guy the victim, he was being accused of the crime. Jim's unease with his own feelings multiplied. He was going to get this woman and put her away if it killed him. But he had to know if he and Max shared more than Max would ever know. "Did they arrest you?"

"Of course. Who believes the man would be innocent? That *I* was the victim?"

Jim knew that feeling all too well. He and Max were uncomfortably close to kindred spirits. Both falsely accused of rape. And both …

And both rape victims of Sophie Ryan Evers.

"Flip side of this being such a small town out here is my brother-in-law heard quick. He's an attorney."

Max looked Ava in the eye now. Stood his full height. "I'm telling you. I know a Mickey when I see one. The bitch drugged me. Put shit in my drink. Brother-in-law sent me to the hospital, did the rape kit. Tested my blood. It was ketamine."

"Did they arrest her?" Nothing had come up in the searches, but this was a small town.

"When my brother-in-law took the evidence to the police, they went to question the crazy bitch, but she was long gone. Never heard another peep out of her. Flat out disappeared."

Ava stepped away to make a call. Jim heard bits of the conversation. *Latest vic. Signs of Special K.* He knew that was the street name for the drug.

Jim noticed Max didn't wear a wedding ring. He'd said he was married. Now that it was just the two of them, he asked, "The wife?"

"Didn't like the stigma either way. I was a villain or a victim. She couldn't hack the aftermath. It's been years now." Max started back to the task of cutting the evening's limes. "Most people have forgotten or at least don't seem to care anymore."

"And you, you still care?" The importance of the answer was weighty.

"Life's short. And if she's killing folks now, I guess I got something to be appreciative about."

Jim agreed with old Max on the whole *not having your throat cut* thing. He hoped this feeling of helplessness passed soon. Last thing he needed was one more thing to drink over.

"But it'd sure be real nice to know if you get her. Feel kind of like vindication."

Amen. "I'll let you know if we do. Any idea where she might have gone? She ever talk about any family or friends living around here or out of state?"

Max pulled in a deep breath. "Sure wish I could tell you anything useful. I didn't even work in the same department she did. She was sales and project management. I was operations. Only knew her from the few times a big group of us went out."

Jim handed Max a card. "If you think of anything."

He knew he should probably tell Ava about his own experience with Sophie. The thought only lingered a moment. Wasn't going to happen. Unlike the good folks from small towns, Jim could keep a secret. It in no way jeopardized the case or his client, so Ava didn't need to know. If Sophie was drugging vics, they'd figure that out. They didn't need his word for it. Max had fixed it for him, actually.

He would file his experience, that freakish night, away with a few others he'd buried in the *never think of again* file.

It'd be easier to accomplish once the bitch was behind bars.

36

MARY CALLAS'S TRAILER WAS, at one time, pink. Flamingo pink, Jim would guess. Now it was faded I-don't-give-a-shit salmon-ish. A tiny porch was missing half the handrail and the driveway was more weeds than gravel. The surrounding lot had not been mowed all season. Haphazardly placed along the mobile home skirting were crumbling plastic pots with the skeletal remains of long-dead flowers.

A lone red Ram Raider from the eighties sat covered in dust by the steps.

Agent Webb, looking particularly starched and official in this crumbled surrounding, put her hand on the hood. Jim wouldn't have bothered; thing looked like it hadn't moved in weeks given the weed growth around the tires.

"Haven't seen one of these in a while." She looked back. "Dated a guy who had a black one years ago."

Three steps and she was on the porch. Jim stayed on the ground. No room up there for the both of them. Not without being really close to her.

No bell.

Webb pounded. Jim figured she would shout an announcement, a proclamation the FBI was on the premises. *Open up.* But she waited. Silent.

"No appointment here, huh?"

She raised an eyebrow. "No. Someone told me it was best to catch them off guard."

His own words. But she'd obviously made this decision long before he'd made that statement at Heffelmire.

She knocked again.

Jim indicated he was going around back with a head tilt. From the side, he saw a second trailer several hundred feet behind the faded flamingo. No driveway led back that far. The thing was old. Rust stains dripped down the corners and window edges. Overgrown shrubs and trees had taken over to the point he was sure no one had lived in the place for the last decade. Windows were busted out. What was left of the porch was detached and leaning off into the bushes.

But after finding the ex-showgirl in the abandoned housing unit in Dallas, who knew? His thoughts were drawn back when a woman started singing. At least, he thought she might be singing. It also might have been a cat gargling razors. He eased to the back corner of the trailer.

Sure enough, it was a woman in her sixties, squeezed into a plastic lawn chair two sizes too small. Her double chin wriggled as she mouthed the words to a tune he didn't know. She tossed something to the ground and a flutter of crows swarmed to her feet. Bread crumbs? She didn't look to have the income to be buying bird seed.

Webb joined him. "I'll go first. Stay behind me." She loosened the strap on her holster. Ready to draw. Started walking confidently toward the mother. "Ms. Callas?" She walked on.

"You worried an old woman might be killing black birds with a machine gun or something?" Jim asked.

"Given what her daughter's done ... " Which was laymen's speak for protocol. "Mary Callas?"

The woman lost her balance as she reeled back in the chair. Arms flailing to catch herself on a concrete step. Quick as a whip, she recovered and reached for something next to her. Jim was three steps behind Agent Webb. The mother swung a shotgun in his general direction.

Webb drew lightning quick.

Chalk one up for the Fed's protocol.

Jim held up his hands. "Whoa, Nelly."

"Who in the tarnation are you assholes?"

"I'm Special Agent Ava Webb, FBI." She said it calm. Collected. "Put the weapon down and I'll show you my ID."

"Ha!" she barked out. "Put your weapon down an' I might let you live long enough to get your first hemorrhoid."

Jim chuckled. "I think she's calling you a baby, Agent Webb."

"Shut up, Bean."

He poked his head around his female protector. Didn't like the idea of using the woman as a shield. And Momma didn't look too intent on shooting anything but the shit.

"Jim Bean. I ain't got no government ID. Private investigator from Vegas. You're not in any trouble, Ms. Callas. We just wanted to see if you could help us with something." He shrugged. "At least, you ain't in any trouble as long as you put that gun down."

She pointed the gun off toward the woods where there was no immediate danger of killing anything human. She looked at the old gun. "Just for robbers, snakes, and such." She pointed it at the ground, seemingly unconcerned that Special Agent Webb still had her sights dead set on the woman's center mass. And boy, was it a center mass.

Webb pulled out her billfold and flipped the badge out as she let the gun point straight up. But she didn't put it away. "Wondering if you can tell us anything about your daughter."

"Ain't got no daughter."

"Sophie Ryan Evers?"

"I said, I ain't got no young'uns."

"No kids?" Webb asked.

Momma Callas didn't answer. Sufficiently convinced she wasn't getting robbed, she put the gun on the ground next to her chair.

Webb kept hers out. "I have records that say you have three children."

"I popped out three spawn. Give them up, so's they not mine. Hear one's dead, the other two is off somewhere that's not here. They are not *my* daughters. Adoptions is supposed to be private. Seems everyone and their dog been out here about those girls."

"The youngest." Webb stepped closer. Jim followed.

"She's a piece of work, that one." The mother turned her head and spat between two crows that had resettled on the food scraps.

"You have seen her?"

"Suppose I has. Stupid girl came around here few years back." She shielded the sun from her eyes to look up at Jim. Sweat trailed down her face and neck. "Crying about being broke and mistreated by the folks that raised her. Looking for a handout, I reckon." She tossed some more of the scraps on the ground. Crows swarmed. "I look like the handout kind to you, Mr. PI?"

"You're feeding birds."

"I'm littering. The fucking birds is scavengers" She pried herself out of the chair with a great deal of effort. The distortion and near destruction of the plastic made Jim feel the need to go and assist, to prevent a fall, but she seemed the type to be offended by chivalry.

"Sophie?" Webb turned the conversation back to the papers. "So she wasn't working then?"

"Pfft. No good little whore. Couldn't hold no kind of job. Pathetic. Weak. Stupid. That's what I told her too." She shook her finger at Webb. "If she was gonna whore with her stepdaddy, or whatever the man was, she might as well go do it on the street. Make some cash. I wasn't gonna let her come here and use up my check." She shook her head, chin swinging. "Kids gotta make their own way. No one ever gave me a thing in life. Told her that much too. Stupid bitch just cried."

Webb flinched at the harshness. "She's your daughter."

"She's a fucking useless waste of air. Girl got no backbone and no sense. Just like the others. All she wanted was a handout. Little snot wouldn't never bring a thing into my place but trouble. And you being here is proof enough of that, now ain't it?"

Webb took in a deep breath. Her face got that determined look again. "You have any idea where she went from here?"

"Do you think I asked the girl her travel arrangements? That was years back, anyhows." Momma Callas was trying to get up the stairs and into the house. The crows were landing close to her feet, looking for their crumbs.

"She did manage to work her way into college, Ms. Callas." Webb wielded the information as if it were a weapon.

"Did she then?" She looked back from her open doorway. Jim was sure she would have to ooze through the door like the blob. "Should I be proud?" She curled up her nose and her top rotted teeth showed though the sneer. "And the FBI and some PI comes looking for college kids just to congratulate them?" She waved them off. "Whatever trouble that child is in is all on her shoulders. I ain't got nothing to do with it."

"I think you had lots to do with it. But nothing I can charge you with."

Mary Callas flipped the bird to the federal officer and slammed the door with a rickety clunk.

Agent Webb stomped through the weeds back to the car, grumbling under her breath the entire way.

Jim followed. "Can't pick your family, huh?"

37

CARLA TROTTED HAPPILY AROUND the splintered wooden picnic table. She'd pooped and peed and was now sniffing the signatures of a thousand other dogs who had ventured through this rest area.

Sophie took a drink of her vitaminwater. She'd go herself before they got back on the road. Carla was fine moving about in the big van, but the stiff upright driver's seat made Sophie's human back ache. She could take something, but she wanted her nerves calm and her head clear.

A phone in her pack rang. She opened the zipper. Three cheap prepaids lined the bottom of the pocket. Untraceable. Disposable. Then noise came from the project phone. The other two were her work phone and what she referred to at the time as the bat phone. Only a select few had the project line number. People who didn't care what her real name was. People rendering services. Something was happening.

"Yes."

"It's um … Cat." The little homeless girl Sophie left watching the house where the police held Danny sounded unsure she'd reached the right number. Killing the neighbor had been a momentary lapse. She should not have given into the ardor so easily. Cat had been her fallout plan. Using her own brilliant strategy, she'd acquired another dog and set Cat up with some new clothes, food, and a hotel a few blocks away. The poor girl hadn't had a good meal in days. So it was charity as well. To earn her gifts, all she had to do was walk by the house several times a day, blend in, look like she belonged, hang out on the corner like a teenager without enough supervision.

"I think something's going on. They like put an old lady in an ambulance thing and moved her. I followed as best I could."

"You lost them?" Sophie's grip on the phone was almost painful. Having to track them again would burn up time. Sophie was out of patience and the dead sister and dead neighbor really sped up the sand dripping through the hourglass.

"Kinda. Made it to another corner, several blocks away. Was weird cuz they was heading like, *into* the neighborhood, not out of it." She sniffed.

"You're not *using* with that cash are you, Catty?" If the little shit lost Dan …

"Naw. I never really use. Makes you vulnerable on the streets. It's allergies. My nose runs all the fucking time." She sucked in again. Sneezed. "Anyway, then a truck went by. Three guys were in it, all in the front. I thought it was the one from the house. I managed to follow that for a block or so. Then I just wandered around until I saw the ambulance again."

So they'd moved him, but not far. The old woman must be frail. "Nice work, Cat." Too bad she'd still have to die. Poor kid had saved her some legwork, but she was now a witness. "You think the cops noticed you were hanging around both places?"

"I don't think the same cop saw me at any two places. Stayed back, I tried being sneaky." Sniff. "Put a cap on and shit."

Didn't matter. Sophie was on her way. The anticipation, the excruciating waiting, had been eating away at her. She'd started biting her nails again. She needed to take extra vitamins next week. The stress was murder. That's why she'd only stayed two nights at the house. She was itching to go, get her Danny and get back home. In a matter of hours she'd roll back into Vegas.

"The address?"

"375 Harper."

"Thanks, Cat. You stay at the hotel a few more days. It's all covered. And I hid a bonus under the nightstand."

"Wow. Thanks, lady. Been nice eating regular like. I'm gonna hate hitting the streets again."

Sophie hung up.

The hotel would be a great place to stage the van until she could scope out the new house. Carla jumped up on the bench and curled up next to Sophie's leg. Her fur felt like satin under Sophie's fingers.

"You look tired. Ready to go nap in the car?"

Carla raised her head and gave Sophie that ridiculously cute head tilt, eyebrow lift thing.

"Okay. Let's go."

At the word *go*, Carla was up and pointed at the van. She stayed right by Sophie's side until Sophie herself got up and started moving.

"Good girl."

The phone rang again. Irritated, Sophie punched the green button. Nothing. Another ring. It was another phone. She pulled one of the other two out.

"The bat phone." Her heart fluttered. This phone was connected to her real self—or as close to a real self as Sophie could get. She'd set it up under the name she'd decided would be her hidden identity years ago. She wasn't sure what to expect. It had caller ID, but she didn't recognize the number. Texas.

"Hello."

"Hello your dammed self."

Sophie looked down at the electronic device with a dizzying mix of hate and curiosity.

"Well, you gonna say anything, stupid?"

"What do you want me to say?"

"'Hello, Mother' would be nice." Her voice dripped with the same malice that barraged Sophie with insults and disdain in her head. The voice was Sophie's own, but the content was all the venom that this woman could spit. Sad, seeing as they'd only spoken a few times in her life.

"Hello, Mother."

"I'm not your mother, you cunt."

Sophie spun around, as if she would find her birth mother sitting on the bench. If she had been, the bitch wouldn't have an ounce of blood left. Teeth clenched so tight her jaw popped at the hinges. Her temples throbbed as a blood-red haze clouded her vision.

Carla nosed Sophie's free hand. Her mother was bitching about something related to damaging her reputation. As if she had one worthy of protection.

"I really wish I had just gone to the clinic and been done with the three of you. Only the first of you has had the decency to die."

What the fuck was she so worried about this woman for? Nothing but a birth canal. She held no power over Sophie. No power.

"Maybe you should have. What do you want?"

"No trouble on account of you're in trouble."

"That makes no sense, birth canal."

"What?" She coughed again. "Whatever. Cops came looking for you."

Holy crap. They'd traced her that far. Good thing the plan was getting close to culmination. Outsmarting the cops was not a problem. She'd done it a hundred times before.

"And you told them what?"

"None of your damned business, you ungrateful shit." The birth canal started coughing again, but this was not from allergies like little Cat. That disgusting hack rang of heinous lung damage, sprawling cancer from years of chain smoking. The red eased away some more. Sophie may not have had the nerve to kill her, but fate would intervene on her part.

"Fuck off," she said.

"Oh, so you do have some backbone. Imagine that. Fancy education and little baby balls."

"What did you tell them? When were they there?"

Get the facts and get off the phone. Should have never left her a number in the first place. Ignorant, youthful hope. Had she really wanted to make a connection when the birth canal had been a bitch to her?

"A while ago. Took me forever to find that thing you wrote your number on."

Sophie remembered. She had to turn and pace back toward the table. "You mean the copy of my birth certificate?"

"Oh. Whatever. Can't read the small print no more. Been in the junk drawer. So how come the cops are looking for you?"

"But you kept it? How sweet."

"Don't go looking for a Hallmark from me, honey. Knew trouble would come from you someday. Only kept it so's I can tell you I don't want your shit to bring no trouble on me."

"Lose this number then."

"Lost." The line went numbly empty.

38

JIM'S STOMACH FELT LIKE an abandoned well. Empty and dusty. He glanced around the area surrounding his hotel as they approached. Slim pickings. "Anything better around here than the Arby's?"

Agent Webb pulled to the curb. Didn't put the car in gear. "I'm heading to the Grove. It's a cop hangout. But it has a good beer menu and the burgers are as big as *your* ego."

"Good for you. Arby's for me unless you have a better idea. Is there somewhere around here?"

She gave him a weak smile. "I'm asking if you want to come."

"Oh." That was a genuine surprise. "With you? Sure you want to be seen with the likes of me, Agent Webb?"

"My reputation might survive this one time. And call me Ava."

She put the car back in gear. They drove in silence. She was playing with her bottom lip. The mindless action was hot. And now she was Ava. Like a real girl.

He looked out the side window. Ava Webb was the kind of woman he always figured he'd end up with. Strong. Independent. Only one thing... He'd lost his opportunity to be in the bureau back in college, so now the whole FBI thing was a deal breaker. He'd spent a good deal of time being angry at life and at women since then. And he drank too often because of it.

The betrayal, the bitch slap to his life's plans. It was the first thing he thought about in the morning and the last thing before slipping off to sleep. He'd gotten better, but he was still bitter. So it didn't matter what he wanted. Or what the guys thought he needed. Ava Webb would remain Agent Webb to him. No way he was going there. Not now. Probably not ever.

They slid into a booth. Several other men in uptight Fed suits were scattered around the bar. A couple off-duty cops as well. Irish joint, not a surprise.

"What is it about the Irish? Even down here in Texas, the cops hang with the Irish."

She smiled. "I've wondered about that too. All over the world, it seems the same everywhere. I have no idea why. Maybe the casual feel of Irish pubs?"

They ordered off a flip menu standing on the middle of the table. Burgers and beer.

"Maybe because the Irish are either cops or criminals themselves."

She chuckled. An uncomfortable silence took over. If it wasn't case related, what else could they talk about? Maybe dinner together had been a bad idea.

After a moment of silence, she said, "Tell me what happened in Ohio, exactly."

And there it was. Dinner had been a colossally bad idea. He had been looking at the cardboard coaster advertising a local brew. His gaze slowly went to hers. She didn't blink.

That information was *his*. His history. "Rather not. You read the file. Sure it's all in there."

"Couple lines. Basic facts. Reality is usually longer, and way more interesting than a blurb in a file."

"More interesting?" Oh god, was she right. But he was in no mood to go over the nightmare simply for her curiosity's sake. He was still reeling from his encounter with Sophie in Fort Worth. No way he wanted to churn through pain and anger from his past to add to the growing acid reflux of his present.

"Why do you have those facts anyway, Agent Webb? No reason for my history to be in the Evers file."

"We get as much information as possible before an interview. Can't imagine your technique is much different." Her brows rose, but she only hesitated for a moment. "You were almost in the academy when things went south, weren't you?" She twisted a napkin without looking away from him. Might as well be a knife in his gut. She looked into his eyes as if she knew his secret without his telling her or without that file to give her hints. No judgment there either.

He suddenly wished he'd picked Arby's. Sliced beef and curly fries didn't sucker punch you with questions about your past.

Thank whatever beer gods hover around Irish bars, her phone rang. She dropped her catlike stare to grab the call. His shoulders relaxed a bit. He didn't lean forward, but could hear a muffled male voice on the other end. Obviously Fee Bee business. Probably the partner in Vegas. All she said was *yes* or *okay* for five minutes. No hints for him. Thankfully, the beers came. Distraction number two.

Now that the irritating subject had changed, he was hoping to get something, anything that would help them get closer to Sophie. Time was passing by like a stock car. The maniac would be back to get Dan, and it would be ugly when she showed her face.

All day, Jim had been torn in different directions. On one hand, he wanted to leave the legwork to the Feds and get back to personally protect Dan and his mother. On the other, he didn't trust that Agent Webb would keep him in the loop if he wasn't by her side. Then there was the *third* hand: he wanted to be there. To be the one to strap Sophie's hands behind her back. Cuffs or tie-wraps, he didn't care which. She might not be left unmarked before her trip to the station either.

O was back in Vegas by now. He'd be watching Dan. No one better. And Miller and his team were on the job. Plus the Feds. No worries in Vegas, he told himself. Again.

She disconnected the call with only a stern, "Okay." She took a long drink.

"And?"

"The neighbor was drugged. Ketamine. ME says there was a mark on his shoulder that was made by one of those auto-injectors. You know, like an EpiPen?" She didn't wait for his answer. "Found the same mark on Cynthia Hodge when he went back and checked." She spun her glass between her fingers. "Makes sense. Sophie's a smallish woman, right?"

Jim nodded, remembering her straddling him, whispering in his ear. He bit his tongue. He hadn't been injected, that he remembered, but she'd had control of his drink when she was at the bar.

Webb kept talking, unaware of what was racing through his head. She never would be either. Now that two vics had come up drugged, there really was no benefit to Dan or the case to share his experience.

"Some ketamine would make the bigger guys much easier to manage, her kills cleaner. And the sexual assault of Max ... I can only guess that was a power trip."

Jim's heart was pumping again. The feeling of loss and violation churning with anger forced the acid in his gut to climb toward his throat. "Why do you say that?"

She shrugged. "Fits the profile of a serial. Sex and killing get all tangled up in their minds. Rape is just as much of a power trip as slicing that throat, maybe more. For male perpetrators, rape is more about power. Maybe it's the same for her. Unlike the drug dealer killings, there's no financial gain. No theft, no drugs to take. No higher moral ground for her to cling to." She tucked an errant hair behind her ear. "I bet she's done it more than we know. Maybe that's what she used to placate the killing urge when she was holding down that job. If she did, it wouldn't have satisfied her lust for killing for long. Not enough violence. She was far too into the act of killing by then. But the fact she used ketamine for both the killings and the rape is telling."

Every time she said *that* word, his stomach pitched like he just ate a dozen raw chicken livers.

Webb hadn't noticed. She kept on with her theory. "If she's injecting strangers, she can't know their weight up-front. Right?"

Jim nodded. He should contribute to the conversation, but his mouth was dry, numb. His throat thick.

"Dosing is usually figured by weight, so the doses are not quite accurate. Bigger guys probably don't get as fucked up. Maybe remember a little more. Max was a big guy—240, would you say?"

Jim was very aware his own weight hovered around 230. Maybe more, not like he had scales in his place. He breathed in through his nose. Agent Webb was looking at him as if she expected him to speak. Had she asked a question?

"You okay, Bean?"

The burger was set in front of him. No. He wasn't okay. The burnt meat smell convinced him he wanted nothing to do with a medium-rare hamburger. He wanted to crawl under the table, straight into a deep hole. He wanted a shower. A long, hot shower. Did not like feeling so weak. Out of control.

"I think I might be a little jet lagged." It wasn't a good lie. He didn't care. "I think I need to head back to the hotel, get some sleep."

She didn't need keen special agent senses to see he was lying, and she was not going to let this go. "Jet lag?"

He nodded.

An overt sigh. Her expression was not anger, no. Disappointment maybe? Too bad. He had that effect on women more times than not.

She looked over toward the huge bar. "Hey, Jake." The bartender looked around. "Couple to-go boxes and the bill."

"No problem."

Jim guzzled down the beer much faster than he had intended. One beer wouldn't cure what ailed him. But scotch might.

39

JIM PACED THE LENGTH of his hotel room. Eight strides in depth, thirteen in length. He'd made that journey fifty-seven times. Not that he was counting.

His computer sat open on one of the two double beds, notes and pictures scattered around it. He'd hit a dead end. Everything stopped with Elizabeth Stanton. Nothing beyond that. She'd gotten another name, started over. He glanced at the copied images of the IDs Agent Webb had been able to get. He had to hand it to her, Sophie had found a fantastic source for IDs. They were perfect. To start over completely, new name, new social security number, new you—that shit wasn't cheap.

Jim Bean knew that, and not just from tracking lost kids and cheating husbands. More than once he'd considered starting clean himself. But he'd stopped short of doing it illegally. When he was accused of rape in college, he'd lost everything. His life, his friends, his shot at the FBI or the force. Not to mention the money of defending himself against that kind of lie. But he couldn't clean up a past that lived in his head. He'd moved, changed his name. It had been enough. No one was looking for him. No one cared where he'd gone to hide. He wasn't hiding like Sophie anyway.

He picked up a sheet that included the timeline of Sophie's name changes and location changes. That made trip fifty-eight across the room. Grabbed another slip of paper. Fifty-nine. He compared it to the timeline of known vics. Again.

Usually he or Ely could find the trail, the electronic signature of name changes, money moving, auto registrations, utility bills, *something*. But right here in Dallas four yeas ago, she left. Elizabeth Stanton fell off the face of the virtual world after she... attacked Max. And she'd set him up first. Why?

Jim had to be missing something. Maybe it was just a power trip for Sophie, but why a coworker? He'd consider that very close to shitting in her own kitchen. That one act had her scrambling out of town. Had to be something else there. He made a mental note to call Max tomorrow. Maybe the man had stumbled onto something that would incriminate Sophie. Maybe he didn't even know it. Or maybe she just lost control one night. Like in a bar in Texas. There was no reason to... assault Jim either. Except ego.

Jim sat on the paper-covered bed. There was nothing worse than failing. The idea of this trip was to find her before she had a chance to attack Dan. Not finding her meant sitting and waiting for her to come to Dan. Bug in a web, waiting on the spider to get hungry. That could take a while. She'd been planning and waiting seven years as it was. Waiting weeks, even months, would wear down his protection detail. Dan's mom couldn't take moving around to keep Sophie off their trail. And for that reason, fully going under witness protection wasn't a good option. Not without a hit to her health.

Jim paced back to the bathroom counter.

Thirteen steps back to the door. Sixtieth time.

His gut tightened. This time it was a bad feeling, not anger or misery over the crummy life that twisted his insides. This was about the case. About Dan. The clock on the wall ticked off a countdown.

Sophie had waited this long. Hiring him had to be to speed up the process. She was so close to her goal. Staying away must be torturing her. Nope. She wouldn't wait much longer. That meant Jim couldn't wait either. He needed to do two things right away.

40

"**FIRST FLIGHT TO VEGAS** in the morning?"

There was some key chatter as the reservations agent put in his request. "Five a.m., Mr. Bean. Would you like me to assign you to that flight? There's two seats left."

"Yes." No sleep for him tonight.

She rattled of a confirmation number. He'd get the email with the details, he wasn't worried.

"You're set. Thank you for choosing—"

He disconnected before she finished. The cab hadn't showed yet. He'd called them first. Thirteen minutes. The clock ticked in his mind. He shouldn't have let O insist on returning the rental. Tricky way to stick Jim with Ava ... Agent Webb. Should have known he'd go out on his own at some point even if Agent Webb wouldn't be happy.

He waited. It was after eleven. A few shots of scotch had cleared his brain and dampened his tormented emotions.

Lights swung across the drive, the cab rolled to a stop.

"Haskel and 2nd," Jim said.

"This time a night, gringo?" A Mexican driver looked concerned through the mirror and the glass divider. "Not a good place for a man like you."

A man like him? What kind of man was he? "There was a restaurant around there. Good food."

"Ah. Tres Hermanas?"

"Yeah."

"Still. Bad neighborhood. I can take you to good restaurant closer. Less chance you get shot."

"Have a crush on one of the waitresses." Jim shrugged. "Take me there."

"As you wish, señor." He shook his head with an *it's your neck* look and put the cab in drive and pulled off.

Jim stared out the window and watched the streetlights go by. In the beginning it was all about the money. What would a prostitute do to save money? All the way to south Dallas Jim struggled with his bad feeling. He texted Miller. EVERYTHING OK?

OTHER THAN MRS. HODGE IS KICKING MY ASS IN SPADES, YES. ANYTHING NEW THERE?

Jim said "no" aloud. The cabbie looked back at him.

No.

Traffic was much better late at night than it had been in the afternoon. Cabbie said they were lucky not much was going on at the fairgrounds.

"I not stay here, señor."

Unlike the traffic, the area looked much worse at night. People hanging around. Drug deals going on. Girls in salty clothing on the corner.

"You be on duty for a while?"

The cabbie handed back a generic card with his number handwritten on it. "Be driving till the bar crowd goes home." He looked at the closed restaurant. "She might be gone. You sure you want to stay?"

"I'm okay." Jim checked for his slap-jack in his pocket. The weight of the small metal weapon was reassuring as he got out. The thing would break a jaw bone in an instant, but there were guys with guns out here. No doubt about it, he'd have to take care not to offend the natives. Just a guy looking for a girl.

Jim banged on the front door of Tres Hermanas. Nothing. He waited. Two young black guys walked by. They stared him down. He made eye contact but tried not to threaten their alpha standing in this neighborhood. He jerked his head back slightly. It's cool. Keep going, dude. The guys returned the gesture and walked on.

He banged again. This time Alejandra peeked around the closed sign. Once she recognized him, she opened the door. "What are you doing here this time of night?"

"Wanted another taco?"

"Liar. You still looking for Elizabeth."

"I am."

She put her hands on her hips. "I have been thinking about her since you left. But I can't imagine anything that might help you find her."

"I appreciate that, Alejandra. Do you know many of the girls working tonight?"

She looked down, then behind her. They were still alone. "After Elizabeth left, I did start to give them food sometimes. Like she did. Leftover things that are not going to last, you know. Here and there, I patch a few of them up after their man get too rough."

Jim smiled. Maybe Elizabeth Stanton did have one positive legacy. "You think there might be one of those girls who would be old enough to have been around seven years ago, when Elizabeth worked?"

"You know they don't last long on the streets."

"Think for me. That would be someone twenty-five to thirty. Maybe the one the rest of the girls are afraid of."

"There is one. Um ... Jelissa. I bet she was around." Alejandra worried at the polish on her finger. "But you can't tell her I sent you. She's mean. Last I saw her was a couple months ago. Works a couple blocks west, I think. She has mean-ass boys too. You better be careful."

"Anyone who would put girls through this shit is mean. I'll watch myself though." Jim pulled a twenty out of his wallet and tucked it in her apron. "Thanks."

"You'd be surprised 'bout who is working for who with her. Good luck, mister."

She locked the door behind him.

41

THREE BLOCKS WEST LOOKED more like a blown-out Middle Eastern war zone than a good place to pick up johns, but there was a four-lane street and an abandoned ball court. The hoops were rusted rings standing guard over a lost court. Three benches lined the far part of the tarmac with three girls lounging on one. They noticed him coming.

"We don't usually get white boys walking up around here."

The one who spoke was not a pretty girl. Skinny. The way her shirt hung off her shoulder showed deep hollows around her collarbone. Her teeth needed work. But her clothes were clean and her makeup was freshly painted on light black skin. She didn't smile or make any offers.

He must look too coppish tonight, even in jeans and a black T-shirt. The other two didn't bother to get up, just shot him skeptical looks and went back to an animated conversation.

"I'm looking for a girl."

"Aren't you all?"

He smiled. "I mean I'm a private investigator from Las Vegas. I'm looking for Jelissa."

She shrugged and looked back at the other girls, who'd stopped their conversation and were now paying attention. "Don't know no Jelissa."

Jim pulled a twenty out of his pocket. "She's not in trouble. I think she might be able to help me find a missing girl. That's all." He waggled the bill in front of his principal interviewee.

She glanced back. One of the girls shook her head and turned to face the four-lane. A couple cars went by. They didn't slow.

Jim pulled out one more twenty. "More than you get a trick, I would guess. All I need is a place."

She snatched the money. "You shouldn't flash bills around like that." She tucked them in her shorts. "Do you know where you are? Gonna get yourself knocked over."

Unfortunately, he did know where he was. "Surprised you care." He held out his hands. "Where can I find her?"

"You better not be making trouble."

"Scout's honor."

"No scouts round here. But I'll tell you. Other side of that warehouse." She tipped her hip to the right. No pointing. "There's a little yellow door. She stay in there. You don't tell her I said so, okay?"

Jim peeled off one more twenty. "Eat a sandwich."

She huffed and pushed up her tiny tits. "Some like it thin. You want a fat chick, Candy over there is your girl. But I can take care of whatever you need, white boy."

"I bet you can." He knew there was no need to give these girls any advice. No need to try and talk them off the street. If their man was watching, just talking too long could get them beat. He'd seen enough of that in Vegas.

"Thanks," he said loud enough for them all to hear. "You girls be safe." He walked back across the empty courts to the dark warehouse. "Why does it always have to be a dark warehouse?" he asked no one.

But it was true. If he were to buy and renovate all the empty warehouses he'd been through in the last two years, he'd be a freaking billionaire. He slowed as he made his way alongside the building. Two stories at least, gray metal siding. No windows facing the side street.

He looked around the corner. Several men were hanging out in front of a faded yellow door. All looked to be bangers.

He was alone, without transportation. He texted the cross streets to the number on the cab driver's card. Ready to go. And then he walked around the corner as if he belonged. He kept his head up, his stride loose and easy. One of the guys had gotten up and was already heading his way. The thug actually laughed when he realized what was walking his way. White man with no business on this block. He shook his head as Jim approached. Still smiling.

"Good evenin'," Jim said as the kid came alongside. Didn't keep eye contact, didn't avoid it.

"Might be." The kid kept walking. The kid's gait slowed, probably turned to check out the interloper. Jim didn't look back.

The other two thugs had already stopped whatever they had been up to by the time Jim reached them. One was sitting on a tattered folding chair. The other was on an overturned bucket. That one stood and faced Jim. He was very thick. And tall. So was Jim. His slap-jack was in his back pocket. Easy out if he needed it, but he prided himself on talking to people to get what he needed.

"Jelissa in there?"

Big boy took a step forward. "What the fuck you want with her?"

"Well, a visit, I suppose." What else would a guy be looking for her for? Not really good business for a pro to have bodyguards outside turning away potential buyers. Unless she was on a known-customers-only basis these days. Happened.

"She ain't seeing visitors. Go on outta here before I make you a stat, bitch." A threat. A stupid one, but the big guy stepped closer to show he was serious.

Jim supposed he should be afraid. The moose had his hand behind his back. But then again, so did Jim. If he carried a gun, Jim would have only a second to act. *Re*acting would be too late.

If this guy wanted trouble, he was sure hesitating. His body language was all wrong. He was still standing head on. Open to all attacks. The man glanced back at the guy in the chair.

Jim addressed him. "I want to talk to her. That's all. I'm a PI from Vegas. Just looking for a lost girl she might have known. Not a cop or anything."

He eyed Jim. Assessing. "No lost girls around here."

Jim huffed. "Nothing but lost girls around here." He stepped to his right, around the big boy to address the man with the power. Guys with power never got up until their muscle had failed. "This is ancient history in your world. Seven years ago."

"I said—"

"Who you want from that long ago, darling?"

They all jerked around. A beautiful woman stood in the yellow door. She was in a bright green wrap with African designs. Her makeup and nails were immaculate. She glowed compared to the dank and dirty of everything surrounding her.

Jim gave her a little bow of the head. "She went by Elizabeth." He pulled out the picture of Sophie and Dan. The big guy took it and handed it to Jelissa.

She held tight to the door frame. Her wrists looked thin. All of her looked thin, weak, though well-disguised in cosmetics. Not skinny like the girl on the bench. This was gray and hollow thin. Jim recognized cancer when he saw it. Yet she held a lit cigarette. Time must be running out for Jelissa.

"She got out."

Jelissa nodded. "She did."

She shooed the man from the folding chair. "You two go down the corner."

They balked, but she insisted. Her word obviously carried some weight. "Why you looking for her?"

"Her family's looking for her."

"That a lie, baby."

"So you knew her pretty well?"

She took a long toke. "You got one more chance and I call the boys back."

Hard ball. Sometimes the truth can be an ally. It was hard to tell when. But this time the choice was easy.

"You're right. It was a lie." He folded his hands in front of his jeans button. He would deliver the information as if it could be bad news for Jelissa. "She's wanted for killing about fourteen people. Some from this neighborhood back then. Now she's stalking a boy from her youth. We're trying to stop her from killing him."

"So you *are* a cop?"

"Nope. Just a guy who fucked up and needs to set something straight."

She eyed him carefully. "That is the truth. Probably in more ways than one."

He wasn't sure if he reeked of a fuck-up or if she had immaculate people skills. Perhaps both.

"He's not a pusher?" she asked.

"The guy she's after? No. Simple cowboy. She killed his sister too."

Jelissa looked down. Flicked her ashes to the dirty concrete at her feet. "I learned a great lesson from Eliza." She took out another cigarette and lit it, offered Jim one. He took it. She lit his too.

"Thanks."

She nodded. Cool. Collected, she was. "She told me how to take back what belonged to me."

Jim almost laughed. "Didn't go telling you to kill your pimps, did she?"

She gave a quick raise of the eyebrows but didn't answer. "Things have changed in this neighborhood over the years. I can now keep the really bad element out. The girls get a bigger take. It's safer. As safe as this life can be on a girl." She looked back at Jim. "Eliza told us how to do that."

Dang, crazy bitch did have a soft spot for the downtrodden. "And it looks like you've done a hell of a good job. Whatever she said to you was good advice. But she's off the chart now. Killing anyone in her way. Cut the throat of a guy in his backyard." He let that sink in. "Another couple young girls who were just out for a party. Now she wants this guy because he was nice to her when she was a kid."

"That don't sound like her."

"She's changed. Very delusional. She's switched identities several times." He turned to face her. "Jelissa, I'm not a cop. I'm just trying to get her trail. None of the work you've done here"—he made a circle with this finger to indicate the neighborhood—"is in jeopardy."

"You gonna kill her?"

"No." *If I get the chance, hell yes.*

"Killing people for no good reason ain't right. I done a lot of talking to kids and parents in this area to make that point. We are getting better." She stood and gingerly paced a few steps back toward the door. "But I don't know where she at. Haven't seen her in years."

231

"You made this place safer." Even if it was by killing off the worst of the bad element. But that wasn't his business. "Tell me this. Takes money to make these kinds of changes. "

She looked away. Had she gone to the extremes Sophie had? She was trying to clean up her neighborhood, save some young girls, and he respected that. Small-time vigilante like Jelissa was okay with his moral code. Too bad Sophie had not taken the same road.

"She teach you to protect your cash?"

She shrugged.

"How did she teach you to hide the money? Can't leave it around here in boxes."

"In the bank, of course." She smiled. "In my momma's name. High-interest CDs."

And the woman still lived in this bleak neighborhood? Maybe she just worked down here now. "In your mother's name?"

"Yep." She took another hit and blew slow, dancing smoke rings. "Sure you ain't a cop?"

"Nope. No interest in what you've accomplished here, Jelissa. I just want to stop a guy from getting dead."

"Okay. It was mamma's name, only I switched that up too. Flipped the names around. Easy enough nowadays to use it without ever going to the bank. Use my iPad to do all the banking. Cash goes in the ATMs."

"Brilliant." He dropped his cigarette butt on the ground, stood, and stomped it out. "Thanks, ma'am."

"You want an escort out?"

Car lights turned off a side street. The cab. "No thanks, my ride is here."

He gave her a pantomimed tip of the hat and got in the cab.

42

SOPHIE SAT IN THE van watching the new age diner. The lot was empty, and the only lights on were the safety lights above the back door.

She'd decided to snatch the waitress on the morning drive in. After talking to momma, Sophie realized that she'd left a very troublesome loose end dangling in the wind. She needed insurance. Bean had seemed rather taken with the little blonde during their initial meeting. It made her valuable.

Sophie waited in the beginnings of the new day, parked behind the diner, assuming the staff parked here as well. Between the drive and the waiting the hard van seat was killing her ass. Carla was restless.

"You need to pee?"

The pup whined. No way to tell her she had to hold it, was there?

"Oh all right, but you have to make it quick." A stretch of the legs wouldn't hurt. She got out and made sure Carla's leash was attached. She tucked an injector pen in her waistband. Always prepared, right?

Carla sniffed around the gravel lot as if there were gold to be found. Or bones. They must be the doggie equivalent of a rare metal. Given the mush and vegetarian fare that Bean had been eating in that diner … "Probably not a bone in sight, sweetie."

A tiny red Honda popped into the lot. Old enough Sophie figured it for an eighties model. Behind the wheel was the little blonde. "How fortunate." She'd supposed the cook would show up first, requiring a plan for getting the girl out back alone, but fate had helped her once again.

Carla barked.

"Why yes, little one, you may help me take our prisoner," she cooed to the dog.

Sophie nodded to the waitress as she got out of the car, and then let the leash drop. Carla, as if following mental instructions, ran to the girl.

"Carla!"

She meant it to sound panicked. Urgent. The girl spun back to them, saw the situation, and placed herself in the line of fire. Not that she needed to do much. Carla was heading right toward the girl. She abandoned her things, swept down, and caught the pup as Carla bounded up.

"I got her."

Sophie limped a little as she took a step toward the waitress. In response, the girl hurried to bring the dog over. People were cattle.

"I got her. I'll bring her to you."

She made her way right to Sophie and stopped within two feet of the van. Cow to the slaughter. Except this particular cow would have to wait for her appointment with the blade. Dead hostages aren't worth much.

"Thank you so much." She reached out to get Carla, but stumbled and quickly reached for the girl to steady herself. In the process, she smashed the injector into the girl's shoulder. The girl caught Sophie and prevented her from hitting the ground. Even though she didn't let Sophie falter, she did let out a little yelp at the pinch of her flesh.

"I'm so sorry." Sophie tucked the spent syringe away while acting as if she were trying to regain her balance. "My ring does that occasionally." She held out her hand to show the girl that there was a silver ring on her middle finger. It was designed as a butterfly with two stone encrusted wings with pointy ends.

"I'm constantly pinching myself … and everybody else. But my daughter gave it to me for Mother's Day and I can't bear to not wear it at least occasionally. Didn't break the skin or anything, did it?"

The girl rubbed the spot. "I don't think so. I'm fine. Don't worry about it."

Carla jumped up on the girl's leg. She reached down and rubbed the dog. Carla wallowed in the attention, rolling over, kicking happily as the girl scratched the pup's belly.

"She's such a cutie. What is she? A Yorkie?"

Shit. Sophie had no clue. That sounded as good as anything.

"Yes. A mix." That should cover it. "I recently adopted her and we've bonded so well. The rescue people said she was with a dreadful family before. I haven't had a friend like her in ages."

Carla came back to Sophie's voice. The friend part was true anyway. Sophie had no clue how the people before had treated the dog. They had left her tied up outside a coffee shop, so how good of doggie parents could they have been?

"I love her so much. But with my injured hip, I'm having a heck of a time traveling with her today."

The girl swayed, trying to hold her balance. Lost to the effect of the drug, she stumbled backward. She caught herself on the van.

Sophie had filled all the syringes on hand for a man-sized dose. This little blonde was short and thin. Shit must be hitting her pretty hard.

"Could you help me get her into her crate?"

"Sure." The girl touched her front teeth. Pulled her hand away and then looked at her fingers, wiggling them out in front of her face. Poor thing must be feeling a little numb. Sophie needed to hurry before she began to hallucinate.

"Great." Ignoring the girl's obvious altered state, Sophie limped the few feet to the back of the van. The waitress picked up her bag and her apron where it had landed in the short altercation when she got her injection. That would save Sophie a trip back to retrieve it. Someone else should be showing up soon. Prep had to be done in a kitchen before the day started, and light was now visible on the horizon.

Sophie waited by the back of the van. The girl wobbled as she took a few steps, shaking her head as if she could shake off the growing effects of the ketamine. Not a chance, girl. You're toast.

"Right in here." She thought of the witch in the fables who tempted children to her house with candy and then cooked them. Sophie didn't even need to include Carla in the charade anymore. The girl wouldn't know a dog from a dishwasher in less than a minute.

"I think I'm gonna be sick."

"Oh dear. Here ..." Sophie opened the van door. She'd had the interior of the van custom built. For business travel, of course. One side of the cargo area was a deep plush bench covered in outdoor, cleanable carpet. It was wide enough for a nap and narrow enough for a seat. The wall behind it was cushioned with lots of matching pillows. "Have a seat. I'll get you some water."

The other side had a small mounted table for working and several built-in cubbyholes for storage of ... things. Like knives and injectors, bandages and food—stuff she might need on the journey to bring

Danny home. She was very happy with how it had turned out. Comfortable and practical.

She helped the girl in.

"Thanks," she said, not at all concerned that the van was decked out like a killer's lair.

Sophie reached to the cubby that held her knife. She unlatched the drawer and pulled it open. The metal shone up at her, begging. "What's your name, dead ... I mean, dear?"

The girl's head smacked the back wall of the van a little harder than Sophie had intended when she tried to turn her attention to Sophie's voice. Her eyes were glassed over. She was almost gone. "What?" Her head drooped to the side.

"Your name?"

"Name. Name. Sa ... Sandy." She tried to touch her face again. Her hand never made it past her chin. She missed completely. Her eyes rolled back.

Sophie closed the back door and locked it. Carefully, she latched Sandy's legs in the cuffs built into the base of the bench. They were in plain view. If not for the drugs, the girl would have surely seen them and questioned their reason for being.

Sophie smiled as she tucked the seat belt across the girl's torso and snapped her in. No argument. Sandy was smiling as Sophie tied her hands in place.

Her arms were hanging awkwardly, so Sophie fixed that. No need to make her uncomfortable. She would be a guest until Sophie got Danny safely to the house.

If Bean showed up in the meantime looking to thwart the master plan—and he might—Sophie had a card left to play. She couldn't resist tracing her fingers down the girl's young face. Her complexion was perfect, her skin tight, her lips full. Her life had been spent around people who loved her.

How do you know that? Stupid girl. Just kill her now.

"Hush. I need her."

You need to see her blood flow across the floor of this van. You need to christen the mobile retreat. You need to feel her pulse stop as the life leaves her perfect little body!

Sophie closed her eyes. She could very well visualize all that, looking at her pretty face, holding her graceful neck. *So much lovely skin to slice.* She fought back the images, tried not to let the urge take over.

Her heart pounded in her chest with anticipation. She did *want* to kill her now. She did *want* to feel the life flow out of that girl as Sophie held her, feeling her pulse, counting in time as the beats dwindled into nothing.

She shook her head. It was harder all the time. Not killing. But this girl was important to the plan. She bit into the inside of her cheek hard enough to tear flesh, her eyes watering from the stab of pain. She fell back.

"I'll need her later," she said to convince herself she was right. It was time to go.

She got up and made her way to the driver's seat, buckled herself in. She gripped the steering wheel with all her might. Carla followed and took her place in the passenger seat, all perky ears and bright eyes. No judgment from her.

Fighting the urge to kill was always a battle.

43

STYLE WISE, THE NEW safe house looked incredibly like the last one. From the first scan of the windows, it simply had one more room downstairs. Miller's car wasn't there yet.

Jim showed his ID and passed by the undercover at the door. Dan was standing in the kitchen in only pajama pants, which showed off a tattoo of a rearing stallion on his left side as he leaned on the counter. He held a small white mug close to his lips. One leg was crossed over the other, the top one wagging back and forth like an excited hound's tail. But he wasn't happy to see Jim like a loyal hound might be. His annoyance was clear to see.

"Please tell me you found something."

There was a bay window and a sliding glass door across the back wall of this living room/kitchen combo. Not safe. Who picked these places?

"Ready to spring this joint, huh?"

"You have no idea. This place has some extra room and all, but I want to get out. I'm used to big open spaces. I feel like I'm in a fish tank. Diner, gambling, titty bar. I don't care at this point."

Lynette rolled her chair into the room. "You mind that mouth, Danny." She looked up at Jim. "Well?"

She wanted info. He didn't have what she wanted.

"You catch my girl's killer?"

She was lucid today.

"Sorry, Mrs. Hodge. I didn't. Not yet."

Her articles were hung on the half wall between the eat-in kitchen and the living room.

"What good are you then? All you po-po hanging around here. What good are ya? Go out there and find her."

"Mom." Dan pushed her toward the kitchen table. "Sorry. Stephen's nephew was here for a couple of days. Having a kid around did her some good, but now she wants to talk like she's from the hood." He looked down at her. "It's irritating. But I'm glad to have her this engaged."

Jim handed her a book. He'd seen it as he paced the terminal last night waiting for his early flight.

"*This Side of Paradise*. More crappy F. Scott?"

"You might like this one better."

"Doubt it." Her lip curled up like a teenager facing cooked spinach. "His books are all about the same things. Men whose failures are the result of their own shortcomings and the influence of women with low moral standards." She scrutinized him. "Or is that why *you* like them, Mr. Bean? Hmmm?"

Dang, that was an arrow right on target. "Maybe I should give up the classics and stick to a good mystery?"

"Ah. No good," Miller interrupted as he joined them in the bright kitchen. "As a master investigator, wouldn't you always figure out who-done-it well before the end?"

Jim wouldn't count on that. "You're the detective."

They exchanged a vigorous hand shake, but his face was a bit pinched. "Oh. And, thanks for not pissing off Lady Fed."

Heavy sarcasm. Had he pissed Agent Webb off? "You're welcome?"

"She was in my ear first thing this morning. Cursing up a storm because you'd left without permission."

"Permission?" Jim shrugged. None of her business, really. "Not on her payroll. No reason for her to be upset. Told her I had jet lag."

"Then you went out to the fairgrounds."

Damn. "How did she know that? Did I have a tail? If her uptight agents go out to visit my informant ... " He didn't want them bugging Jelissa or making any trouble after he'd promised.

"She's on her way here. Says she knows you know something. Threatening to charge you for interfering in a federal investigation."

Lynette cackled. "I knew you were trouble, Jimmy." She chewed on the edge of a placemat. Dan took it from her.

Jim checked his phone. "She didn't call me. Went over my head to you ... oh wait. I don't work for you either." He glanced past the FBI agent quietly lurking in the hallway to Dan. "Except you. I work for you. But that's just a formality. This is my case too. And, yes. I got a lead on the money trail. But it's just a lead."

"She was sharing, Bean. You have to return the favor. You can't sneak out in the middle of the night."

"I did not sneak out. I took a morning flight. It's only ten a.m. now, for Christ's sake. I did share with her what we found on Sophie's birth mother. I shared that." He had planned to share this too, but it had been the middle of the night. He didn't think it was urgent enough to wake up Agent Webb. "I'm going to go home and then over to Ely's to follow this lead." Jim squatted next to Lynette's chair. "Look at me, beautiful."

She did, in her addle-minded honest way.

"I expect things to get a little crazy around here soon. I want you to listen to Dan and the po-po and do *exactly* as they say."

Miller's phone rang. "Gotta take this."

"Do you all have to treat me like a child?" She crossed her arms. "I'm no child."

"You are in danger, Lynette. Think of it as being treated like a VIP. If you were the first lady, you'd get the same handling. Hidden away at the first sign of trouble."

She seemed to consider. But her eyes were getting glazed. He touched her arm. It was frail and cool. "I mean it, woman. Follow orders."

"Fine. Get on outta here and scrounge me up some pomegranate marmalade."

He stood. "Yes, ma'am."

Miller's face said bad news. A detective really should have better poker face skills. He was still on the phone, but he covered the receiver and said, "I'll run you to Ely's. But we need to go now."

"Okay." Jim's curiosity bone was tickled. "Lynette, follow instructions. Okay?"

"Yes, my love." There was a warmth in her eyes for just an instant that made Jim feel like she meant it.

He smacked Dan on the shoulder. "If this lead pans out, we're golden. Once we have a money trail, it usually takes us right where we need to go. Just like the yellow brick road."

"Good. I want out of here. And I want to take care of Cynthia."

"I know you do."

Miller coughed and picked up what passed as Jim's overnight bag. "Really, Bean. We need to go." He gave a head fling as if no one would notice.

"Okay, Captain Subtle. Giddy up."

As soon as they pulled the door shut, Miller continued his phone conversation.

"Diner. Keys. Unlocked car in the lot. No one's seen Sandy." Miller kept talking but Jim couldn't wrap his head around the fact Miller was talking about Sandy.

"When?" They got in the car. Jim shoved his belt into the catch with difficulty. "Who the hell did this?"

Miller hung up. "Don't know for sure. They think she went missing this morning." He started the car and turned on lights and sirens when they were a couple blocks away from the safe house.

Jim's blood pressure was rising. "What do we know?"

"Her car's there. Manager is sure he saw her leave last night. Silver van was exiting the parking lot when the manager got there this a.m."

"Silver van? What kind of van?"

The cruiser blasted through red lights, the suspension tossing them like a small boat on high seas. Cars pulled to the side, some faster than others.

Miller laid on the horn to insist traffic yield to the mass and momentum of the Charger as it careened through Vegas back streets. Jim closed his eyes. Not in fear of Miller's driving ability. That he trusted. No. His mind was centered on one thing. Sophie Ryan Evers. If that woman hurt one little blond hair on Sandy's head . . .

"There is a good chance this isn't related." Miller said the words, but Jim knew better.

"Sophie knows we're getting closer. We visited her mother in Texas. Maybe her mother contacted her afterward." Maybe she was just a sadistic bitch and wanted to hurt Jim for not following her instructions and making her job harder. Maybe she wanted to use Sandy to keep him quiet about the rape or off her tail. He clenched his fists. Who knew with her?

"How much time did you spend with Evers?"

Jim didn't want to say exactly. "Just a couple client meetings, phone conversations."

They spun to a stop in front of the diner. Jim only took a momentary glance toward his place in the townhouse community across the way. Two uniforms were at the front of the diner and pointed them around. The back parking area was cordoned off with crime scene tape. Another uniform there. Miller logged them onto the crime scene. Two techs in white lab suits were dusting Sandy's car.

"You have anything?" Miller asked the tech who stood. He motioned them back a few steps.

"Several prints, no sign of forced entry. There's some disturbance in the gravel that appears to be a rushed departure. But gravel won't give us tread imprints. Her keys were on the far side of the car." He nodded in the direction as his hands were full of the powder and the brush. "And one small dog poo that looks fresh."

Jim carefully made his way over to the tire impressions. "You guys already shoot these?"

"Yep. Measured and photographed."

"Bigger than a minivan, wider. More like a panel van or a delivery truck."

The tech came and glanced over Jim's shoulder. He was a tall dude. "I thought the same thing. I'll be able to narrow it some, so maybe the manager can point it out from some pictures. Get us a little closer."

244

"Good."

The dog shit was marked with a plastic yellow evidence tent. Number 7. Poo number seven. "Is the shit part of the equation or just in the scene?"

Miller leaned in over it. "Hard to say. No sign of a dog at the last scene. I'll have someone reread the canvass statements. You never know."

"Can't imagine Sophie is the dog type."

"What the fuck type is she?"

Jim said the only thing that came to mind. "Snakes?"

Miller headed inside. Jim followed. They'd closed for the moment. The owner, Todd Haig, stood at the far end of the room, looking at his phone display. When he saw Jim, Todd brushed by Miller and grabbed Jim in a bear hug, the force almost taking them both back into the bar.

"I saw that van and didn't think anything of it. She's been coming in early last couple of weeks while Bobby's out with a bad back. Helping me get the prep work done." He let Jim go. "What do I do?"

"Do?" Jim ushered the tree-hugging vegan onto one of the counter stools. "You're going to relax. Take a deep breath." Jim went behind the counter and poured the man a glass of water.

Miller sat beside Todd. "What was the first thing you saw when you pulled in?"

"Her car. The van was pulling out before I got in the lot. I didn't have to wait for it to leave the driveway, but it was close. The burger joint around the corner gets deliveries back there all the time. I saw there was no logo on the van or anything but figured it was one of their vendors. Then I saw Sandy's car and I didn't think any more about it." He scratched his ear, then started thumping the inside of his palm. A tiny punishment. "The first sign anything was wrong was when I realized the kitchen door was still locked. She usually leaves it unlocked when she gets here. So I had to dig out a key. I looked back at her car. But it all seemed okay."

He stood and paced to the front door. "But it wasn't okay cuz she wasn't in here. I went back out and saw her keys out there. I knew. Called you guys." He looked at Miller.

Nothing really helpful. "You did everything right, Todd. Can you remember anything else about the van? Was it a man driving?"

"I think. Maybe. You think it was those human traffickers, Jim?"

"Doubtful, but anything's possible. The van, was it more like a delivery truck than a minivan?"

"Yes." He wagged a finger. "A good-sized one cuz it took up almost the whole driveway. Or the way she was driving made it seem that way."

He'd said *she*. Not he. But Jim wouldn't push it right this second, given he'd just answered that question. Give it time for the memory to start putting things together. He was calming a bit.

Miller had his pad out. "And you didn't see a plate?"

Todd shook his head. "I was coming in, he was going out."

Now *he* again. That was no help.

Miller handed Todd a card. "Call us if you think of anything. We'll have your business back to you in a little while."

It occurred to Jim that if Sophie had snatched Sandy from the lot without leaving a body to be found, that was a good thing. It gave them some time. But the bitch had some kind of nasty agenda. Whatever it was, Jim had no intention of letting her play it out.

44

JIM WALKED HOME FROM the diner after the last of the crime scene people had left. He was exhausted. A couple hours' restless sleep on the flight was all he'd had in two days. The heat and humidity of Texas had drained all his energy.

If Sophie took Sandy, the possibility of an imminent attack on Dan was high. And it was clearly a message to Jim. No other reason for Sophie to target a twenty-something waitress who had nothing to do with Dan or the case. Sophie had seen him and Sandy interact at the Coffee Girl the day of the initial case meeting.

No question about it. Miller could investigate however the book told him to; Jim only had one suspect. He fumbled in his bag for the key fob to his apartment door. The beep sounded as he deactivated the automatic door lock, but he heard no latch click open. Jim edged closer and noted the door was slightly ajar.

He pushed it open, using just his fingertips while he protected himself behind the wall, out of the line of fire. Nothing seemed out of order from that angle. He stuck his head in.

Annie rushed out. The little black ball of fur wound between his legs. Her attention nearly tripped him as he stepped inside. Ely had dropped off the cat. Jesus. Glad that was nothing, he went in without further concern. He glanced on the office desk. There was a note from Ely.

Thought you might like some company. Be back over as soon as I track down anything related to the mother's name.

Take a nap.

~Ely

There was nothing he could do to find Sophie without Ely's information. Maybe he should search himself? His legal databases paled to what Ely managed to find in most cases.

He sat in the recliner. Without invitation, Annie hopped up on his lap. His girl wanted some loving.

He leaned back, slouching in the deep chair so she could stretch out on his chest. Her purring and soft fur lulled him. The familiar leather seat, cool.

Jim woke to searing pain in his chest. He leapt to his feet and took a defensive stance, ready to swing or kick. The house was silent. He'd dozed off rubbing Annie.

He found two small punctures where she'd dug in her back nails as she'd jumped off. His phone was on the counter. From the angle of the sun casting weak shadows through closed blinds he guessed late evening. He needed a shower.

He checked for messages. None. Not from Miller or Ely. Jim made his way back to the office instead. He needed to get a pad of paper out and think through this situation. Write out what he knew. There was something lingering that he hadn't put in the right place. Something that would make Sophie's latest move make some sense.

Turned out there was not. There was no rhyme or reason to a psychopath like Sophie Evers.

He slid into the worn office chair and found his reading glasses under a pile of unfiled paperwork. He did need some help around the place. O had been on him about expanding, hiring some people, making his jack-leg operation into something respectable.

Sometimes he wanted that, other times he was happy being able to take on the cases he wanted and walk away from the ones that seemed like too much trouble or not enough money. He'd missed the mark on this one, hadn't he?

His phone rang. Unknown number.

"Jim Bean."

"PI Jim Bean?"

"Yes."

There was a nervous pause. "This is Max."

Interesting. "Hello, Max. What can I do for you?"

"I was thinking. You know, about what she's been up to."

"Yes." Jim waited, but Max didn't say anything. He needed prompting. "About the night she attacked you?"

"Yes and no." A light cough. Clearing of the throat, a classic sign of trying to summon courage. Saw it in kids all the time. Jim bet the man was looking at his feet too. Maybe he'd had a drink or two before dialing the number. Maybe dialed and not connected more than once. This should be good.

"I wasn't exactly truthful with you and Agent Webb."

"No?"

"Not sure it's relevant but, I umm ... I had ... spent time with Elizabeth prior to *that* night." He waited for Jim to say something.

Jim decided to withhold comment, hoping for more information. This time it came without the prompting.

"We had seen each other several times over several months, I reckon. The thing is, I had broken it off three days before. You see, my wife found out. She gave me an ultimatum. You know, her way or the highway kind of thing. She was right, you know. It was wrong. Well, Elizabeth took it bad."

"So the harassment accusation against you at work ... "

"Revenge for me dumping her." He paused again. "I think the ... attack was to prove a point. One of the last things I remember was her saying that I shouldn't have ignored her. I shouldn't have treated her just like the rest."

Still didn't explain why she'd done the same to Jim, but it explained why she would give up her steady job and safe home. She got mad and snapped and made a mess in her own bed. But it left Jim no closer to figuring out where she was now or what her immediate plans were.

"Anything else?"

"It's all still really fuzzy. More now than then. But I remember something weird."

Weirder than getting raped? Jim didn't say it aloud.

"She said I was just practice anyway. For real life."

"Real life?"

"Yeah. It didn't make a lick of sense then, not sure it does now."

"Everything adds together to make a puzzle complete, Max. Let me ask you this. She ever talk about a favorite vacation spot, or someplace she wanted to retire?"

"Not that I can think of. It wasn't a talking, sharing kind of relationship."

A real personal relationship was probably way far outside of Sophie's skill set. "You think she was practicing while having sex with you?"

"She was real awkward at it at first. Kind of mechanical. Not to brag or anything, but she'd gotten much better. She'd learned to relax, explore some as we went."

"Thanks for the call, Max."

"Yeah."

That did help make sense of things. She left Texas because she'd fucked up with Max. She had to start all over. Create another life somewhere else. She was practicing on how to be a girlfriend or a wife, planning to build a life for her and Dan all this time. Too bad he wasn't in on her delusion.

Jim was sure Dan would decline that particular invitation. And surely Sophie knew that too. Maybe she'd been practicing with the drugs as well. How to kill versus how much to keep a man just messed up enough so he was willing and happy. Great way to build a relationship.

He pulled out his laptop. There had to be at least one more alias she was using. Jim had to find it. He logged into his database.

Mary Callas. Texas

Two came up. One, the mother. The other too old and in jail.

He tried a national search. Thirteen.

He searched through those not in Texas. No one close enough to Sophie's age or ethnicity.

Callas Mary, backwards as Jelissa suggested. None. He searched nationally. Zero.

He grabbed his phone. Had a hunch. It was a long shot, and she was probably still mad.

"Special Agent Webb."

"Agent Webb. Heard you were looking for me."

"Hold on." Her muffled voice came through the speaker like she was finishing another conversation. Maybe she hadn't headed this way. Sounded like she was in an office.

"Mr. Bean. You left town without so much as a goodbye. And after I bought you dinner."

"One that gave me food poisoning."

"You didn't take one bite."

"I needed a night in my own bed."

"Uh huh."

No more excuses. "I have a lead. I talked to an old pro out there in Dallas. Evidently our Sophie was quite the philanthropist to the streetwalkers. Taught them how she moved up in the world. How to make their lives better."

He heard her let out a long breath. "So there's more than one pimp killer?"

"Can't say for sure. By the way, I hope the very nice woman I met while in Texas continues to live a happy, federal agent–free life."

"I didn't send in the dogs, Bean. How does this help us?"

"Miss Jelissa also said Sophie gave her advice on how to hide her money in the bank. She told her to use her mother's name. I've searched but don't see anyone using an alias that fits our profile."

"Callas. Callas. Mom was Mary Callas, right? Damn. Elizabeth Stanton was a famous activist."

Jim leaned back, hoping the wheels in her pretty little brain were churning. He wished he could see her face. "Yeah."

"You have your computer in front of you?"

"I do."

"Look up Maria Callas instead of Mary. I can't remember, but that seems familiar. I bet it's someone famous too."

"You're really on it when it comes to women's history." Jim typed in the name.

"Yeah. Just don't ask me for anything about European history. Took the women's study class to get out of that."

Jim scanned the screen quickly. "Maria Callas was a famous opera singer. Looks like this chick had a rough time of growing up. Managed to come out a star on the other side." He typed in the name in his database. Twenty-two. Skimmed the basic info on the list. "Two of these have no previous address or known associates."

"Where are they?"

"One is in Washington, D.C. The other is California." He hit the expand search key on that entry. "Not much on this one. Address is a PO box in Bakersfield."

"I used to go skiing not far from Bakersfield with my grandfather. It's pretty secluded, not far out of town. Not surprised to see the PO box. If she's set up with an address, it might be more than a disposable identity."

"Great skiing." Jim had no clue about skiing or the area, but said it anyway.

"Oh, you've been?"

"I have not."

He enjoyed the silence created as she decided how to interpret the obscure statement. "Okay."

"I bet all those secluded cabins make it a great place to play a creepy game of house."

"Hang on. I'll be there in two minutes, we'll finish this in person."

Jim stood. Glanced around his house. He hadn't been there in days and the mess reflected that. He was still covered in the filth of Texas and traveling. "Where are you?" Why did he care?

"At the diner. I had my guys go back through the crime scene, just in case."

"You're checking up on Miller's investigation?"

He could tell she was moving around.

"Most locals like having Federal resources these days, Bean. It's no longer the Wild West out here. Any turf wars we get are due to ego, not politics. We have big labs and big budgets."

"I guess." He didn't care one way or another if it helped find Sandy. "That girl is my first priority now, Agent Webb." Dan was protected—two officers and Stephen were with him. "Sandy is out there. Alone with a lunatic."

"Understood. But let's do this within the boundaries of the law, Bean, so when we get Evers, we've got her."

Jim didn't immediately answer. Maybe that's why he never moved his business into the next level. The bigger the organization, the harder it was to play by his own rules. He liked his rules.

"I'm leaving the diner."

"Give me ten minutes." He wanted to clean up.

"Be there in five."

45

AN HOUR PAST SUNSET and it was still hotter than snot, but at least there was a decent little breeze. Perfect for her intentions this evening.

Sophie pulled the pack of matches from her homemade attack suit. It looked like a SWAT team Halloween costume with its black cargo pants and a long-sleeved black shirt with vented underarms to keep her cool. Or at least as cool as one could be in Nevada in August.

She'd bought a tactical vest on eBay and altered it so it fit like a second skin. The pockets and straps held all the tools she would need for this mission. As if there would be another one like this. This was *the night.*

Butterflies danced in her stomach as she struck a match. The thing cost her less than a penny and it would kick off the rest of her life. She fanned the little flames of her diversion, a paper grocery bag packed with dried twigs, leaves, and some thicker sticks she'd brought from the mountains. In seconds she had a nice little flame burning under a propane tank. These silly people had left that tank a little too close to the house. Accidents happen.

She backed off, heart pounding as she made her way through two backyards and settled behind a covered boat to wait for the fireworks. Her watch read 9:01.

She cleaned under her nails. Missed a bit of blood from the business with the homeless girl, Cat. She bit her lip and counted back. Number fifteen.

Her whole body shuddered with a tingle of pleasure as she remembered the rush of that struggle. That little thing fought harder than most of the men Sophie had X'ed out.

Seemed the drifter was far cleverer than Sophie had given her credit for. It was an actual fight. There'd been no drugs for her. She had to subdue the girl with a chokehold and split open her midsection instead of her throat. Messy. Very messy. The hotel room would never be the same. Oh well. She only needed it for a few more hours.

Sophie wiggled her toes inside the combat boots. They were a half size too big. Stupid tank should have blown by now. She stood and peeked over the back of the boat. The distant streetlight helped her make out a thin trail of smoke as it danced up the side of the house. No one would be alarmed by it. That house was empty. Neighbors on the far side were out as well. Everything was going her way. It wouldn't be long.

She sucked in a deep breath as she sat cross-legged and closed her eyes, visualizing a perfect future with Danny. The mountain house was amazing. They would enjoy peaceful, sunset dinners on the deck overlooking the valley, chilled wine, and the scent of the little blue flowers out by the lake. The positive visualization made her smile.

The PI will be coming for you, stupid. You had to go and hire him.

"Shut up. That's under control," she whispered through clenched teeth.

What if he doesn't care about that waitress?

"He'll still try and save her. Him and the police."

Your plan has holes in it.

"All plans have holes in them. Ever watched a movie? Of course you have. I suppose you've seen every movie I've ever seen."

You will fail. Just like you have always failed.

Sophie opened her eyes. She had to eliminate that chattering. She wanted to be free of that voice forever. She should stop engaging, ignore it.

How stupid can you be? I am part of you. I know you, your thoughts, and I know your failures … all of them. So many of them.

Sophie closed her eyes again and imagined making a toast with Danny while laughing over some overly decadent dessert. He loved plums, so it would be something plum.

The voice started laughing.

Louder.

And louder.

46

JIM MADE IT THROUGH the shower in record time. He was pulling on his pants when the bell rang. His front door. No one used the front door. This time he would have a shirt on. He had a couple clean black T-shirts left in his drawer. That was about all. Not that he cared.

She knocked again as he got to the bottom of the stairs.

"You impatient"—he opened the door—"Agent Webb?"

"As a matter of fact, I am." She pushed by him, scanning the surroundings. Her training was probably better than his. She'd have found the back hall, assumed it lead to another entrance.

"I've been out of town a lot." He was not sure why he felt the need to justify a bachelor's state of living.

She turned by the kitchen counter. "I'm aware."

Annie rushed onto the counter to investigate the new arrival. Webb bent down and let her smell her face. Annie approved and gave a fine flick of her tail.

"That's Annie."

"After Annie Hall or little orphan?"

Jim huffed. "Oakley. Annie Oakley. She was a tough little kitten. You think I'd name a cat after a character in a play?"

She shrugged. "You knew it was a play. And you have a pretty, long-haired, female cat. Not exactly fitting the macho image of a rugged PI."

"Of course I knew it was a play. I went to school." He decided to ignore the blow to his image. "Everyone had to sit through at least one mind-numbing middle school performance of that god-awful thing."

She laughed. Her face lit up. It made him glad she was here. Hated that. He needed to get back to business. With a hand motion he offered her a seat at his kitchen table. She took it.

"Beer?"

"Haven't eaten, better not." She pulled out her note pad.

"Water?"

"So I called into the office and asked for everything they could find on Maria Callas. We should get a call soon."

After putting a warm bottle of water in front of her, he sat across from her and showed her what he'd found. Not much. But he had been able to generate the fake social security number she'd been using as Maria.

"They probably already have it, but ... " She texted the number to someone.

"So what all can you search that I can't?" He wasn't sure what data they could really get these days, post 9/11.

"Stuff. Taxes, banking."

"Can you find her phone number? Maybe trace it from her mother's phone? Assuming her mother called her after we visited."

She shook her head. "TV FBI can do that. I need a warrant or at least a subpoena."

Ely could track the phone number if they had it. Of course, that was supposed to be by consent too. But Jim was fortunate to have the freedom of not worrying about playing by the rules and not having to deal with the government restraints.

"We need this all above board, Bean. We have to be able to produce evidence that stands up in court."

He knew that. "It amazes me that she's killed at least ten people and we still need to build a strong case."

"She's been clean, given how messy the crime scenes are. It's like she's great with the crime itself, but then turns around and makes horrible decisions about how to go about daily life. She doesn't really fit a serial killer profile. She just kills when and where she wants. I think it's usually associated with the end goal of becoming a better woman for Dan, but not always. Either way, she's gonna implode when Dan doesn't live up to her expectations. Hell, I don't think *she* can live up to her own expectations, not sure how she expects a kidnapped man to do so."

Jim's phone chirped. It was Miller's ringtone. He grabbed it off the counter. "Talk to me."

"Fire across the street from the safe house." Miller sounded out of breath.

Webb's phone rang.

"Fire at the safe house," Jim said to her. Back in to the phone. "We'll be right there."

47

THE LITTLE FIRE FINALLY generated enough heat for the tank to exceed its tolerance levels. The liquid of the propane turned to vapor faster than the release valve could handle it. The explosion was louder than she'd expected. The wave from the blast reached her even behind the boat. It blew the hair from her shoulders and made her scream just a little. The sensation thrilled her to her toes.

As people started moving toward the house and the fire, she crept around to the other side of the cul-de-sac. The officer from the front porch of the safe house was in the driveway of the burning garage. Something else exploded. She almost squealed in delight to have the help. Joy. It was elusive in her world, but she felt it as the house burned.

She reached the next-door neighbor's yard. They were outside too, in their driveway, keeping their child close. No one was looking her way as she skirted through the backyard. Someone else came out of the house as well. A big black man she'd not seen before. He ran toward the burning house. Must have medical or fire experience. No one else ran towards danger. They were banging on the doors, yelling, looking for signs of any possible occupants. By her best judgment, that would leave Dan and possibly one other cop in the house. It was time.

She jumped the short fence, her mind racing and her heart pounding. How would he take seeing her? It would be a shock. She had to remind herself that he would need time. She'd read plenty on Stockholm syndrome. She had all the time in the world to stick to the plan.

She emptied a potted plant from the back porch as she passed and made her way to the small bathroom window on the far side of the house. It was cracked open a bit. In her narrow experience, men like some air while they make a major bathroom transaction. They certainly don't want to leave the noxious aftermath of a big dump for others in an impersonal environment.

She jimmied the screen off and pushed the sash open as far as she could with her feet on the ground. The sill was too high for her reach to get it all the way open. But she would manage. She set the planter upside down under the window and was then able to work it up a few more inches. It was just enough.

She knocked a candle off the back of the toilet as she climbed over. She stood stock still and waited, listening. Only distant clamor from the fire. No noise from inside the house but the yelling from the excitement across the street grew by decibels as she opened the bathroom door.

She peeked into the hall. The kitchen and part of the living room looked abandoned.

Even though she preferred a knife fight, she gripped her blade in her left hand and pulled out the gun she'd bought last year. She took lessons for that as well. A little time and a good instructor and a girl could become proficient in about anything these days. Instructor said she was a natural.

She eased around the corner. As expected, all the occupants were looking out the front window, including the old woman in that same rolling office chair she'd used to wheel herself around the rest home. It was odd, but this was Danny's mother. She'd always been independent, strong-willed. Sophie had liked her for that even though it sometimes felt intimidating to a girl with few opportunities to express such qualities in her own world.

No way was she good enough to outshoot a cop, but she was smart enough to take one by surprise. She had a plan for that too.

She pulled one of the smoke bombs she'd bought off the paintball supply website. The things produced a huge amount of smoke in about twenty seconds. She pulled the pin and left it just inside the living room entry, backing away.

First to the hall was the female cop. Sophie tripped her as she ran past the hallway opening. The cop fell to her knees, losing her advantage. Sophie knocked her in the head with the gun handle and then used her blade to slice her tight throat. Sophie caught her slumping, jerky body.

Using the wall for support, Sophie eased the convulsing officer to the ground. Blood bloomed from the neck wound. She sucked in, inhaling the steely fragrance as the stain swelled and made its way down the woman's chest. The pathetic woman struggled to reacquire her dropped weapon, but her heart had slowed so much she had no ability to complete the intended movement. Blood was exiting her brain too fast.

Number sixteen.

She stood when she heard the heft of the front door slam into the wall. Danny came through, shouting about the fire department. He stopped suddenly. Looked at the body through the smoke and then up to Sophie as she loomed over her kill.

"Holy mother fuck, Sophie." He didn't look particularly happy.

That was expected and, frankly, part of the plan. Surprise always worked in her favor. She drew and pointed the gun at him. "Come with me."

"You really are insane."

"From you, that hurts, Danny. You'll understand. It's time to go home."

He turned and tried to back away, but the move did little more than back him against the kitchen counter. He was trapped.

She needed to be quick. The old woman rolled her chair into the area. Sophie pointed the gun at his mother.

"What do you expect to happen here?"

Sophie held up her free hand to calm him. "You'll understand everything soon." She pulled the auto injector from its pocket on her nifty vest and stepped toward him. "Turn around."

He didn't.

"I will shoot her."

As he turned, believing her words, he kept his head facing his mother as long as his strained muscles would allow. Sophie hit him with the big dose as soon as he was facing away. She got him right at the base of the neck under his ear. Her aim was good and she was sure she hit the carotid.

"I'm not going to do whatever it is you want me to do, Soph."

He said it the way he'd used to, back in Texas when she was a kid. Hearing him say it took her off guard. Made her weak in the knees. Her stomach fluttered. There had to be a chance for them.

"Let's go, Danny. It's time."

"I'm not going."

"What is this mess all about?" His mother was looking at the dead cop.

Danny eased in front of her. "Nothing, Mom. Go read your articles."

"Is there a fire here too, Danny?" She pushed herself off to the side, her chair rolling where she directed it with her dangling feet. "Something's wrong with Miss Edwards, Danny." She rolled right up to the cop, her wheels making tracks in the fresh blood. "We should do something."

"You do as Danny says." Sophie motioned with the gun toward the back of the house. "We're all going that way anyway. Move, Danny."

"Don't hurt her. She's so out of it today, she won't even know you were ever here."

Having his mom there to manipulate him with made things a little easier. It was all working out much better than she'd expected.

"I have no intention of doing that. *If* you come with me, you and I will be on our way and she'll be fine."

"Promise?" He pushed his mother toward the living room, the chair leaving an interesting pattern of blood behind. The cops would love that.

"Do you? Promise? You'll come with me?"

He nodded. His eyes were starting to glaze a bit. She needed to get him moving before he was too out of it to handle.

"I'd like some tea. Where's Stephen?" She looked toward the stairs "Stephen, we have company. Come make us some green tea!"

"Hush." Sophie still had the gun pointed at Danny, who shook his head. "Back up to me. Hands behind your back, but close together."

He stood there.

"Don't make *me* do something *you* won't be able to recover from." She let the gun's business end sway slightly toward his mother.

Man, that made him mad. He glared daggers her way. While he was making his mind up, her internal clock was thumping hard. She pushed the pistol close to the momma's head.

His face softened in resignation, marking the moment he understood it was best to follow her instructions. They needed to move fast. Back in the hotel room, she'd started a big loop in a tie wrap and attached it to her vest with a little duct tape. Now it easily yanked off when she needed it. She slipped it over his clasped hands and drew it in. When it was close to snug, she tucked the gun under her arm and used both hands to quickly yank it tight.

"Let's go." She pointed to the sliding glass door.

He lifted the safety bar with his foot and opened the glass. She followed. He stumbled a bit taking his step over the threshold.

Before she made her first step into the night, something slammed into the back of her legs. The impact was a hard blow to the back of the knees, like she was taken down in judo class. Her toes went tingly and she felt herself fall backward and over his mother's lap. Sophie landed uncomfortably and twisted onto the floor.

Dan turned. He tried to do something, but his bound hands and altered state made it impossible to do much more than fall on his knees.

Blows rained down on her head. Sharp, spiky pain lambasted her as she tried to stop the old woman. Four more good blows with the wood spoon landed on her head. Her temple smarted, but adrenaline was pumping. She didn't want to kill the woman after she'd promised Danny. He *was* doing what he said, even if it was because he was tied and drugged.

"Stop." Sophie tried to get up, but the crazy woman swatted her straight across the cheek. It stung like hell.

"Enough." Sophie grabbed another of the injector pens from a vest pocket and pressed it into the bony leg by her head. The old woman howled.

"Mom!" Danny got up.

Sophie met him and shoved him toward the backyard. The fire truck was getting close. The last of the sand had slipped through the hour glass.

"Go. Go." She pushed him.

"My mom ... "

"It's just tranquilizer, she'll be fine. I didn't shoot her."

"Bitch!"

It was slurred. She forgave him for saying it at the moment. All he needed was time. Right now, this was traumatic, painful. For them both, really. Like a new life coming into the world. It was the birth of their new life. Nonetheless, they needed to hurry. Everything would be fine in time.

She looked back as the other cop rounded the corner of the kitchen. He was wide-eyed and sweating. Young.

She pushed Danny down and raised her gun. He had drawn his, but it was by his side. He seemed somewhat confused, looking over the scene, which made him a little slow to find his target. Stupid cop. Sophie was not slow. She inhaled and took an instant to aim and squeezed that trigger as she exhaled.

Bang.

She'd aimed for the chest, but managed to hit him square in the face.

Number seventeen.

The old woman lay in the doorway behind the faceless man. With any luck she would die. A dizzying wave of nostalgia threatened to ruin her plan.

Dan grunted. He was losing it. She pulled him from the ground and ushered him on. He was almost too groggy to make it on his own. His anxiety had expedited the onset of the drugs. She pulled him past one more house and then she caught sight of the van down the block. Her heart was thundering and her body pumping with adrenaline. She gave a look back to see if anyone was following.

She'd done it.

48

"My car's across the street." Agent Webb headed for the door of Jim's apartment.

The rage in Jim's gut was back to levels he'd not felt since before his first anger-management class. At first he'd only gone because the court mandated it, but he soon realized the time with the group did him good. Like AA for people with shitty lives. But none of the stupid exercises were going to help with the absolute fury he felt brewing at the moment. When he got his hands on Sophie's knife he would be slitting *her* throat. Eye for an eye, a tooth for a tooth, and a slit throat and dust to dust.

"I'll meet you there."

Agent Webb hesitated but then flew out the front door. He calmly walked through his converted garage office and grabbed the small key hanging by the back door. His bike sat there, dusty and unridden for months. It roared to life with a turn of the throttle and a little ignition. He was closer to the neighborhood than Miller. He knew the back roads and the cut-throughs. The advantage of hour after shitty hour of surveillance in this town.

He whipped that bike through the side streets, ignoring stop signs, until he found a familiar path.

The dirt path cut from one subdivision to another. Kids used them to go from the smaller subdivisions and sneak into the pools of the larger. At the end of the third path was a narrow opening between fences. Six-foot chain link. He'd walked it before but his bike was bulky. At this speed, if it was too narrow, the consequences would be ugly. Pucker factor high.

He gunned it and zipped up the sidewalk and righted the bike as fast as he could so the machine would be straight up when he reached the gap. From this vantage point it looked like he was never going to make it.

He twisted the throttle. Grip it and rip it. The front wheel bounced when he hit the dirt.

"Never gonna fit," he yelled as he went through. A jerk yanked the bike to the right as the handle bar brushed the metal fence pole. The fishtail pulled the rear tire to the left. Gripping the bars like his life depended on it, he did his best to minimize the oversteer. The dusty path didn't help, but he'd made it.

Without slowing, he kept going, popping out at an intersection close to the new safe house. Cut a good five miles off his journey. He slammed on the brakes in time to skid up to the driveway. There was a fire truck across the street. People lined the sidewalks, taking pictures with smart phones. Everyone wanted the shot to post on their Facebook or Instagrams.

He rushed in. First thing he saw was a female face-down in her own blood in the hall. Must be Miller's plainclothes girl. Jim stopped to check her pulse. None. He moved into the open living area.

Stephen was holding up Lynette's limp little body. Her chair was lying on its back next to them. The back door was open to the night.

"Is she ... " Jim didn't want to say it.

Steven was crying but shook his head. "She has a thready, weak pulse. I called for help."

Miller and his team came in with guns up, ready to shoot.

"Officer down. Repeat, officer down," Miller shouted when he saw the woman on the floor bleeding out. He glanced at Jim. "Momma okay?"

"Not really," Steven said.

Miller signaled two men through the back sliding glass door. "See if they left a trail. Anything!" Two officers went into the night. He pointed at two others. "Check upstairs, see if Dan's up there."

Jim hadn't bothered to check. Dan was gone. He knew in his bones that Sophie had taken him. He was long gone. Along with Sandy.

"FBI agent down out here." Jim and Miller left Lynette's side. The officer checked for a pulse. Too dark to see the blood on his jacket. With the shake of the officer's head, they all knew the agent was dead.

Jim squatted back by the table. From that angle, he saw the young agent's face. No open casket for his family. Fresh blood ran in streams along the scores in the concrete patio. Lynette shuddered violently in Steven's arms. Her labored breathing got thicker with the struggle.

"Was she shot?" Jim didn't see any blood on or around her. Maybe she'd be okay. That would be a miracle from the looks of this place.

"Help me get her to the couch." Stephen lifted her upper body. Miller grabbed her tiny legs under the knees and helped move her. Sirens were approaching, but with all the commotion across the street Jim had no idea if it was the medics or more fire equipment.

Steven checked her over, careful not to cause any further damage to her frail body. "I don't see anything."

She coughed, gagged.

"Heart attack from the stress?" Miller headed back to the front room. On the radio. "Where's my medical? I need at least two."

"Could be something like that." Steven straightened her dress as she struggled to breathe. It was automatic for him to do his best for her, to make her comfortable.

Medics came rushing in.

It was too late.

———

The life had drained out of Lynette as the EMTs tried to assess her condition. They started CPR, connected a mask to help her breathe.

Then she was gone, right before Jim's eyes. Lynette Hodge's obituary would join the articles on the wall.

If Jim didn't find Dan, who would write her story? No more than seventy-five words. How could the life of a firecracker like her get wrapped up in seventy-five words?

Jim's rage shifted gears. Sorrow, deep and profound.

He sat back on the recliner across from the medics. The sounds of their voices muted. Miller was screaming away in the front room, but that was white noise as well.

One of the medics went out to check on the FBI agent lying just outside the door on the patio.

Agent Ava Webb walked slowly into the room. Her weapon was drawn but she quickly holstered it. She headed straight for her guy on the porch. The medic shook his head.

She said his name. "Foster." Ava knelt by his side. She touched her guy's back. She too was now wrapped in a wet blanket of sorrow. Anger.

Jim's anger slipped away, lost in yawning anguish as he watched Ava kneel there beside Foster and shed a tear for him. The medic returned and covered him with a sheet.

After a moment, Ava stood, her tears gone, her game face back in place.

Jim had moved in her direction without realizing. She found his gaze and looked down. Maybe she didn't want to share the moment of sorrow. He understood.

The carnage around him was raw, fresh. In his line of work, the closest he came to a fresh crime scene was when defense attorneys hired him. His arrival came long after the fact, often when the tape was gone and the area clean of all signs of bloodshed. His job was digging to uncover missed clues and follow up leads. Not this.

More police showed up. More FBI.

Jim made his way to the front room and looked out the window. The yard and the fire scene across the street were both being roped off with yellow and black tape. He wished he had a cigarette. Some scotch.

Miller came out. "How'd you get here so quick?"

Jim pointed to the bike. "Took a couple off-road shortcuts."

"You see her?"

"Nope." Jim leaned against the rail. "Didn't hear any shots either. She was gone."

"Dan wasn't upstairs."

Jim knew that. Didn't say anything.

They moved back toward the kitchen and the dead police officer on the floor. Ava approached and stopped before the bloody floor. Her body was slack with shock and pain. "She never used a gun before. With her profile, I'd have never thought she would." Ava looked back to the porch. "Foster had drawn, finger not on the trigger. She had to be damned good to hit him."

Miller tilted his head toward his officer, the woman on the ground with the slit throat. It was as if he didn't want to look back at her. To see her again. "Kahill was a marksman." He picked up the spent smoke bomb with a gloved hand. A burnt chemical smell lingered in the room. "But we'd said the perp was a knife wielder. And Sophie used the fire and smoke for cover."

"Dammit!" Ava kicked the side of the counter then paced the length of the small kitchen. "I have to go make a phone call I don't want to make. Foster had a wife and two young kids. I need to get someone to his house before this hits the news."

She walked away without waiting for a reply. Jim gave into the desire to follow. He managed only as far as the front porch, and then his legs stiffened. He hadn't the slightest clue how to comfort this woman. So he watched her climb into the big FBI car and drive away.

Miller walked up behind him. "Thank god my captain makes those visits."

A job Jim wouldn't want. He kept watching as Ava's car turned at the end of the street. "Lynette?" he asked.

"They think she was hit with the ketamine. Too much for her." Miller shook his head.

Jim's throat closed from the acrid taste of how much that pained him. Hard to breathe. All he could do was push that shock and sorrow to the back of his throat and try to swallow it down. He thought of Sophie Evers. Got mad. Anger was much easier to manage than pain. Always had been.

49

THE GIRL WAS CRYING. She was awake enough now to know she wasn't where she wanted to be. It was a pathetic whimper, really.

Sophie needed to pee. It was midafternoon and she'd driven for hours without a break. Dan would be rousing soon too. She needed to stop and manage all three.

"You ready to stop, baby?"

Carla jumped up from her comfortable pillow on the passenger seat.

"Okay. Give me a minute." She'd seen a sign a ways back for a rest area. "Should be able to stop in a sec." She patted the dog on the head.

You are more stupid than I ever imagined. Changing things up like this ...

"Shut up. Shut up." They approached the exit sign. "It's only minor. Besides if Bean found my birth mother ... our mother ..."

No response to that taunt. The voice was not her. Or it was separate from her, but it was her. It had started with talking to herself as a kid. Trying to make herself feel better. It never worked. Eventually the internal conversations changed, and one day she couldn't turn it off. It was all very confusing. The kind of thing that could give a girl a headache. Pinching the bridge of her nose didn't help clear things up.

Sophie now figured the voice was her mother. At least the last few years it had been that cranky old shrew. Always there. Always nitpicking. That was a mother, right?

"It's better this way. Plan C."

If she could figure out how to do it, she'd get rid of the voice as well.

Nothing's ready at that house. It's all in Cali.

Sophie ignored the nagging and pulled off the highway, parking in the most remote spot in the rest area lot. Many cars were parked down around the bathroom and that meant lots of eyes.

She twisted to the back. The girl was still crying but out of it enough that she wouldn't be any trouble. Sophie put Carla on the leash.

"You go. Then I'll take care of our passengers."

The dog hit the grass and squatted.

"I wish I could do that."

After the dog was empty, Sophie did her own business, bought a vending machine coffee, and returned to the van.

"Where am I?" The girl was struggling to sit up.

Sophie patted her head. "Not to worry. We'll be there soon and you'll get to be in a much more comfortable position."

Dan also moved, probably in response to the conversation.

She touched his face. His cheek twitched. The movement was cute, like a mouse wiggling whiskers. He had a tiny bit of gray coming on his temples. Mrs. Hodge's hair was all white. Maybe the premature gray thing ran in the family. She imagined him salt-and-pepper with his rough face weathered and wrinkled from years in the sun. She smiled and carefully injected his neck with more of the tranquilizer. His eyelids fluttered.

Sandy whimpered again, breaking the tender moment with Dan.

Sophie chose another syringe and plunged it hard into the girl's neck. It was the third or maybe the fourth time. There would be a few more. Hopefully it wouldn't kill her before Sophie was able to play this out. It wouldn't work without the waitress, but Sophie'd had a great idea on the road that made the girl much more useful. Another change of plan.

Stupid.

"No. Genius."

50

THE MEETING ROOM WOULD have been drab under the best circumstances given its tiny putty-gray tables and folding chairs with chipped brown paint.

The walls were decorated with a poster reporting some Vegas crime statistics, a picture of a missing kid, and several other memos. All taped to the wall. They reminded Jim of Lynette and her articles. It was downright depressing.

Ava looked ten years older than she had the day before. Yep, he was thinking of her as Ava all the time now. It didn't really matter. What mattered now was getting Sophie. But Ava looked beat. Her neat hair was in a ponytail and mussed a little on one side. She'd not bothered to fix her makeup from the tears.

But then again, Miller looked like he was in need of a good stiff drink, and a clean pressed jacket. The one he wore looked like it had been tossed in the back of the car more than once that day.

"We got a hit on Maria Callas." Ava tossed a sheet of paper on the table. "No address other than the PO box in Bakersfield, but we found an employer. Medical software. High-end stuff. I have the address."

California. Miller was stuck. Out of his jurisdiction.

"Our office has the address and a supervisor's name. I'm flying out in an hour."

"I'm coming." Jim figured that was going to be a no-go. Not that it mattered. At this point he'd find a way to get there on his own. He wanted Sophie himself and if he had to admit it, he didn't want Ava facing this freak on her own. Of course she was FBI, she wouldn't be on her own. But Jim didn't want her facing Sophie Ryan Evers without *him*.

She almost smiled. "There's an FBI flight scheduled. I managed to get you on as my witness. In reality, you are the only one who has seen her in person. My director wants a confirmation on her ID since this is such a high-profile case now."

No shit? He'd expected to be left on the tarmac as she flew off like the heroine in an old romance flick.

Miller looked pissed. Jim knew the drill. Las Vegas police had a dead Cynthia Hodge, a dead neighbor, a dead cop, and Sandy was still missing and all Miller could do was sit on his hands while the Feds chased down the out-of-state leads.

Jim felt for him but was once again happy that he could play by the seat of his pants.

Miller was stuck. He might not even get to prosecute Sophie for any of his warrants. Feds would choose the charges that would be the easiest to make stick. Probably not even in Vegas courts.

"When do we leave?"

She glanced at her phone. "Thirty minutes."

"That's barely enough time to get to the airport."

"Then we should go."

51

MEDIBRIDGE RESIDED IN A midsize building in Bakersfield. The receptionist was cheerful. The decor was a mix of bright orange and teal that gave the visitor the impression that the place was crisp, the business intelligent.

Jim leaned over and gave the receptionist his best smile. "Do you have pictures of your employees on your website, miss?"

She straightened her headset. "We do." She held up a finger. "Mr. Layton, some people from the FBI are here to see you." She paused to listen. "I'll tell them." She disconnected the call with the push of a button. "He'll be right here."

Ava moved closer. "Can you show us a picture of Maria Callas on the site?"

She typed away and then turned the screen in his and Ava's direction. A professional-looking photo of Sophie Ryan Evers took up the left half of the screen. Her credentials were listed on the right side. It was a boring picture. Hair pulled back so you had no idea how long it really was. Beige suit, white shirt. Not like the yellow she was wearing when she came to him and started this ride. But it was definitely her.

Ava asked, "That her?"

"Yes, ma'am." His stomach did a little flop. His brain immediately supplied the memory of the night in Texas.

Before he could get too worked up, a man came striding into the reception area in a very expensive suit. Jim was familiar. He'd seen plenty such on the big-time players on the Strip.

He greeted Ava first. "I'm Dave Layton. How can I help you?" Dave was typically handsome with a tight jaw and stubble just enough to make him look rugged. His fake, overly white smile and surgically perfect nose made Jim immediately think car salesman.

Ava was on her feet, showing her credentials and giving her name. Her suit was looking a bit better than it had that morning, but this guy and the receptionist had both out-labeled her for sure. Not that Jim gave a rat's ass about fashion. He didn't. In his business he would often use clothes to get a read on a person. See what they thought of themselves. How they wanted others to see them.

Jim was still in jeans and a black T-shirt and didn't care what anyone thought of his fashion sense.

"We're investigating a case and think one of your employees might be able to assist us," Ava stated as matter-of-factly as possible.

Dave's expression faltered for an instant. "Wow. The FBI? Really?" He glanced at the receptionist, who was still listening even though her head was facing the computer screen on her desk.

"We should pop into a conference room." He gestured through the glass doors separating the reception area from the rest of the business and led them to a small conference room with a table that would accommodate eight attendees.

They all stood. He took a position at the far end of the table.

"Tell me about Maria Callas," Ava said before he had a chance to ask her any questions.

"What about her?" He crossed his arms. Defensive.

"Where does she live?" Ava kept her arms limp at her sides. Relaxed.

He huffed. "Not sure how much I can divulge about her, you know, legally."

"I assure you that, legally, you can tell me her home address and her phone number." Jim wasn't sure that was true. But the FBI had more leeway than regular Joes thanks to the national security umbrella of changes.

"Not sure I want to." Dave was trying for tough, but he just looked smug. Jim wanted to punch this guy right in his perfect nose.

Ava strode over to him, stopping right in his face. "If I want to, I can charge you with interfering with a federal investigation, Dave."

Something told Jim that Special Agent Webb was not impressed with the pretty boy in the expensive suit.

"Harboring a fugitive." One side of her lip rose as if she were thinking hard. "Maybe even accomplice?"

"Hey!" Dave put his hands up as if to surrender and took two steps back before his butt hit the wall. "Not so fast. I'm just saying that HR might not like me giving out personal information. What's this really about anyway?"

"National security. Can't tell you." She opened her jacket. "Now am I arresting you, or do you have the information I've requested?"

"I have her number on my cell, but I'll have to get the address and shit." He dialed the speakerphone on the table. "Helen, I need Maria Callas's records in first floor, conference two, ASAP." He hung up after the woman confirmed the request. "So really, Maria is my best salesperson. Brings in about seventy million a year. Is she in trouble?"

Jim ignored the last part. "She works commission?"

"Oh yes." He grinned. "And she's good."

"You sell hospital supplies?" Ava asked.

"No." Dave's face lit up. "Software that integrates all systems in the hospital. Accounting, ordering, inventory, HR, even patient care and records. A portal. One-stop shop."

"But she's in hospitals all the time?" Jim asked.

He shrugged. "Yeah."

So she had plenty of access to drugs, assuming she had the talent to get by security. But then again she'd gotten by a cop and federal agent in the safe house and evaded getting caught for about umpteen murders.

Dave continued, "She travels all over the world visiting potential clients. She's gone all the time. I've only seen her in person maybe five times."

A woman knocked on the door. Another young, pretty, upwardly mobile person stood on the other side of the glass.

Dave opened the door for her and she beamed her whitened teeth at him. "Here you go, Mr. Layton."

"Thank you, Helen. That will be all."

She hesitated after seeing the strangers in the room with her personnel file.

"Really. I have this."

She backed out.

He opened the file. "Breckenridge." He made a surprised sound. "I didn't realize that. Strange, she never said she lived up there."

Jim figured it wasn't so strange at all. Lots of ski cabins up there. Lots of privacy to do whatever she wanted.

He read off the address. Ava typed it on her phone. Jim memorized it.

Dave also rattled off her number. Jim would remember that too.

"Her area code is Bakersfield?"

"Yeah. Company phone. Company car." He shrugged. "You make the sales she does, you get all the perks."

"How much you figure she earned last year?" Jim asked.

He looked up at the ceiling as if to add in his head. "Can't remember exactly. Probably close to a million."

Well. That was certainly enough to bankroll all her activities. "And she works her own hours?"

"I thought you said you wanted to talk to her as a witness. This sounds more like she's in trouble for something." His bright smile was gone, replaced by tight eyebrows that were also perfectly shaped. Jim wondered if he had them tweezed.

"If she calls, please don't tell her we were here, Mr. Layton. That would be grounds for charges. You understand?"

Dave nodded, his smugness exchanged for a hint of fear.

Ava handed him her card. "You keep the conversation to whatever normal business you'd conduct and then call me if she calls in."

"*Is* Maria in trouble?"

"You could say that."

52

THE ROAD TWISTED UP to Breckenridge. Back and forth, winding like a snake with a bellyache. It was summer, so there was no snow to fight, just vacationers in their oversized campers taking up both lanes. Jim supposed it should be a pretty drive, but the circumstances distorted the beauty of the scenery.

When she got a clear bit of asphalt, Ava pushed the Town Car along far above the posted limit. She bit her bottom lip and tapped the steering wheel with her index finger. Anxious. Worried. Pressured from her boss to get this psycho before she made more headlines.

No one had been told of the connections to past killings. The media was focused on the brutality of the Cynthia Hodge murder and was unaware of the depth and breadth of Sophie's killings. It wouldn't be long until someone leaked something. Secrets were not long kept in Vegas, no matter the city's slogan. It should be *Whatever will make news in Vegas will make the news.*

They came to the fork in the road. Ava eased left. Before long the pavement gave way to a white-graveled path that would take them to Sophie's hideout.

The driveway was long and tree-lined. Postcard material. The forest was too thick to make out any structure from there. Too dangerous to drive up to the house, and their backup was still on the way.

She pulled the car off just past the drive. Foot power from here on out. Ava opened the trunk, loaded, and cocked a shotgun. She offered it to Jim without words.

He considered it, then shook his head. "Not for me." He looked toward the house. "Shouldn't we wait for the SWAT team?"

"We're just going to take a peek. Assess the situation." He liked her style.

Twigs, pine cones, and other material crushed beneath his feet no matter where he placed his big boot. A particularly loud snap made Ava stop and glare at him. He cringed. How Native Americans used to be so quiet was beyond him. Maybe that was historic urban legend.

Sneaking up like this had his heart flopping around in his chest like a super ball. This much tension was bad. Made him nervous. Jumpy. It was dangerous. He attributed it to the fact that he wanted Sophie too bad and was worried over Sandy.

Personal investment was doubled down in this case. Bad mojo made for bad outcomes. Declining the gun had been a good idea. He was ready to jump out of his skin. And just like O said, a squirrel could run by and startle him enough to shoot Ava in her cute little ass.

She glanced back as if she heard his thoughts but pressed on. The sapling trees and vines tripped them up, slowing progress. A bead of sweat had rolled down his back and more would follow. He had his slap-jack in his right hand. Ava had her handgun at the ready and the shotgun hung over her shoulder.

She eased through the woods with a grace Jim would never possess, as if the branches and twigs were intentionally not in her way. That wasn't possible. The bottom line was his mass and momentum carried a volume hers did not.

She stopped and braced with her back against a tree. She pointed ahead. There was a narrow cabin at the end of the gravel. Two-story, given the height of the windows. Nice. Something a family from L.A. would rent for a week of skiing in December. He could picture a large Christmas tree covered in fat multicolored lights reflecting onto new snow through the wall of windows. Of course it was the middle of the day in August and nothing twinkled. Regardless, not the kind of place a murderer brought her victims to be tortured and killed. His gut told him something was off.

"No cars." It was a very low whisper.

"Maybe around back?"

Ava nodded. She pointed to the right and to him. "On three," she said without sound.

"What about the backup?"

"They'll be here."

Not what he meant. She held up one narrow finger. No polish. No rings.

One.

She would go to the left, he to the right. But the place looked deserted.

Two.

She didn't look back at him. Her brain was already on her mission. Jim's brain was deciphering what his gut was screaming at him. Would Sophie leave her hostages unattended after so much careful planning?

Three.

Ava moved out. That left him no choice. He turned and headed in his assigned direction, skirting just inside the tree line.

The yard was narrower on his side, bringing him closer to the house. Glare from the sun blocked his view inside the tall front windows. A cheerful spring wreath with white birds on it adorned the front door.

Maybe this was the wrong place. Maybe she'd used a false address with her employer. That would make sense.

He crouched and ducked behind the front bushes to try for a glance inside. He stopped just short of the floor-to-ceiling windows. He peeked in quickly, saw nothing, and then waited a few seconds before a second look, this one longer.

Bright, open, and airy. There was cabin-themed decor everywhere. A bear rug and log furnishings with heavy plaid fabrics. The kitchen was at the back of the large two-story room. No one in sight.

He headed back the direction he'd come and continued to the back of the cabin. That side of the building was logs all the way up. One small window, shoulder height. Bathroom. It was covered by a curtain. Nothing to see. He made it around the back.

That was better than expected as well. Multi-level deck. Hot tub. Grill. Flowers decorated the area. It was only ten yards from a large pond. High-dollar for a hideout.

Ava stood at the back door, weapon lowered. "I didn't see anyone."

"Me either. Looks like we might be in the wrong place."

She shook her head. "I don't think so. May look pretty, but it feels creepy as hell."

He looked in the back door window around the drawn curtain.

She tried the door. The knob turned.

"Thought you wanted it all by the book?"

"That would be best. But..."

"Sandy's clock is counting down," he said, glad she was using his line of logic today.

She nodded. "Dan's not exactly safe either."

A low chirping noise repeated several times. Not a bird. Electronic. He looked down, following the line of the bottom rail of the deck. A small round device was screwed to the post closest to the door. That was some kind of trigger. Triggers meant things going boom.

"Motion detector."

"What?"

He grabbed Ava around the waist. No time to explain. He pulled her away from the door. Tangled legs made them both stumble down the two levels of deck steps. He recovered first and pulled her toward the pond. She caught her footing and started running with him. They were about five feet from the water when the world ended.

53.

No sound.

Jim was deafened. His legs were numb and he couldn't breathe. No way this was good.

He tried to breathe, drew in water. In a panic his lungs coughed out the fluid. Jim tried to move his arms. They answered.

In an instant his body returned to the normal responses to his mental commands. But his hearing was still off. He realized he was in the pond, one leg pinned under a large piece of timber. He sat up and his head was above the water.

Heat pressed against the back of his head. He twisted around. The cabin was ablaze. All of it. Immense logs of the framework had folded in on themselves like a Boy Scout campfire on steroids. The yard was littered with the shards, large and small, of the exploded timbers.

"Ava!"

He didn't see her. He dug in the mud, pulling at his leg. It didn't feel broken, only trapped. This was going to leave a mark. He held his breath to fold forward and dig at the mud holding him under the wood.

Ragged shards scraped his trapped leg. His foot twisted first, then his calf. He pushed up with all his weight and the timber rolled off. He stood in the water, testing his steadiness. His shin would carry a nasty bruise for a while, but he'd live.

"Ava!" Strange to listen to himself yell and not hear a thing.

He started out of the water and saw her sit up in a tall patch of reeds a couple of yards away. Her hair was a soaking-wet mess, her head was bleeding and her arm hung limp and twisted in an impossible direction. Her shoulder was dislocated or broken. Either way, she would be in a great deal of pain when the shock of the blast wore off.

Smoke billowed past, obscuring his path as he waded in her direction. The cabin burned like dry kindling.

"You okay?" He said it but was sure her hearing would be as dampened as his.

Her reaction was neither positive nor negative. But she did mouth something he could understand. Her hand went to her head wound first. She gently tested the cut and then inspected the blood it left on her fingers. Then she tried to move her left arm. He barely made out the screech of pain that accompanied the action.

"Keep it still."

He dug for his phone. Wet. No bars. No signal. They had passed several other cabins on the way in. Surely someone heard the explosion. Backup was on the way. He took off his shirt and wrapped it around her body, tucking it under her arm with the least amount of movement to her shoulder as possible. She cringed again.

"Sorry."

He tied it off, making a sling of sorts. Would hold it better than nothing.

54

THE CELL PHONE ON the dash started talking. A ring tone. The cartoon. Marvin the Martian. *"Where's the Kaboom? There should have been an earth-shattering Kaboom."*

No need to respond. It was an electronic message sent from the device planted under the cabin.

She closed her eyes, ignoring the road. The bastards had found her happy place. Her retreat. The thought was a soul-sucking wound in her stomach. There wasn't much she was attached to in this world. That cabin had been about it. Since they found her birth mother, Sophie had suspected Bean may be good enough to find her.

She was right. He would be punished.

She took in a yoga breath. Long, deep, it filled first her chest and then her belly with fresh air.

Good thing she had trusted her intuition and headed northeast.

"Fucking PI."

A horn blared. She opened her eyes. She was half in the right lane. Who cared? Calmly she steered the van back into her lane.

She envisioned the explosion. The creep she'd bought the C4 from promised spectacular. Even setting them up she'd been torn. That plan was a double-edged sword. If it worked, the cabin—her dream home—was gone.

Not what she planned. No.

Told you so.

"Shut up."

You should have just found Danny yourself.

"Not now."

The nag was right. There had been no lack of trying on Sophie's part. For months she had searched for Dan. She sat taller so she could see him through the rearview mirror.

He was sleeping, his body laid out on the bench as if he was in his bed, a peaceful expression on his angel face

Sophie sighed. She should have kept at the hunt herself. Instead, she'd lost patience and hired that irritating PI. Bean was supposed to be a loser only after a quick buck. He had even acted like a loser both on the phone and at that pathetic diner. No professionalism. No receptionist. No office building.

She gripped the steering wheel. With any luck Bean was right there when the house blew. Standing on her porch, or even better, inside. She closed her eyes again. She'd loved that house and had looked forward to living her perfect life with Danny there. Fucker. He'd been nothing but trouble.

She turned up the radio and let the music fill the rolling metal box. It was loud. Violins echoed off the walls. It was not a proper sound stage for Schubert, but it would help soothe Sophie's worn nerves. Carla raised her head for a moment and settled back down.

Let it go. Move forward. She tried to push the rage away. Send it down to that place where it disappeared in her gut in a tiny ball of shit to be flushed away. Anger did her no good. The house was just full of *things*. Nothing she couldn't replace.

The bigger problem was that Bean and his helpers were so close on her tail. Digging in her business. She wasn't used to people knowing about her, knowing her history or her details. A strange sense of anger and shame filled her. Not that she was shamed by any of her actions. No. Only the few loose ends she'd left behind caused her any embarrassment. One day she would go back and eliminate *all* those loose ends.

A situation like this called for going on the offensive. No running for Sophie Evers.

She glared at the waitress in the back. She didn't look as comfortable as Danny. She was sitting, her head at an awkward angle. Good. It was time to use that leverage.

The GPS unit said she had one hour, twenty-three minutes until arrival. Sophie needed to hold it together that long. She needed to get those two unloaded, count her losses, and then solidify a new plan. There was lots of stuff at the cabin that could be evidence. But she was sure there was nothing about Indiana. And if there was, the explosion and the incendiary devices should have destroyed all of it. Still, you could never tell with fire. It did what it wanted.

55

A MAN CAME RUNNING around the back of the house. He was tall, red-headed, and had a dry phone in his hand.

He fell to his knees beside Ava. It was clear he was talking. Some sound was drifting through the haze of Jim's hearing. Not enough to understand completely.

Call maybe. *Others?* Jim shook his head no. At least he hoped there was no one in that cabin. God, he hoped Sandy wasn't in there.

Jim pointed to his ear and shook his head. The universal *I can't hear you* gesture earned a returned sign for *I called for help*.

The man opened up a fanny pack medical kit. Johnny-on-the-spot this guy was. He rinsed Ava's forehead with water from a squirt bottle. She closed her eyes to keep from getting fluid in them. The cut wasn't as bad as Jim had first thought.

Jim got up and strode to the burning structure. All he could think of was the bonfires his buddies used to throw in college. In his past life. Before his world fell to pieces. He'd gotten it together since then.

Some. But now he found himself in the middle of what looked like a war zone.

Then it hit him that if Sandy was in that massive bonfire, his heart would break once again.

He was pushed back by a wall of heat as the front of the structure collapsed in on itself. Everything was burning. The place had been rigged to be totally destroyed if disturbed.

He heard the pop and searing of the wood push through the empty numbness of his ears. He could make out the muffled sound of a fire truck coming down the drive. The driver swung it wide, rolling through the shrubbery along the path, to spin it around so he could back closer.

Behind the fire unit was the ambulance. They followed, stopping short of the walkway. Jim's vision blurred as two men and a woman filed out, large plastic cases containing all manner of medical equipment in tow. Ava would be fine.

Behind them were three black SUVs. Backup. At last.

Jim felt a little wobbly. The female medic stopped by his side and tried to steady him.

"I'm good."

She pointed at the grass and pushed him into a seated position. Seemed reasonable. He let his legs give way; she eased him down. "Anything hurt, sir?"

"I couldn't hear."

"Explosion?"

Jim didn't say anything, just gave her a small nod.

She shouted, "Common. Should return fairly fast unless there's damage." She looked in his ear but didn't make any proclamation as to the future health of his eardrums. "Anywhere else hurt?"

"I just had a piece of wood fall on my leg. It's okay."

Without permission she cut straight up his pant leg, all the way to the knee, and yanked it open. There was a large round area that was trying to start a bruise already.

She felt around the wound. "Nothing feels broken." She checked his eyes and had him follow the path of her moving thumb a few times before she left him to go see if the others needed help.

The firemen worked in a choreographed dance with water and time to put out the flames. Jim watched for longer than he intended and then got up to go check on Ava.

56

AGENTS, COPS, AND FIREMEN were scattered over the lawn like ants. The house had burned hot and fast. His hearing came back in increments. The last guy Jim spoke to figured there was a large amount of accelerant expelled during the explosion. No one there was a bomb specialist, but that much was obvious.

He sat beside Ava on the tailgate of the fire marshal's truck, drinking off-brand bottled water and waiting as the crew searched the smoldering structure for any remains. Jim's gut told him Sandy and Dan were not in there.

Neither of them had spoken for a few minutes, both staring at the remains of the house.

Agents had found two other triggers. The bomb could have been set off from the front porch or a trigger by the pond. The entire property had been booby-trapped.

"That was close, Agent Webb."

She let out a little laugh. Her hair was free and dangling in her face. Mud drenched her white shirt. She'd lost one of her shoes. "Again, I think you can call me Ava. After all, you saved my life."

Jim said nothing. He wasn't sure how he felt about being on a first-name basis with her. He'd been calling her by her given name in his mind since the scene at the house. Out loud was another matter. She was strong, beautiful.

He took another drink of water. It was good. Soothing.

"Now what? Where would she take them?" She shoved her hair back again. It seemed to irritate her.

"Why not cut it off?"

"Cut what off?" She didn't look at him. Just watched the men moving around with hoses and long pry bars.

"If your hair bothers you, why not cut it off?" Easy enough. He liked it, but he could understand why a woman in her position would keep it short.

She looked down at her hands. "I don't want to come off too mannish at the office. I have enough trouble because of my job as it is."

"Trouble?"

"Never mind, Bean." She stood. The paramedic rushed over.

"You need to sit, ma'am. I wish you'd let us transport you. That's a bad dislocation." He'd iced and wrapped it but didn't have the skills—or the pain meds—to reset the joint. Agent Webb—Ava—had refused to go to the hospital until she was sure no one was in that house.

One of her agents approached. "For you." He held out the phone to Jim.

"Hello?"

"Hey, my man. Hear you're having a blast up there."

Ely always had a way with words. "Not funny."

"You guys okay?"

299

"Head hurts. Ava has a few cuts and a dislocated shoulder."

"Ava? Must be getting cozy."

"Shut up. What do you have?"

"Well, I think I know where she might be going."

Jim straightened. Ava turned her attention away from her agent and was obviously eavesdropping. He held the phone out some so she could hear.

"There's one little cross-reference from a car sale. Elizabeth Stanton sold a 2009 Toyota and traded it in on a cargo van. One like the caterers and shit use. The dealer remembered the picture I sent him because the woman said she was buying the van for her aunt. She insisted the title be put in the name Eloise Fowler."

He looked at Ava. "That name ring any bells for you?"

"None."

Ely broke back in. "It shouldn't. Eloise Fowler was a single woman, no kids, who died in a car accident four years ago. But I found where she got a ticket driving from California to Nevada last week."

Ava stood, holding her arm, and looked at her guy. "You find any of this?"

He shook his head.

"You have an address, Ely?" she shouted a little too loud at the phone.

"Why yes, I do, Miss Lady Fed. And for you, I have one other little treat."

"You do?"

"I found an online veterinary medical distribution. I called and said I was working for Dr. Eloise Fowler and needed some ketamine. That I didn't have my account log in. They wouldn't let me order, of course, but I managed to find out they sent a large shipment just last month to ..."

This had to be where she went. It was her drop location. It may not have been her first choice, but Sophie had been numerous places. "Where is she?"

"Knoblesville, Indiana."

"Text the address to this phone." Ava was still loud talking. Evidently, her hearing wasn't all the way back.

"Yes, ma'am. Right away, ma'am!" The phone dinged. The text was there.

"Nice work," she said. "If you ever need a job, give me a ring."

"Already did my civic duty, ma'am. I like my ... recreational activities way too much for government work."

Jim laughed. "You have Annie?"

"I do, indeed. She's sleeping on the eagle as we speak."

"Eagle?" Ava asked.

Jim eased off the tailgate. "Ely has some rather impressive hanging sculptures in his place. Annie likes them."

Into the phone she said, "Later, Ely. Let me know if you find anything else."

Jim paced away. "Sophie changed her plans. Why?"

"We got too close. This was her plan. To make a perfect home for Dan. She got spooked, took the waitress, and changed her destination. She's unprepared. Probably angry. My bet is Dan's not going along with her scheme. She's going to get off-balanced in a hurry."

"As if she's not now." Jim paced back.

"She's been calm and collected for years. Her killings had been planned or at least convenient. Now she's running. I bet she never considered what to do if we caught onto her. Psychopaths assume they are correct, even justified in everything they do. They have no respect for the police. Or you. Probably picked you because she thought you weren't capable of figuring her out—no offense. Now that we've tracked her, she's got to be in a panic. Or worse."

"That makes her even more dangerous." Jim thought of Cynthia Hodge, disfigured and dumped. The dead agent on the back porch of the safe house without a face. A limp Lynette Hodge in Stephen's arms. He didn't want to think of Sandy and Dan stuck with Sophie Evers as she fell apart.

And again, all because he'd found Dan for her. Fuck, he wished he hadn't taken this job.

Jim looked at the young agent standing beside Ava. "Can you get us a ride to Indiana?"

He didn't answer. Just looked over at Ava.

"Do it."

57

JIM EASED BACK IN his seat. They should be getting close to the small town where they believed Sophie was holed up. Locals had done a drive by and someone was in the house. That's all they were asked to do.

The fruity smell of the Tahoe made his stomach turn. He was in the back seat. Maybe this had been a K-9 unit at some point. He couldn't narrow down the offending scent. Using stinky shit to cover the smell of stinky shit confused him. The vehicle was thick with the strawberry perfume. And not the fresh-picked strawberries like mom puts on shortcake kind of smell. No. It was the medicine-ish, kid's cough syrup kind of strawberry.

Ava's face was pale. A military medic on the plane had popped her arm back into the proper position. It had to hurt like a motherfucker. She now had a brace, a better sling, and a little pain medication. She'd refused anything stronger.

"You shouldn't be here."

"I'm the agent in charge, or have you forgotten?"

"Wow. Um, no, I have not. I was just worried—"

"Don't worry."

He looked out the window. A light rain. Clouds. That was good. Made it darker. Easier to sneak up. Of course, a SWAT team would be doing that.

It churned his gut being so out of control. What if they fucked it up and Sandy was hurt? But no one was concerned about his worries. They were all following some book on tactical and hostage situations. Jim wanted to follow his gut, go in there and strangle that bitch with his bare hands.

They pulled up into the parking lot of a long-ago closed gas station. How a gas station went out of business with the price per gallon so high, he'd never know. There were several police units, five FBI cars, and a tactical van there.

Ava climbed out gingerly and addressed the officer in charge of the Knoblesville police.

Jim hung back. She'd told him pretty clearly that she was in charge from here on out. He leaned against a police car and watched. Still within earshot, of course. The house was a doublewide, north of town. At least fifteen yards from any other structure.

"Well, brother. Looks like Lady Fed doesn't need the likes of us any longer." Double O strolled up and leaned on the car right next to Jim.

"What the hell are you doing here?"

He shrugged, put a toothpick in his mouth like a lollipop. "Was in the neighborhood and thought I'd stop by."

"The neighborhood?"

He shrugged, lit a cig, and handed it to Jim. He needed it. The nicotine wouldn't ease his problems, but it sure made them easier to swallow.

"Ely called. I was at the airport, changed flights." It was good to have one person he could depend on. "The SWAT team decided to wait until full dark to go in."

"Great idea. As long as you aren't being held hostage by a maniac," Jim muttered.

"Look at that. Fifteen cops, at least that many agents." O spit out the toothpick. "The crazy bitch will see all that coming a mile away. She was smart enough to booby trap the house in Cali, she'll have done the same thing here." O situated his jeans by pulling up then down on the waistband. "You know, a couple smart guys could probably get in there quieter and easier than that big SWAT team."

"You think?"

"I do.

"Rental's back there." O motioned behind the mess of official vehicles. "Got GPS and the address."

Ava would kill Jim if they moved in first and messed up her perfectly planned rescue. Only, her plan left one thing to be desired: the element of surprise. Sophie Ryan Evers had time to prepare for it.

"Let's go."

58

"OH MY, BUT YOU do looked pissed."

The waitress had been awake a while. She'd screamed her fool head off for about an hour. Now she was quiet, her red-rimmed eyes hard. Her cheeks flushed with fear that Sophie guessed was quickly turning to anger. She didn't want the child to be resistant; she wanted her crying and pleading.

The girl didn't answer.

"I'll be killing you soon enough, no need to be getting yourself all worked up. I just need to make sure your friend doesn't show up and try to ruin all my plans."

She looked confused, but still didn't speak. Sophie hadn't asked her a question, had she?

"You hungry?"

She paled. So much ketamine would have been rough on her. Puke bucket Sophie had left nearby was half full as it was. She shook her head but still didn't speak.

"You have a bad-ass hangover, girl. You should sleep that off."

"How long?" Her voice was very scratchy, hoarse.

"Ah. No wonder you weren't speaking." Sophie had added it up on the way here. She'd kept the poor girl out for almost two days. She was surprised the girl survived even though Sophie had tried to keep the doses weak enough to keep her alive but strong enough to render her incoherent. "A long time. Too long. Your head will hurt and your stomach for a while. But I figure you'll be dead before you feel better, so you sure you don't want some food?"

Her bound hands shook in her lap as she sat on an old cot, her back against raw boards.

Dan was up at the trailer. Sophie had brought the girl out to the shed so Dan wouldn't hear her. Didn't want him distracted. He was stirring as well and she wanted to be there when he was in that twilight stage so she could give him just the right amount of the shit to make him accommodating.

You should have him kill the girl. Make an official bonding between you two. A marriage of sorts.

"Shut up."

The waitress looked confused again, but if she refused food, what the fuck? Less work for Sophie.

Seriously, if he kills her when he's under the influence, then he'll be better off staying with you because you can keep him away from the law. It's what you do.

It could work. He could use her blade.

Dan was moving a little bit when she got back inside. Trying out his legs, his fingers, but his eyes were still closed. That last dose had been a big one. It was all she'd had in the van. But she'd stored a good bit of the ketamine in the dreary kitchen of this shitty trailer. She'd used it as a warehouse of sorts, only coming here to restock. The neighbors thought Eloise dead, her relatives fighting over the land.

Pffft. The land wasn't worth a shit. It stunk. The thirty-year-old trailer was moldy. She'd passed herself off as a realtor and asked them to call her if they saw anyone hanging around. Now she was the one hanging around.

"What are you doing, Soph?" Dan's eyes didn't open.

Her heart stopped for an instant. He was still calling her Soph. Maybe … She was afraid to think of maybe. "Getting you some water."

His eyes opened. "Where are we?"

"Indiana."

He sat up, pausing to realize his leg was shackled to the bed and his hands were still bound. She helped him up then handed him the water.

He wiggled his foot. "Why am I tied up?"

She shrugged. This wasn't going too easy. She'd expected yelling. But his head probably hurt too much.

"You need to be this way to start. You'll see soon. You'll want to be here and … Then I can untie you."

"I need to piss."

Cowboys. She pushed an empty paint can closer to him.

"Really?"

"It's the best I have. This is not where I wanted us to start up, Danny. I had the perfect spot in the mountains, a little lake. It was magical."

"What happened to it?"

Rage filled her again. She needed to move. She got up and walked to the door and leaned on it. "That private eye. He found us. Well, it. He got there first. It's gone." Her belly knotted at the thought. "I hope he burned up with it."

Dan just nodded. He didn't look upset. He wasn't happy either. He was just there.

"Are you feeling okay?"

"I feel like I drank all the beer in Austin last night."

She couldn't help a hint of a giggle. The last time she giggled was when she was a kid. "I, um … I want us to be … "

"Happy?"

He looked her in the eye when he said it. She felt his sincerity, but she knew better than to trust it. Too many men had used that ploy on her before.

But for the moment she'd enjoy the possibility that he could love her without going through her *treatment* plan. The fear that the plan would fail and she would have to slash his throat had faded some. But she would do it if need be.

She remembered playing cowboys and Indians when they were kids. She was the Indian, of course. He tracked her down. He held that cap gun to her stomach. Looked her in the eye as he pulled the trigger. Over and over.

You shot me, she'd said. Easy to remember the hurt and surprise.

You've committed nineteen crimes against god and humanity, he'd replied with a smile. *It's what I do.*

And that was it, wasn't it? It was what *she* did too.

Looking at his stern face, she thought she might kill him anyway. He'd hurt her so many times. And all she'd ever done was love him. That was not how she expected to feel. She thought once he was here, he would fight and she would convince him … of what? That he loved her?

The cops and that fucking PI were closing in. Her throat was tight.

"Drink. You have to be thirsty."

He looked down at the glass in his bound hands. "More drugs?"

She gave him a small smile. "No," she lied.

If he killed that girl, that would make Sophie happy. She wanted to see him do it with the same smug look of the cowboy who shot little girls with crushes in the stomach.

"Are you happy to see me?"

He took a sip. Good. "I'm worried 'bout you, Soph. You've caused a truckload of trouble."

"It's what I do."

He nodded. Did he remember the words he'd uttered to her all those years ago? Did he remember that he'd laid his body on top of her and kissed her hard right after that? She'd felt his desire for her. Did he remember that? Did he remember acting like it never happened the next day?

"Talk to me." He took another sip.

"About what?"

"Why are we here? What do you really want me to do?"

His hair was a mess, his clothes rumpled and twisted on his body. She'd waited so long for this moment and now she wasn't sure what she wanted out of it. She'd pined for him. Wished for his attention. She knew he would complete something that was missing, some huge piece inside her. But now all she felt was ...

"I want ... wanted ... But you're not."

"Not what?"

Not what I remember. Not what I really want. Not worth a shit for fucking around all these years.

She needed to think.

"Drink your water."

There was a soft bong like a doorbell several rooms away. She jumped. He tried to move.

"Stay put."

59

"YOU STOLE A BATON from a cop?" O shook his head.

They made their way past the property at 11103 Southwest Highway. Its driveway led into the dark. No way going in the front door was going to work.

They had gone to the next farm road and cut through the woods on foot. O held his gun at the ready. Jim had managed to find a police baton lying on the hood of a car before they left the checkpoint. "He left it laying around. You know how bad crime is these days."

"Right."

The SWAT team need not have waited. The forest was so dark Jim had a hard time negotiating the stumps and roots. Again, there was no way to be quiet about it when the damned blackberry bushes were reaching out and grabbing his clothing. Did not help going in stealth mode one bit.

They headed toward a couple of lights twinkling through the trees. They eased closer, doing their best to be quiet. Again Jim wondered how the hell he made so much more noise than everybody else. O had at least forty pounds on him and he was ghostlike as he moved around the trunks and over the dried leaves.

They stopped and hunched down behind a couple of downed trees. The trailer wasn't the only building on the property. Closer to them was a shed large enough for a car. A small outdoor light burned on the corner, revealing an ancient tractor rusting behind the shed. The seat and steering wheel were gone. The tires were flat and cracked by time.

For the second time in as many days, Jim was hit by the shockwave from an explosion. This one was smaller, farther away. In the front of the trailer. He and O both ducked for cover.

Jim peeked over the logs. Fire and smoke rose over the trailer.

"Cops came in the front. So much for waiting till dark."

Jim saw movement off to the side. Three men in assault gear were creeping through the woods, moving in unison around the back of the trailer. Jim suspected the formation was mirrored on the other side. They hustled into the yard.

Mistake.

Within seconds one stepped on a mine. The explosion was loud. Jim's not-quite-back-to-normal ears complained.

Guys came in and retrieved the screaming men and dragged them to the relative safety of the woods. They would fall back. Call for more help.

"They'll reconvene," O whispered.

"Probably send in a negotiator."

Ten minutes passed. Nothing moved. Not a curtain. Nobody crossed in front of the back windows. "You think it's another dead end?"

Jim thought about it. Remembered her smug look the morning after she'd ... He closed his eyes. The sooner this ended, the sooner he could forget Sophie Evers and move on with his life. Dan wouldn't be so lucky. If he was still alive, he'd lost his mother and his sister to the crazy bitch.

"She's arrogant. She may have had one backup plan, but I doubt she has two."

60

SHE CHEWED HER FINGERNAIL. Dan was looking at her, his eyes sparkling as if he were amused. She considered slapping him for his smugness.

"You know how this ends, don't you, Soph?"

If she didn't know better, she'd say his expression had changed to pity. She didn't want his fucking pity. She was in control of this situation. Regardless of the number of police in her backyard. She peeked through the curtain.

"Why don't you turn off the lights if you don't want them to see you?" His eyebrows rose. "You know they'll cut the power soon anyway. Just like they do in the movies."

She spun back and slapped him. "This is not the movies, you bastard. I *am* in control."

No, you ain't.

She ignored the voice and rushed to cup his face. "I'm sorry. I have to think." She had nowhere to go. No way to get away from his disappointed gaze.

The party's over, stupid. Might as well slice these two. You have a better chance of getting out through the woods alone.

She didn't want to be alone. All the planning. All the struggle.

The whoring. Fucking old, ugly men. Those nasty pimps. You whored yourself all the way up to a cush job and still no one wants you. Your boy sure don't.

NO! Dan did want her. He was here. He wasn't fighting her.

He thinks you're trash.

He didn't. And she would prove it. He was on the bed. Sitting there with that water glass still in his hand. It was half gone, so he'd drunk most of it. He was a little fucked up, not all the way.

"Danny."

He looked at her.

She inched forward. Schoolgirl butterflies performed a complicated dance in her belly. Gently she cupped his face again. His expression was blank. She was sure that would change. She leaned forward, waiting to see if he did the same. He did not.

She eased down to her knees. She'd loved this man since she was nine. And this was the last chance they had.

Leaving her eyes open, she tilted her head and made up the distance to his lips. They were warm, soft. And she was sure he was kissing her back.

She pulled back an inch.

He was looking at her, face still blank. She was filled with joy and he was blank?

"That's the last time you do that." Cuffed hands and the water glass flew at her face. He faltered backward, flailing. Trying to get his hands around her neck. Comical almost.

She shoved him. "Asshole."

"Whacko." He kicked out at her.

Well, that settles that, doesn't it?

"It does." Her heart broke. There would be no time for the treatment. To convince him. She retrieved her gun from the counter. She unlatched his foot. "Move."

"Where to? The FBI is out there."

"So is someone I want you to meet."

She assumed he didn't remember seeing the waitress or he would have asked about her first thing, with his cowboy ways.

"You doing the suicide by cop thing?"

She laughed. "Hardly. I have insurance. And you'll probably like her. She's cute and young. She's our ticket out of this hellhole. If you're good, I'll let you watch me kill her. If you're not, I'll make her kill you."

61

"Lights went out," **O** said.

"Time to move." Coming from inside, her night vision would be lacking. They'd have a few seconds before it adjusted. "Stay on the gravel path. Less likely to get blown up. She had to leave herself a path out of here." Jim hoped.

He went first, running low. Staying in line with the shack so she couldn't see him. Moving as quiet as his clumsy feet would take him. He made it to the tractor and realized the farm equipment was hiding a small car between it and the building. Some kind of all-wheel drive, all-terrain thing.

O pointed two fingers to the right. Jim went left. He made it around the corner just as Sophie and Dan closed the shack door behind them. Sandy screamed. It was worn, tired sounding.

He approached the door, O pointed the gun and just before Jim's hand landed on the handle, the door flung open.

Jim stumbled back. Sandy stood there, crying. Sophie was behind her with a long, shining blade at her throat.

"Hello, lover," she cooed at him. His skin crawled. "Come back for more?"

"You can put the knife down now."

"And then we'll talk about this? Hardly." She cut Sandy's neck, enough to make her screech and blood dribble from the wound. "You and your buddy will get up and walk away. You'll tell all your cop friends out there to let us drive away. Otherwise she dies." Sophie quickly glanced back. "Danny. Come here."

Dan stumbled through the opening and onto his knees. He was under the influence of the ketamine and she'd crudely taped something around his waist.

"I'll blow him up and cut her. By now you know I'm more than willing."

Dan tried to stand. He made eye contact with Jim. Winked.

He then stumbled forward, knocking Jim backward. Jim landed on something hard. Metal. The downed SWAT team member had dropped his weapon in the explosion. Jim easily scooted it behind his back and then helped Dan to sit back beside him.

Two hostages, cops, explosions: the scenario was too much for Sophie. He could see it in her fidgety eyes. She was losing control, her mental state degrading just as Ava said it would.

62

SOPHIE TRIED TO BREATH normally, to calm and assess. Dan was too far away for her to manage without dropping the knife. She had the detonator for the explosive, and the charge was large enough to take herself out with it. Maybe that was the way to go. Take them all out.

Blaze of glory, really? Stupid girl.

Rain started to fall. Hard. Cold. Running down her face, into her eyes. She didn't know where to focus. Her gaze darted from the PI to the big guy, to the girl, and landed on Dan.

"What other choice do I have?" Her voice sounded weak in her head.

O inched closer. "You can let the girl go and give me that thing."

She laughed. "Yeah. That would be smart."

Just do it.

Numb fingers curled around the detonator as if they were part of someone else's body. Under someone else's control.

63

DAN STAGGERED, STRUGGLING TO make his way to his feet with his hands tied. He was still looking at Jim.

Jim mouthed, *Now*.

Dan flung himself backward, into the girls. Sandy screamed, probably assuming her death was imminent. Sophie scrambled up, still holding the detonator, and glared down at Dan. If she pushed that button, they were all goners. She hesitated, her face softened.

Jim grabbed the gun he'd been lying on. Prayed to the heavens there wasn't a safety on it—he had no idea where it would be—swung it, and aimed for her middle. He squeezed the trigger. Several rounds blasted from the barrel.

The force of the bullets pushed Sophie back a couple more steps. Her eyes went wide. Her arms slack.

She looked down at her stomach; it was blooming blood from her right side.

She dropped the detonator.

O grabbed it.

Agents and police rushed up, careful to remain on the path. They were shouting.

Sandy scrambled to Jim, crashed to her knees, and buried her head in his chest.

STUPID GIRL. YOU SHOULD *have killed them all.*

"I couldn't kill Dan."

LYNETTE HODGE DIED TRAGICALLY Wednesday the 18th
of August.

> *Born in 1928 in Austin, Texas, Lynette received a M.Ed. in*
> *Nursing Education from Texas Christian University in 1955. Hers*
> *was an entire life spent putting others first, even perishing to protect*
> *her son. Lynette was a beautiful individual, a jokester, Fitzgerald*
> *hater, and a dear friend.*
>
> *She is survived by her son, Daniel Hodge, who brought her great*
> *joy and cake in her later years.*

Dan read the text, nodded, and handed back the words Jim had scribbled on a legal pad. Had taken two hours to get the wording just right. It mattered.

"Seventy-five words. Perfect." Dan smiled, though his eyes were dull and lifeless. "She would love it. I've got to get going. Have a date with a mortician. Thanks. For this"—he held up the obit—"and for everything."

Jim stood as Dan did.

"My guess is I still owe you money even after that retainer."

Jim waved him off, not sure what to say. "You going back to Utah?"

"Yeah. I fit there and I don't have to hide anymore. So, who knows?" He saluted with the folded paper. "Anyway. Thanks again."

Special Agent Ava Webb entered the Coffee Girl about fifteen minutes later. She was in jeans and a dark blue T-shirt. Nothing fancy. Long legs were all the accessories she needed. Jim shook his head at himself. Always wanted the things he couldn't have.

"They'll be filing tomorrow. She's going up for nineteen murders."

She eased into the booth.

"That's what Dan told me. But he put it a little more dramatically. He said 'nineteen crimes against god and humanity.' I think it meant something to him. Does it to you?"

"Nope. I like it, though. Sounds more applicable than Murder One."

They both sat for a moment, not speaking.

Nineteen souls gone, just so Sophie could try to play house with a boy from her youth. He wanted to ask about the rape charges and Max, but he kept his mouth closed.

Turns out his shooting did suck. He hadn't killed her. Once Sophie recovered, she would be on death row. What difference would an additional rape charge bring? He would deal with his mixed emotions on that subject at a later date. It might involve a great deal of scotch.

"Sandy doing okay?"

"They're going to keep her one more day, just to make sure there's no lingering aftereffects of the ketamine. It could have killed her."

"Should have."

Another waitress showed up. Her name tag read Lou but Jim was sure her name was Louise. She was new. "Would you like to see a menu?"

"No thanks. I'm not staying." Ava smiled at the girl and then looked back to Jim. "Flight's in two hours."

That was a problem too. Ava lived in Dallas.

"She's coming back to work soon, so you get your morning routine back?" Ava gave him a wink, as if knowing his routine was a major accomplishment.

"No. She's not. I talked to her last night. Offered her a job."

That brought a surprised look.

"She's almost through with school. The girl needs some real experience. I offered her an office management position with a reputable detective agency."

"Reputable?"

"Yes. Do I detect disbelief, Agent Webb?"

"If you mean like having the reputation of a guy who would move into a hostage situation, disregarding the tactical plans and orders from FBI agents and police officials, then no."

Dang, she was cute out of that suit and the pressure that came with it.

"It turned out I saved your ass out there and you know it. But I bet that's not what's in all the reports."

She gave him a shrug. "Did you manage to find a home for that dog, Mr. Reputable Detective?"

"I did better than that. I found its owners. Turns out Sophie stole her from outside a café. A young lady was very happy to have her princess back."

"Too bad I can't get the dog to testify."

"I think you'll make the case, Agent Webb."

She gave him a little grin. "If you're ever in Dallas, Mr. Bean," she said as she stood, "I would still like to hear your story. I have a friend with a similar one. I understand how tiny ripples can disrupt an entire pond."

She walked away.

Never looked back.

Damn, he liked her.

Acknowledgments

As with most books, many people helped with the development of my writing and the creation of Jim Bean and his world. The dream of being a writer was my own, but fulfilling that dream would have been impossible without writer's groups whose members and programs taught me how to hone the craft. MWA, Sisters in Crime, RWA, and others have all helped mold me, teach me, and nurture me. Thanks to Tony Parkinson, Nancy Kattenfeild, Kris Froehlich, Jeffrey Deaver, John Gilstrap, and Art Taylor, who've read and eagerly supported my work.

To all the wonderful friends and acquaintances in the mystery / thriller community who have welcomed me with open arms and a deep glass of wine, I thank you. My parents always supported my storytelling, starting before I could imagine writing them. They were saddled with rehearsals and attending plays way back at Casa Manana in TX. Acting shifted into making up my own dialogue, and eventually stories and then books. My dad would have been thrilled to see all this come to fruition.

Many thanks to Gina Lamb for editing the dyslexia out of my first draft. Kelli Collins for teaching me to stay in the story and where the right place to start is. Usually, three chapters after I started it.

To Terri Bischoff for believing in the Sin City series, to Nicole Nugent and the rest of the Midnight Ink Crew for all their hard work making it read well and look good.

Thanks to Raleigh PI Gary Richardson for helping with interesting stories and technical information, and Chris Grall for weapons accuracy. Any mistakes in these areas are all mine.

And mostly to Shaun, who courageously dug his way out from under the crippling stigma, personal toll, and financial ramifications of a false accusation of rape. Through the struggle I watched him become a stronger man, a loving husband, and an adorable father.

Good thing he handled it better than Jim Bean. Thank you for letting me ask you the hard questions and making you relive those memories to answer them. I hope we'll open a few eyes as the series progresses.

© Dreamlight Studios

About the Author

J.D. Allen (Raleigh, NC) attended The Ohio State University and earned a degree in forensic anthropology and a creative writing minor.

She's a member of the Bouchercon World Mystery Convention National board and president of the Triangle Chapter of Sisters in Crime. She does workshops on the basics of crime scene investigation, voice, and public speaking. You can visit her online at www.JDAllenBooks.com.